Under
the
Bridge

Printed by:
Haines Printing, North East, PA

To order additional copies contact:

Emily Steiner
155 Memorial Gardens Rd.
West Liberty, KY 41472

Phone: (606) 495-8090
email: jemstyle01@icloud.com

Printed in the United States of America

ISBN 978-0-9997295-0-2

To my cousin Lyndon
who believed in this book from the beginning
and who spent untold hours
doing what he does best—criticizing.
Thanks!

Part 1

Chapter one

Her father was a tall, spare coal mine man who carried himself with an unconscious, shambling sort of grace; and her mother a woman of sinewy toughness who seemed made from the mountains she lived among. Lilly Burchett had taken characteristics from both of them. She was a slim, brown-haired, brown-eyed girl of thirteen, with long legs and arms, a thin mouth, fine straight eyebrows, a pointed nose, and calloused feet that rarely felt shoes.

She stood in the middle of the narrow trail that crossed and re-crossed Sand Lick Creek on its way into the hills, poised, glancing first up the trail, then down. Her younger siblings thought she was right behind them on their way home from school, but she had intentionally loitered. By now they must be well ahead of her, near the cabin at the forks of Upper and Lower Sand Lick. She couldn't see the cabin from here, but a thin tendril of gray smoke showed the spot where it crouched back to back with the end of Peter's ridge. Upper Sand Lick, where almost nobody lived save old Hester Sue, went off to the right of it; and Lower Sand Lick, where most of Lilly's kin on the Burchett side had settled, off to the left.

High, domineering ridges and hills hemmed in both creeks, and dozens of others like them, running alongside each other, twisting and turning, merging and separating at odd angles. Already now, in the middle of the afternoon, the ridge to the west threw long chill shadows over the path and the ancient bridge that spanned Sand Lick.

Lilly stood close to the bridge, in shadow herself, but shivering more from eagerness than from cold. She took one long breath of the air that wasn't yet spring, but hinted at it, one long look to be sure she was truly alone, and then slipped down the creek bank and under the bridge.

The creek flowed rapidly, tumbling over half-submerged rocks and pouring through stony crevices. Usually the mountain roads ran directly through the creeks, but at this ford the rock walls on the sides of the creek were high, and a pioneer several generations back had sunk logs into the creek bed and built a crude, sturdy bridge. It was high enough that she could stand up straight underneath it, but barely. Here was no smell of approaching spring, but the dank and mold of a hundred floods. To Lilly, this smell, combined with the smell of tumbling water and muddy banks, was a good smell, the smell of a well-kept secret. She let it wash away the unpleasantness from her heart.

The school day just past had been long and full of drudgery. Lilly had annoyed the red-haired, loud-mouthed teacher, Mr. Ferguson, by messing up on her division of decimals. He said that her head must be filled with the corn mush she had eaten for breakfast, and that if she couldn't do any better than that, she might as well stay home and help her ma. Then he slapped down another ten problems for her to work. The extra arithmetic had stung, but not as deeply as what he'd said.

She could take him at his word and quit. Ma certainly wouldn't mind. Although she believed firmly that her children should know how to read, write, and cipher, she said often that there was more to life than what Lilly could find in the old log schoolhouse. And when Ma, not knowing the subtle art of hinting, said a thing, she said it right out, in words like, "A woman's place is getting married and raising a family." Ma would be happy to see her married and setting up housekeeping soon in her own cabin—or a coal mine cottage down in the town—and then having babies, having them one after another as fast as all the other mountain women.

Lilly's upper lip curled scornfully at this thought. She hoped for life to give her more than that. Quitting school would mean no more math, and she did hate math. She thought sometimes that she hated Mr. Ferguson too. But it was his stories that kept her in school: glorious stories of wars and conquests, of vanished kingdoms and forgotten kings, of moonlight on desert sands, of brown-faced Indian women making curry, and black Africans glistening with sweat in their corn fields. She liked him best on the rare days when he took out his copy of Shakespeare and read to them. She could never understand how some of the children fell asleep during those readings.

Mr. Ferguson couldn't understand it either, and it made him angry. He would stop reading, glower at them from under red-blond brows, and tap his ruler sharply on his desk, though Lilly was sure he would have liked to tap it on their heads. "This is literature, children. Literature. Have you no brains for anything but corn fields and coal mines?"

Coal mines were Mr. Ferguson's especial nemesis. He always spat out the phrase with venom as though it left a bad taste on his tongue. Occasionally he resorted to openly making fun of the students' fathers and older brothers who were coal miners. Beulah, who managed to come in for this kind of criticism more often than many of the others, always laughed it off. And sometimes she whispered to Lilly, "He don't like the mines because he had two brothers killed in a collapse. That's all."

It was February and still too cold for Lilly to dabble her toes in the edge of the creek. But listening to the water for a few minutes was enough to calm and refresh her. Then she stepped backwards and reached up into a crevice between a piling and the timber above. Carefully she drew out a small square of paper and unfolded it. From her pocket she took a half-used pencil. She squatted beside a flat rock and wrote quickly, in tiny, even letters to save the paper, adding to what was there from other days.

"February 9, 1918. Today was not a Shakespeare day. It was a math day. If all days were like this, I would quit school right now. I hate to make Mr. Ferguson mad, but he does look so interesting that I almost enjoy it in spite of myself. His eyes get greener and they sparkle, and his eyebrows seem to come alive. I wish he could get mad without saying such biting things. His words hurt. I just stopped listening and thought about my new story idea for a bit. That helped. The story happens in India. Mr. Ferguson told us about the caste system yesterday, and I dreamed about it last night. I wonder if a girl from a lower caste ever loved a boy from a higher caste. I think it would make such a wonderful story. I wish I had about ten sheets of blank paper and two whole pencils and a day from sunrise to sunset to do nothing but write."

Lilly stopped and bit the top of her pencil. She had filled up enough space for today. She flipped the paper over and looked earnestly at the other side, empty except for crease marks and soil smudges. Carefully she wrote across the top, "A Longing Love." She knew just how she would begin this story. "Ramina looked up from stirring the pot of rice, feeling startled." But she folded up the paper again without writing it. She would savor the flavor of it in her mind for now, the thrill of a beginning that could go anywhere, the poetical sound of a name she had made up herself.

She tucked the paper back up into its crack, gently, and whispered, "I'll be back next week."

Then she scrambled up the bank, looked with satisfaction at the empty road, and ran toward home. Mrs. Keeton waved at her from the front porch of the store, but she only waved back. She saw Mr. Greer out on his porch as well, sleeping hound dogs around him, and Mrs. Greer looking out through the window, her face as sour as last week's cream, like usual; but she didn't stop long enough even to say "howdy."

She went around to the back of the cabin and came into the kitchen. Ma greeted her curtly. "I never saw a girl who poked so much on her way home from school."

Breathless, Lilly leaned against the table. "I'm sorry, Ma. I'll hurry faster next time."

"And you've been running, too," Ma added sharply, as she shifted Sonny, from one arm to the other. "Don't tell me you didn't stop somewhere along the way. Gabbing with Beulah, I suppose."

"No, Ma, honestly I wasn't." Lilly wished she had remembered to walk the last hundred yards to get her breath back.

Ma only looked her displeasure. "Here, take Sonny, so I can get something done."

"Where are the children?"

"Out working, like you should be. Vince has got the plow on the first corn field, and the others are smoothing it out. Go and help them. Take an old sack for Sonny to sit on, and be sure you keep an eye on him."

"Yes, Ma," Lilly said. She had been keeping an eye on her younger siblings since before she could remember; first Vince, then Maybelle and Bobby and T.J. and Patty, and now Sonny. She took the plump, blue-eyed baby from Ma and tickled him on his tummy. He giggled and grabbed at her hair.

Behind the house and to the north, the land had been cleared for corn fields, each field steeper than the one below it as they climbed toward the ridge. Vince's plow, pulled by a mule, had made deep furrows across half of the lowest field. The other children each had a forked stick to drag through the dirt behind him, but they were spending most of their time throwing dirt clods at each other.

Lilly might have snapped at them if half her mind hadn't still been in India with Ramina. As it was, she only set Sonny down in a warm place and gave him his own stick to play with. But her thoughts stirred rice with Ramina and watched Abadash, the handsome young man who belonged to a caste far above Ramina.

The story unrolled itself before her eyes, new characters leaped into their places, and the plot deepened and grew more complex. Lilly could feel a tingle in her fingertips, a tingle that cried out, "Give me a pencil and paper." Although other story ideas had come to her before, ideas that had thrilled her at the time, she was sure this was her best yet.

Over the next two days, Saturday and Sunday, the story nestled away into the dreamy part of her mind. There were other things to think about, what with Pa suggesting a trip over the ridge for services on Sunday morning. Ma's eyes lit up at that, for it would mean spending a night and a whole day with the kin on her side of the family. For the children, it meant time with cousins and with the half uncles and aunts from Pappaw's second marriage, who were the same age as them. It meant an evening around the fire in breathless wonder, because Pappaw's second wife knew a fine lot of old tales and could tell them well.

But on Monday, an hour after lunch, Mr. Ferguson held up a stack of paper with one hand and seemed to weigh it and gauge its thickness. "It's time to begin a new project, children," he said. "We're going to write."

A loud groaning protest went up. Jemsey Ratliff, the only other thirteen-year-old student, effected a very realistic-looking faint, his head slumping down on his desk, and his tongue lolling out. Mr. Ferguson ignored them all. "It's time this school has a writing course. We're going to do it every afternoon this week."

Jemsey came back quickly from his faint and looked terrified.

"Raise your hand if you think you can come up with your own idea for a subject."

"What's it supposed to be?" a third grader asked timidly.

"Anything at all. I just want to see if you can write. Write about what you did yesterday. Write a description of your pa or ma, or me, for that matter. Write what you'd like to be when you grow up. Raise your hand if you're ready to start now."

A few hesitant hands went up, Lilly's among them. Mr. Ferguson started down the first row, slapping a piece of paper on every desk. "If you have an idea, begin at once."

When he passed her desk, Lilly put up her hand again, filled with a fluttering mixture of eagerness and anxiety. He looked at her coolly, his green eyes measuring her.

"Can we write stories?" she whispered.

"Didn't I say you could write anything?"

"I think I'll need two pieces of paper." She gazed at the whole rich stack, wishing for all of it, but knew she dared not ask for more than two.

A trace of surprise flickered across Mr. Ferguson's face. Without another comment, he laid down three more sheets.

Exuberance tingled through Lilly. Something—or Someone—somewhere had heard her wish under the bridge. She took up her pencil and wrote "A Longing Love" across the top of the first page.

From then on, Lilly was lost. She vaguely heard Mr. Ferguson handing out assignments and ideas, correcting spelling as he walked up and down the rows, and giving occasional commendation. She was aware that he stopped when he passed her, but she didn't realize that he simply stared down thoughtfully at her bent head and flying fingers.

Lilly had soared out of her desk, out of the schoolhouse, out of the Kentucky coal fields, out of the whole United States. Ramina and Abadash lived on the paper in front of her.

When Mr. Ferguson rang his bell for dismissal, she sighed, partly in happiness, partly in the wish to keep on and on and on.

The students spilled out the door and onto the bare earth playground, where they lingered for a few minutes, talking or playing, not anxious for the long walk home and the chores that awaited them. Beulah's sister Eula exclaimed, "I didn't have a clue what to write!"

"Why do we need a writing course anyway?" Hallick demanded.

"When I'm out of school," Jemsey said, "I'll never write another word in my life, 'cept for signing deeds and things like that."

"You could sign with a X for that." Eula giggled.

"That's what my pappy does," Jemsey answered with a shrug. "Don't know why I would have to do any different."

Eula's full red lips parted in another giggle. "Mr. Ferguson finally told me to write about what I want to do when I grow up. That's simple anyhow." She winked openly at Jemsey, whom she had a crush on.

Beulah sauntered up to the group. She had audacious blue eyes and a running tongue, and now she asked casually, "What did you write about, Lilly? Mr. Ferguson didn't give you any ideas, I noticed."

"Yeah," Eula agreed. "Didn't you see how he always tried to read what she was writing when he walked past. What was it?"

Lilly came back to the hard-packed edge of the school yard with alarming suddenness. "I was writing a story," she said stiffly.

"A story?" Jemsey repeated scornfully. "One of them Shakespeare things?"

Lilly satisfied herself with giving him a look from eyes which had lost their pleasant honey color.

"A story about what?" Beulah asked.

"Is it a true story?" Eula questioned pertly. "My ma says we shouldn't be listening to no stories that aren't true. I suppose she meant we shouldn't write them either."

"Shakespeare's stories aren't true," Lilly answered slowly.

"Ma didn't never hear of Shakespeare," Beulah retorted.

"She couldn't understand half what he writes either," Eula added. "Just like me."

"If you wouldn't sleep—" Lilly began angrily.

"Cut it out," Jemsey said. "No one can understand that Shakespeare stuff. I don't think even Mr. Ferguson himself understands it. He just wants us to think he's smart."

"You didn't tell us yet what your story is about," Eula insisted. "Is it about a girl?"

"Yes."

"What's her name?"

"Ramina."

Eula and Beulah both giggled over this. "That's a made-up name. Ramina."

"Is there any marrying in the story?"

"I haven't gotten very far."

"Can I read it when you're done?"

"No."

"Why not? Please."

"Tell you what, I'll. . ."

"No." Lilly turned her back on them and headed toward home, keeping her eyes on the toes of her shoes. When she was well out of hearing, she whispered to herself, "Ramina and Abadash." The names didn't hold the magic they had in the schoolroom; not after Beulah and Eula had said "Ramina" in that mocking tone of voice. More than that, they had dared to giggle over it.

When she came to the bridge, she hesitated for a long moment. She had promised Ma that she would hurry, and she had fully meant not to stop. She felt now like she needed the solitude, the sensation of dry weeds brushing her ankles, the plash of water against moss-covered stones. But she shook her head and hurried on.

Vince, Bobby, and Maybelle made sure they told Pa about the writing course as soon as he came home from the mine, while Ma and Lilly set supper on the table.

"Writing, is it?" Pa drawled.

"He said we're going to do it for a whole week, every day." Vince sounded thoroughly disgusted.

"What they don't teach these days in the schools," Pa mumbled through his two-day's growth of black beard. "I could say that I need you to stay home and plow the fields."

"Yes, sir. It will be time to plant—"

Pa interrupted him in an unhurried fashion. "But there's no rush yet. Maybe next week. Your time will come soon enough to work the whole day long. I don't know why you should wish for it sooner."

Lilly knew that Pa had only gone half way through third grade before he had begun to take a man's place on the farm. He could stumblingly read the Bible, he could sign his name, and he could do simple math. Lilly couldn't imagine him ever putting a pencil and paper together in the way she did.

"What did you write about?" Ma asked.

Bobby shrugged. "I didn't know what to write about, so Mr. Ferguson told me to write down what I wanted to do when I grew up."

"What was that?"

"Work in the mines," Bobby answered briefly. "I'd a heap sight rather do that than farm."

"Is that what the rest of you wrote about?"

"I did," Vince and Maybelle said together.

"And you, Lilly?"

Lilly slid the pan of cornbread onto the table without looking at anyone. "No," she mumbled. "I wrote a story."

Ma's faded blue eyes, surrounded by the wrinkles of a hard life, widened slightly. "Do you know how to write a story?"

"I don't know. But I want to try it."

"How's a story going to help you live?" Pa grumbled. "You would have done better to be spinning some thread. Let's eat."

Lilly breathed a sigh of relief when the subject was dropped. She took her place on the bench between Bobby and Maybelle.

As soon as Pa had finished his supper, he slid his chair heavily across the wooden floor and stood up, saying, "I'm tired." He kneaded his perpetually blackened knuckles against the muscles in his arms and rolled his shoulders back and forth. "I'm going to bed."

He crossed into the front room, the one that also served as a bedroom for Pa, Ma, Patty, and Sonny, and almost immediately they heard deep rumbling snores. Ma looked worried. "He come in all wet this evening," she said. "Said he had to work lying in water most of the day."

In the lean-to kitchen that adjoined the eating room, Lilly and Maybelle washed the few dishes quickly, put them away on the shelf, and threw the water out the back door.

Maybelle went to join the younger children for a game of Frog in the Meadow, and Lilly watched them from the front porch. Then her gaze drifted from them to the cabin. She had lived there all her life, and so had her father before her. His father had built a one room dwelling, then added the narrower room with the table, and later the lean-to kitchen out the back. It had not changed since then, except to weather and settle.

The front room, where Pa still lay snoring, held two beds, a small table, the spinning wheel, and half a dozen chairs around the fireplace. The eating room was dominated by a long table down the middle and another fireplace, from which ruddy light spilled out onto the porch through the half-open door.

It was a cabin well-suited for life just outside a coal mine town—well-suited for a life where people had little time for anything other than work. The chairs were comfortable, but not plush; the floors sturdy, but not rug-covered. And since no one had time to read, there were only two books— a family Bible, and a thin volume of writings by famous men like George Washington. Pa and Ma read the Bible occasionally, but none of the children were allowed to take it down and page through it. No one showed any interest in the other book.

Ma's voice came suddenly from the corner where she was rocking Sonny. "Getting late. Time the little ones were in bed. Go call them in, Lilly."

The books didn't belong to Lilly, but her thoughts did. When everyone was in bed, either in the front room or the loft, and the childish wigglings had subsided into deep-breathed slumber, Lilly could dream. No one told her now that she needed to redo a whole page of division with decimals. No one called her to come and stir the mush. No one reminded her that there was more to life than books. She always fell asleep shaping her airy fancies into stories.

Chapter two

Writing every afternoon, it took Lilly nearly a week to finish her story about a longing love. Abadash ended up marrying Ramina against the wishes and protests of all his clan. There Lilly ran into a problem, since she had no idea what Indian weddings were like. She spent some time biting her pencil and thinking hard, and settled the problem by custom designing a wedding radically different than any she had ever attended.

Mr. Ferguson had kept her supplied with paper as long as she needed it, making no comment or criticism. He only gave her strange, questioning looks from his green eyes.

She handed it in when she finished, laying it on top of a pile of smudged and wrinkled manuscripts from other hands. Mr. Ferguson leafed through her piece. "Five pages," he muttered. "What are you trying to do, girl? Write a book?"

Lilly blushed scarlet. But in spite of Mr. Ferguson's dubious tone, the words "write a book" haunted her. She caught herself looking again and again that school day at the row of old blue and black and red books on Mr. Ferguson's desk, and wondering—not for the first time—about the people who had written them.

How long would it take to write a whole book? How much paper and how many pencils? She spent a delicious half hour that night before falling asleep, imagining it. She knew she had no ideas good enough for a book yet, but surely one would come. The story of Abadash and Ramina had been better than any before it, and maybe in a few more years. . . If only she could find enough pencils and paper and time.

Mr. Ferguson had the compositions laid out on their desks the next morning when the students arrived at school, liberally marked with red spelling and grammar corrections. Lilly grabbed hers up, quickly, and folded it up to stuff inside the covers of her math book before any of the others could see it. In her haste, she almost missed the note at the bottom of the first page. "I need to talk to you at the end of the day."

Dread coiled in her stomach. Interviews with Mr. Ferguson were never pleasant experiences. The air in the room seemed suddenly stuffy, and she rushed outside without looking at anyone else.

She knew she did poorly on her math. Mr. Ferguson knew it too, and compared her work with Jemsey's, even though Jemsey was working in a lower-level math book. She hung her head and let her hair hide her face and her embarrassment. Then she dared a peep at the clock. Only four more hours until the talk with Mr. Ferguson.

It was the day for spelling tests, and Lilly did badly on that too, spelling words wrong that she could normally spell with ease. This time Mr. Ferguson didn't scold; he only looked, and his eyebrows told of his displeasure. Again Lilly looked at the clock. One hour.

Her hands were so cold that her fingernails had turned dusky lavender at the roots by two o'clock. Mr. Ferguson rang his bell and dismissed the students. Lilly slowly reached into her desk and felt for her math book.

"What are you doing?" Beulah demanded. "Let's go."

"I'm getting the paper Mr. Ferguson handed back this morning."

Beulah walked past, jauntily, one with the crowd of students who rushed to evacuate. In the suddenly empty, echoey room, Mr. Ferguson stood up and stretched slightly. One glance at him assured Lilly that he wasn't angry. Then she kept her eyes on her papers, smoothing the edges with her fingertips.

He sat down in a desk just across the aisle. Lilly, with her head bent again, was only brave enough to look at his long legs and the patch over one knee.

"I read your story," he began, and paused. Suddenly his voice sharpened. "Look at me, would you? There are some things I need to understand about you. You make it hard when you won't even look at me."

Still uncertain, Lilly looked up and met his gaze more frankly. His eyes weren't sparkling with anger, and they looked different than she had ever seen them before.

"How many stories have you written before this?" he asked.

"None."

"How many stories have you read?"

"Not many," she faltered. "We don't have books at home. But Ma tells us tales sometimes, and Mammaw Lewis does often. And you read us stories at school."

"That's all?"

"No. When Miss Sparks taught here, she read us stories every day." Was that when she had started thinking in story form? She honestly didn't know.

"Why haven't you written any stories before this?"

"I don't have enough paper and pencils. And there's always work to do at home."

"So-o-o-o." Mr. Ferguson put his fingertips together as he drew out the word. "If you've never done it before, how could you do it so quickly and easily when I said you should write?"

"I had thought of that story just a couple days before."

"How many other stories have you *just thought of*?"

"I don't know."

"So there have been others?"

"Oh, yes. Lots." Lilly dropped her eyes again, momentarily abashed by how easily she had shared this bit of private information.

"Now, about this story," Mr. Ferguson went on. "What do you know of India?"

"You told us about the castes."

He laughed. "So that's what you wrote your story on? Hardly enough information. I don't know much about India myself, but I don't think you're on track with their marriage customs."

"I had fun writing it," Lilly defended herself.

"Oh, I've no doubt you did. But if you want anyone to read what you write, you have to write convincingly. That means you have to write about what you know."

"I don't know—anything."

"You know about coal mines and living in log cabins," Mr. Ferguson said severely.

Lilly winced when he mentioned coal mines and braced herself. But for once he didn't start his diatribe against them.

"There's nothing to write about that," she protested.

"Isn't there?" Mr. Ferguson picked up her story and waved it carelessly in the air. "There's more material there than in this. I laughed when I read this."

Lilly wanted to grab the paper and cry out, "How could you?" He was, after all, no different than Eula and Beulah.

"But at the same time," he went on, "I got the feeling that I had at least one student listening when I read Shakespeare. I'd like to see what you can do writing a story about what you know best."

"If I write about something in the United States, does it have to be right here at Sand Lick?" Lilly pleaded. She remembered quite vividly another idea about a girl on a southern plantation—a girl who had run away with her little brother, been recaptured, beaten, and chained in leg irons every night.

"Yes," Mr. Ferguson said sternly. "You've never traveled out of Harlan County, so it needs to be something that could happen right here. And right now, in 1918. It's Friday. You have until Monday to come up with an idea, and you'll find the paper on your desk when you come in the morning. I'll shorten your math lesson, and you can begin as soon as you have time."

Lilly's face flushed with pleasure and excitement. She would do anything for the promise of a shortened math lesson. "Oh," she breathed. "Can I have as much paper as I want?"

"Of course. But write small."

Lilly fairly danced from the schoolhouse. The yard around the log building lay silent and drowsing in the mellow afternoon sunlight, dreaming of the time when children's feet would pound it again. Lilly set out on a dead run for home. When she reached the bridge, she slid down the bank, still gasping for breath, and straightened up under the heavy planks. She took the story from her dress pocket, folded it into a smaller square, and squeezed it into the crevice where the other single sheet had been.

On her diary paper she wrote hurriedly, "This is the best day of my life. I finished 'A Longing Love' yesterday at school, and Mr. Ferguson laughed about it. That's not so good. The good part is that I'm supposed to write another story, something that could happen in Kentucky. And the best part is that he will shorten my math lesson so that I have more time to work on it. He's going to give me all the paper I need. I wonder if it would be very wrong to pretend that I need more than I do, and hide the rest here under the bridge for other stories."

Carefully she erased the penciled title from the back side of the sheet and hid everything away. She didn't think that anyone else spent time under the bridge, but she would not chance her treasures being seen if someone should happen along.

She ran again, until she came in sight of the cabin, and then slowed to a walk so that she could come in calmly. Ma didn't question her but simply said, "Sonny's sleeping in the cradle. I'm going out to the field, and you can watch him and make supper. There's some mending in the basket too."

"Okay, Ma."

Chatter and song drifted in from the field along the creek. Lilly peeked into the front room and saw Sonny sleeping on his stomach, his legs pulled up under him so that his diapered bottom stuck up in the air. She left the door between the two rooms open a crack and sat down in Ma's rocking chair with a worn dress, a needle, and thread. No hurry to start supper yet. Mending would let her mind run free to plan the story she was to start next week.

After five minutes she decided that this was definitely harder than coming up with Indian stories, slave stories, stories about ladies in England, or stories of battles in the west. But Mr. Ferguson had told her to use coal mines because she knew about them. She settled at last on something about a coal mine accident, and then, almost before she knew it, the people involved were developing personalities and coming alive, all the while that her needle moved steadily around the patch on Maybelle's school dress.

When Sonny woke up, she changed his diaper, cuddled him a bit, and instantly put a baby just like him into the story. When Pa came home, she looked at him, and a phrase came fully formed into her mind. "A miner's face blackened by hours in a dark coal mine tunnel. . ."

I must include that, she thought, and almost burned the pan of cornbread as she tried to figure out how it could be done.

The story went to bed with her and woke up with her. It went along to the field and the spring and the woods when she went hunting for the earliest greens. It traveled with her when Ma sent her and T.J. with a list and part of Pa's paycheck to Mrs. Keeton's store.

Okla Keeton tallied up their purchases and counted the money, but his wife Elzinnie gathered everything from the shelves behind the counter because Okla's paralyzed legs kept him fastened in his chair. "Your ma got any early garden in yet?" Elzinnie asked.

"No, ma'am, not yet."

"Feels like an early spring this year." She went on chatting briskly, relaying the news that she had gathered in a morning of tending store. But although her tone was pleasant enough, she never smiled. It wasn't a thing Elzinnie Keeton did. When she had collected the salt, matches, and baking soda that Ma wanted, she turned back to face them, and Lilly noticed the unbearable sadness in her eyes. It was always there.

"Well, that's it for you, honey," she said. "Reckon there'll be a lot of visitors at church tomorrow?"

"I reckon so."

"Stop in on your way home and tell me about it, won't you?"

This was as close as she would come to saying that she longed to get out and see the rest of the community, all in a pile, and not in trickles the way they came through her store. Lilly could remember before her husband had been hurt, how she would be the first to go to the neighbor's with a pot of soup or a pan of cornbread, and how she loved to go visiting, carrying her sewing along with her. But no more. She was chained almost as securely as her husband. To make a living when he could no longer work in the mines, they had put up this little store and moved out of their house into a single room behind it. But Elzinnie never complained.

"Of course I'll stop in," Lilly said.

"All of you," Elzinnie urged.

When it came to complaining, Mrs. Greer, who lived about half way between the store and the fork, was a different kind of mule entirely. She hailed them from the porch as they walked past, her voice loud and raspy and demanding. "You been down to the store?"

"Yes, ma'am."

"Wish I would have seen you on the way down. I need some salt. You know I can't leave Silas alone for ten minutes together."

This was an exaggeration, since her husband had only lost one leg, and he could still hobble around with the help of a hand-carved crutch.

"Come on up and set a spell," Mrs. Greer urged.

T.J. followed Lilly up the steps and sat down in her shadow on the porch. One of the hounds whined, and Silas reached down to fondle its ears.

"Need a drink?" Mrs. Greer asked, not as though she wanted to give them anything, but because it was the proper thing. Her face hung down in old, sad folds that made her look like one of her husband's hounds.

"Thank you," Lilly answered. "I'm thirsty."

"It's just water. I wanted to make some tea this morning and get it chilled, but I'm that tied up with my rheumatism that I can't hardly move."

"I'll fetch the water," Lilly offered.

But in spite of Silva Greer's words, she walked with surprising ease into the house and came back out shortly with two tin cups, brimming with water. She took the time while Lilly was drinking and couldn't answer to get deep into a list of her present grievances. Some of them never changed—Silas's helplessness "because of those coal mine men who think they're like God and can treat us like the dirt under their feet," his constant cough caused by years of inhaling fine coal dust, her rheumatism, the chinking that had fallen out of their house, and the fear that their well would run dry. Others were new—the dead chicken she had found that morning, and the letter from her daughter telling her that she had given birth to twins.

"I can't imagine what they're going to do with twins," she said, shaking her head glumly, and paring off a piece of Silas's tobacco chaw for herself. She nestled it into one cheek and went on grimly, "It's hard enough to raise a normal-size family. I've tried it and I should know. And her other children are two and three. She needs me to help her, of course. But she's away off in Johnson County, and everybody knows I can't leave Silas."

Lilly listened to her patiently. Ma always did, and once she had told Lilly, "Let her talk. She's had a hard life, and maybe it will do her a bit of good."

But Lilly knew that she would simply re-tell her grievances to the next person that chanced along. She hated a lot of people and things in her life, and seemed to have only one love—talking about her hatreds. Her stringy hair and shuffling gait usually repulsed Lilly, but sometimes the dreary look in her eyes inspired a faint sympathy.

She and T.J. got on their way eventually, and one of the hounds sent a mournful baying after them. The last thing Lilly heard was Silva saying vengefully, "Shut that thing up, or I will, one of these days."

"Which is worse," Lilly asked, "to be paralyzed, or to have a leg cut off?"

"To have a leg cut off," T.J. decided. "If you're paralyzed, you still have them both. And it must be worse, 'cause Mrs. Greer talks about it a lot more than Mrs. Keeton."

Lilly shook her head, but didn't bother telling T.J. that it was a story she was thinking of. Paralysis had more of a dramatic flair than losing a leg, but maybe she would put them both into her plot.

The story even crept into church with her on Sunday morning, and Lilly spent most of the service staring reverently at the preacher while mentally writing.

By Monday morning she was well ready to begin. Her seat-mate, Nola, stared at her when she put away her math book and took out one of the new white sheets of paper. "What are you doing?" she whispered behind her hand.

"Mr. Ferguson told me I didn't need to do so much math today," Lilly whispered back, loftily.

Nola screwed her mouth into a jealous pout. "He did not. You're lying."

Lilly only smiled and examined the point on her pencil. Then she shielded her paper as well as she could from Nola and began writing, "Mystery of the Mine," in her finest script. She knew that she wanted this story, comprised of all the ideas she had gathered over the weekend, to look good. First she described a girl named Lana who had blond curls, blue eyes, red lips, and pretty hands. Lilly glanced down ruefully at her own chipped nails when she wrote this. Then she described Lana's family at supper time, making their cabin just a little nicer than her own. But remembering Mr. Ferguson's stern instructions, she dared not go further than including a lace pretty on the fireboard, and newer chairs around the table.

Almost before she knew it, she had filled the whole front side of the first paper, and Mr. Ferguson was ringing his bell for recess. Already two boys wanted to marry Lana. Both of them were handsome, but one was a fine, honest man, and the other a rogue. Lana didn't yet know that, of course.

Lilly finished this story in a week as well, and handed in the pages with the same feeling of trepidation. Mr. Ferguson wouldn't laugh over this one, would he? "I'll read it tonight," he said briefly. "Stay after school tomorrow and I'll tell you what I think."

When the next afternoon came, he took the same stance as before, sitting in a desk across from Lilly, stretching his legs out into the aisle, looking sometimes at her and sometimes at the ceiling.

Instead of beginning right away with praise or criticism, he took the pages of close handwriting and thumbed through them again, slowly. At last he asked, "You can't get away from writing about lovers, can you?"

"That's interesting. It makes a good story."

"How old are you, girl?"

"Almost fourteen."

"How old was your ma when she got married?"

"Fourteen."

"You planning on getting married soon yourself?"

Lilly felt as though he had slapped her. This had nothing to do with her story. She stared at him, suddenly distant and a trifle haughty. "That's none of your business."

"Oh, it isn't? Maybe not." His green eyes hardened too, until she had to drop her gaze. "I was just wondering why you never write a story about anything but love."

"What else is there to write about? You told us once—" she was suddenly defensive "—that all the best stories have either love or hatred in them."

"Well, yes, I recollect saying that. And it's true. But you're not writing best stories yet. You need to cut your teeth on something else."

"Like what?"

"Write a children's story."

"Is that an assignment?" Lilly asked suspiciously.

"Of course not. School's letting out next week, and I won't have time to look over any more of your stories."

The haughtiness went out of Lilly. In the excitement of finally having enough paper and the time she needed, she had made herself forget that school would soon come to an end. It was time for all available children to be in the fields and gardens, not sitting behind desks. School would not reopen until the blackberries were picked in July. And this was it. She wouldn't be coming back next year; Pa had already thought it unnecessary for her to come this year.

"But if you get it done this summer," Mr. Ferguson added, "I want to see it in July."

Lilly laughed sadly. "I'm not coming back to school then. And I won't have any chances to write this summer."

"What will you be doing in the fall?"

"Getting married, probably." She tried to say it flippantly, but failed. No matter what Mr. Ferguson thought of her, she really didn't want to get married at fourteen.

He stood up and towered over her. From the look in his eyes, she expected his voice to come loud and angry, and she held her breath. Instead he spoke softly and intensely, almost bitterly. "If you get married at fourteen, you're a fool. There's so much more to life than mining and farming in these mountains. I think you have a bit of a talent. Maybe more than a bit; I'm no good as a judge. But you'll waste it all if you get married. You won't be able to think about a thing after that but having babies and doing laundry and working in the fields."

Suddenly Lilly lifted her chin. "My thoughts are my own," she said sharply, "no matter what I'm doing."

He answered coldly, "You'll see."

"Maybe, if I had some paper. . ." Lilly suggested.

Mr. Ferguson just stared at her for a moment longer. Then he walked up to his desk and came back with a stack of paper, maybe ten sheets thick. "I have some for you," he said. "That's partly why I kept you here today."

The paper was thin, browning, and a bit curled at the corners. "My sister gave me this. It's not nice, but it is paper. I'd like to ask you for a promise in return for it."

Cautiously Lilly looked from the paper to him. He wasn't angry, like he got over her fractions. He was—something else, something she couldn't define, and it frightened her more than his anger. "What's the promise?"

"I would like to make you promise that I won't hear wedding plans for you when I come back over the mountain in July. But I won't ask for that."

A blush that Lilly couldn't stop crept up her neck. She had no prospects, but she realized well enough what being almost fourteen could mean.

"No," Mr. Ferguson repeated, "I won't ask for that. But take the paper anyway."

"Thank you," Lilly said simply. "If I have time, I'll try to write a children's story."

"Take these pencils too." Mr. Ferguson tossed down two half-used ones on the desk.

She pocketed them and waited for him to say something more. But he turned away and began writing at the chalkboard, interview obviously over.

"Can I have my story back?" she asked.

"What? Oh, yes. Better than your first, because you knew what you were writing about. Except for the lovers. Better wait until you're married yourself to try that. I wish you had more books to read. It would improve your style."

"I wish so too," Lilly said softly.

He picked up his chalk and again ignored her. Quietly she slipped out.

Her new treasures went under the bridge as well. Her original crevice was full, so she rolled up both stories and tied them with a string. Then she hid them far back under the bridge, where the creek bank met the old wooden timbers. Just to be safe, she laid several stones in front of the new cache.

Chapter three

School ended without fanfare. Beulah and Eula insisted on walking with Lilly the whole way to her cabin after Mr. Ferguson dismissed them for the last time. "We'll never get the chance again," Eula said forlornly, "with you and Beulah both not coming back."

Lilly could not honestly say she would miss these girls much, but she would miss her chances for privacy and dreaming. The three girls crossed the bridge, stopping for a few minutes to throw pebbles into the water and watch for fish, and Lilly thought longingly of the blank sheets of paper and the pencils underneath her. Without these daily walks to and from school, how would she ever find time to use them?

As she had expected, Pa and Ma took it for granted that she wouldn't go to school any longer. With April and May came time to plant the fields. Corn and potatoes sprouted from the warm soil and spread their flourishing leaves to the sunshine. Weeds grew apace, smothering the tiny pumpkins and crowding in among the corn.

Every morning, at pink sunrise, Pa left for his day in the mines; and every evening he came home blackened with coal dust. Vince and Bobby, while wielding hoes, dreamed openly of the day when they could go into the mines themselves. Maybelle shot up very thin and leggy that spring, while T.J., Patty, and Sonny grew so browned and dirty that when Lilly gave them a bath she could hardly tell where the dirt ended and their skin began.

Two important things happened in May, after the crops were in and the pace of life had slowed a trifle. An evangelist, Resvie Craiger, came round to the Sand Lick Valley to hold revivals. He thundered about fire and brimstone, nearly bringing it down himself on the heads of those who had not been baptized and had their sins washed away in the crimson flow of Christ's blood.

Pa and Ma took the whole family to every service, and Lilly listened to this hysteria again and again. Every night a goodly number of sinners or backsliders confessed their failings, and one night Lilly joined them. She hardly understood why, and yet she felt a moving inside that she couldn't explain away.

The baptizing followed on Sunday morning. Lilly, in her simple, ankle-length dress, joined the other women and girls on the creek bank, just downstream from the bridge. Here the rushing water widened out of its rock-strewn channel and filled a pool the color of deep green moss.

Ma, standing with the crowd just behind the applicants, caught her eye and gave her a slow but radiant smile. She had been unabashedly happy about Lilly's decision, perhaps happier than Lilly herself.

The regular preacher, Brother Holbrook, waded out with Brother Craiger to the middle of the creek. Elias Holbrook was old, white-haired, and stoop-shouldered. He seemed to sway a bit with the current, and Lilly wondered what would happen if he would fall over. Briefly she thought of writing a story with a preacher who tumbled over into the rushing water during a baptizing, and then wondered at herself for being able to think such a thing when she was about to have her sins washed away.

She quit thinking about stories then, and thought about her sins. What did it really mean to have them washed away? Words and phrases that preachers had used longer than she could remember had become a part of her being, without adding much meaning to her life. She knew what sin was, although it seemed distant from her personally; and she knew that somehow Jesus' blood, symbolized by the running water, took it away. But the ideas hung as hazy in her mind as the wraiths of mist that rose off Sand Lick in the crisp early mornings. She couldn't explain to her own satisfaction just what had made her decide to join the sinners and backsliders at the altar on Thursday evening.

One by one the applicants waded out into the deep water. The evangelist did the baptizing, dunking them completely under the water and then helping them back to their feet. They always came up gasping as though they had nearly drowned, and then began shouting out hallelujahs as they splashed toward shore.

Lilly wondered about the gasping. They weren't under for more than five seconds. Did none of them know how to hold their breath? All the same, she shivered a little. Maybe something supernatural happened under water. Maybe the water became like blood—Jesus' blood (all the preachers said the water was the blood of Jesus)—and that's why the people came up gasping. She would keep her eyes open and see.

When her turn came she waded in, and paused for a second, surprised at the chill in the water. It nipped at her legs, but with the evangelist looking steadily at her, she went on. She remembered Ma saying confidently, "No one ever got sick from a baptizing. My own brother heard the call in January, right in the middle of a snowstorm, when the ice was an inch thick. The good brother we had for a preacher then, why he chopped a big patch of creek clear of ice, and they went in there as barefoot as anyone. He stood in that creek awhile, giving his testimony, and he came out singing and shouting and never suffered a bit. The good Lord'll protect those who are obeying Him."

The water closed in around Lilly's knees now, then her waist, her armpits. With the cold came a feeling of exultation.

The evangelist reached out and gripped her shoulders.

"Have you accepted Christ as your Savior?" he asked severely, looking at Lilly out of fiery blue eyes under protruding bushy brows.

"Yes."

"Are you sorry for your sins?"

"Yes."

"Do you promise to walk in the new life?"

"Yes." Lilly thought of her stories, stowed just a few hundred feet upstream, and hoped that the new life didn't mean the end of them.

He had started out quietly enough, but his voice had become louder with each question. Now it rose to a decided bellow. "I baptize you, Lilly Burchett, in the Name of the Father—" he pushed her underwater, and the rest of his words came to her dimly "—the Son, and the Holy Spirit."

He lifted her up and still kept his grip on her shoulders as he shouted out one last command. "Live from this day forward in purity and righteousness, and return no more to the vile sins you have committed before."

What vile sins? Lilly wondered. She thought vile sins included murder, adultery, and such like; and she didn't know how the evangelist thought she had committed such things.

She shook the water from her eyes—just plain water that hadn't been transformed to blood—and waded back to shore.

Ma met her there with a rough towel, which she wrapped around her shoulders. "Don't you feel so fresh and new? With your sins all washed away?" Her voice was strangely soft, almost purring.

For a moment Lilly was embarrassed, not sure exactly what to say. She felt the excitement from all the shouting and singing and praying going on around her, and the remaining tingles from the cold water. But maybe she had missed something that all the others had experienced. "Yes, Ma," she said. "I guess so."

In bed that night she realized with a sensation of guilt that for her the best time of the day hadn't been the baptizing itself, but the church dinner afterward, and the long talk with her cousin Gracie from the other side of the mountain. The memory of Mrs. Greer's words, called out to her on the way home from church, intensified this guilt.

"Hear you got baptized this morning."

"Yes, ma'am."

"Sounded like a right good crowd of you."

"Yes, ma'am."

"Heard you didn't shout like the others. Are you sure you really had your sins forgiven?"

She rolled over in bed, carefully, lest she pull the light blanket off Maybelle. *Maybe I'm still a sinner,* she thought, *with those vile sins hanging over me. But if I am, I don't know what I could do different to be rid of them.*

The second important incident in May happened one evening just before dusky dark when Lilly was drawing a fresh bucket of water from the spring behind the apple trees. She heard hoof beats on the trail, heard them stop, heard the whicker of a horse not far away.

"Hey-y, Lilly."

She didn't recognize the voice, but she headed toward it. When she rounded the corner of the kitchen, she saw Jesse Wright very close to her, his horse already tied to a runt of a dogwood tree.

"Good evening," she said.

"Let me carry that water for you," he offered. "Does it go inside?"

Surprised, Lilly handed the bucket over. "You can set it just inside the kitchen door."

She watched him go, not sure if she should follow him or not. He hadn't yet told her why he had come, and she decided to stay outside and ask him when he reappeared.

He had his hat in his hand, respectfully, when he came around the corner again. This showed his dark hair, and the way it drooped down onto his forehead. He walked with a slight limp, the result of an injury in the war. He had only come back a few months ago, and Lilly hardly knew him.

Without preamble he said, "I thought maybe we could take a walk. Just you and me, you know. It's a pretty night."

"It is," she agreed and fell into step beside him. She knew immediately that this was different than Jemsey sauntering across the school yard with her. Young men of twenty didn't call on girls and go for walks for no reason at all. If the boy was thirteen, it meant nothing. If he was twenty, it might mean. . .

Lilly flushed when she remembered Mr. Ferguson saying bitingly, "If you get married at fourteen, you're a fool."

Then she promptly forgot Mr. Ferguson. It was a lovely night, as Jesse had said, and since he had come along, she could enjoy it as it was meant to be enjoyed. A crescent of moon showed over the ridge, and a hint of breeze stirred the long grasses beside the trail. The earth seemed to be sighing to itself as it relaxed and cooled after a hot day. A breath of wildflowers mixed with pine wafted over them from higher up the mountain.

"Up the trail or down?" Jesse asked deferentially.

"I'd like to go up the right fork."

They walked in silence for several moments.

"What did you do today?" Jesse asked.

"Hoed corn most of the day." Lilly flexed her tired arms. "What about you?"

"The same." He flashed her a white-toothed grin in the gathering darkness. "I have to keep the farm running so Pa and Denzil can work in the mines."

"You'd rather be a farmer than a coal miner?"

"I guess so. I don't think much about it. Pa never gave me a choice."

Darkness spilled quickly onto the narrow, rutted trail. They lost the moon among the towering oaks and maples, and then came out into a clearing and found it again. It gave just enough light to tip the dew-wet grasses with a faint silvery sheen. Lilly lifted her skirt slightly to keep it dry, and was suddenly aware of the patched and faded homespun dress she wore. She looked at Jesse involuntarily, wondering if he had noticed it too. But he was staring at her with a strange expression—one she had never before noticed when a boy looked at her. She blushed under his gaze.

They walked as far as the trail that led to Hester Sue's remote cabin, talking most of the time, but sometimes just enjoying the stillness of the evening.

Back at the cabin, Jesse took his time untying his horse, and then hesitated for another long moment before mounting into the saddle. "Mind if I come back and take a walk again?"

"That's fine by me."

As he rode off, he swept his hat from his head to wave at her, and she waved back. Then she walked into the front room nonchalantly, pretending not to see the younger children staring at her.

"Was it Jesse Wright?" Maybelle demanded.

She nodded.

"Is he coming back?" Vince asked from his spot on the floor along the wall.

Again she nodded.

Pa had not gone to bed, but he sat snoring in his chair. Now he woke up suddenly. "What did he come for?"

"Just to talk to me," Lilly said slowly.

"Call it courting, girl," Ma said impatiently. "You know that's what it is."

"How old are you anyway?" Pa questioned.

"Fourteen."

"Well, I married your ma at fourteen," Pa said complacently. "It's a good age."

May blossomed into a sultry June. Jesse came again and again, and he and Lilly often went for walks along the right fork of the creek. Before long folks like Pappaw, Mrs. Keeton, and Mrs. Greer began to tease her about it. She enjoyed these visits. Jesse could talk fairly well about anything concerning mountain life, and occasionally he mentioned the war. Sometimes he preferred to be silent for minutes at a time, and Lilly liked that too.

Once she decided to broach a brand new subject and asked him if he had ever read anything that Shakespeare wrote. He coughed meditatively. "I'm not sure," he said at last. "Did he live about the same time as George Washington? Was he the second president?"

Lilly still giggled over that one.

Her stories stayed safely hidden under the bridge. She thought of them often and wished for the freedom to slip in and add a few lines to a new one, or to simply touch them and dream in solitude.

Her wish was fulfilled in a very unexpected way. Pa's cronies came over one Saturday night, in jovial spirits because they had gotten their paychecks the evening before. Someone had provided several glass jugs, which they passed around freely. For a short time they could forget the daily fear of mine collapses, the hourly struggle to provide for their families, and the minute-by-minute misery of working in the cramped mine tunnels. With each round of the jugs, they talked and laughed louder, finally sprawling on the porch floor with total disregard for chairs or propriety.

Ma and Lilly took some mending out into the cool evening air, but they stayed on the kitchen porch, out of sight of the men. Jesse had not come calling, but this suited Lilly just fine. She wanted time to think on this humid evening because she had begun to weave another story in her mind—this one about a coal miner's wife. She had made several false starts on a children's story, but never really gotten an idea that excited her. The adult ones were much easier to dream up.

She had gotten to the point in the story where the coal miner's wife lost one of her tiny baby twins, when she heard Jaybird, a skinny, tough old man, begin to speak. "Heard today that the mine boss's wife wants a girl to help her," he said. "She's been right sickly this spring."

Pa laughed raucously. "Might be living in that fine house, way up above everyone else, that makes her sickly."

"Thought maybe your girl wanted a job," Jaybird added.

In the moment of silence that followed, Lilly could hear someone taking a gulping swallow from the jug.

"And what gives you that idea?" Pa demanded. At least, he tried to demand, but he sounded more drunk than demanding.

"He's drinking more than he ever did before," Ma worried out loud.

"Don't know. . ." Jaybird slurred.

"You ever hear of anyone who didn't want more money?" Simon asked. He laughed. "Sounds like you might have a wedding in the family soon. Those take money."

"More money for moonshine too," Jaybird said.

Someone else countered, "One jug would've been a-plenty tonight."

"Not for me," Simon said.

"Yeah," Jaybird retorted, "we all know it's bad news when you come around. None left for any of the rest of us. Why don't you go start you up a still yourself, so you can have all you want?"

There was the sound of a brief scuffle, then Percy saying laconically, "Cut it out, Son. We're not having any fighting tonight. Give him the jug again; that'll calm him down."

Ma and Lilly looked at each other. "It's getting too dark to sew," Ma said, and folded up the pants in her lap. Then she asked abruptly, "Would you like to work for Mrs. Riley?"

"I don't know, Ma. I've never been in such a fine house. Folks say they have nine rooms, and that one of them is a bathroom. What do you figure I would have to do?"

"Clean and cook, I reckon. You could learn. You do good here at home." She cocked her head to see if she could hear Vince coming back from his 'possum hunt. "Tomorrow's Sunday. But why don't you go into town first thing on Monday and see if Mrs. Riley'll hire you? The extra cash would come in handy; you know we never have enough."

Lilly laughed to hide her nervousness at the idea of working for Mrs. Riley and asked, "Will you tell Pa?"

"I don't see why, 'less you get the job." Ma shrugged philosophically. "Those of us who don't drink have to take things into our own hands sometimes."

There was no church on Sand Lick the next morning, and going away was out of the question. Pa woke up late, angry at himself for having drunk so much. Usually he was very cautious, rarely taking more than a few swigs, and most of his friends were the same.

"Maybe it was the roof that came down in the mine on Friday that made us do it," he said dully, sitting at the table with his head in his hands. "Scared us all pretty bad."

Ma looked frightened. "What happened? You didn't tell us, Bernie."

"Why should I? No one was hurt. Too close, though."

Chapter four

On Monday morning Lilly started for town, just half an hour after Pa. She wore her second-best dress, a bright pink calico, dotted over with white daisies. It was a hot morning, with leaves hanging limply from the birches close to the creek, a hazy sky promising thunder, and thick dust covering the road.

Mrs. Keeton stood in front of her store, sweeping off the porch with a stiff broom. "Howdy," she called out. "Where are you off to so early?"

Lilly came closer so that she could step into the shade of the porch for a moment. "Going to the Rileys'."

"Got business there? I hear Mrs. Riley is poorly."

"I hear she wants a maid," Lilly answered.

"Heard that too." Elzinnie sent several twigs flying with her broom. "Reckon you know how to be a maid?"

"I can learn." Lilly did not admit that she had been too nervous to eat any breakfast that morning.

"Heard she's real picky about her furniture and stuff."

"I've heard that too."

"I would like to see that indoor bathroom. But I can't imagine using it. Folks say their front room is as big as our whole store. And they don't call it a front room, neither. They call it a parlor."

Lilly stepped back out into the sunshine. "I need to get going," she said.

"Stop in on your way home and tell me if she'd have you," Elzinnie urged. "It's been dull here this morning."

"I'll stop if I've got time."

Down the road further, she tripped across the bridge spanning Sand Lick, promising herself that she would stop there on her way back home. She passed the church, the decrepit school, and Brother Holbrook's house. Below that, the creek dropped off the mountainside in a series of rapids and tiny waterfalls. Just outside the town, it emptied into the Snake River, which ran parallel to the train tracks. As Lilly came out from the last stand of trees, she could see the whole town spread out before her on the flat and climbing the hill on the other side. The railroad station hulked off to her right, and the coal tipple towered on her left.

She crossed the Snake River on a smaller, newer bridge, and then crossed the snarl of railroad tracks on the other side, being careful not to touch the metal with her bare feet. The rails themselves would already be sizzling on this summer morning.

Straight ahead lay the mine, a huge dark hole gouged into the side of the mountain and surrounded by whitewashed concrete facing. Lilly would have to go between it and the mine office in order to get to Mr. Riley's house, high on the mountain above.

Her heart was pounding from the climb when she reached the house. It was tall, square, and starkly white in a town of gray dust. Large windows stared out from all sides, and a two-story porch ran along the front. Lilly quickly skirted away from that imposing front porch and went around the house until she found what she hoped was the kitchen door. Two wooden steps led up to a tiny stoop before it. But lace curtains covered the windows, even here, and Lilly could see nothing inside.

She knocked, and then stood listening to the thumping of her heart, and a train whistle far away below her. After several long minutes, she heard something else: the faint sound of footsteps inside.

Mrs. Riley opened the door. She had a narrow face; its paleness accented by dull, dark hair that fell from the top of her head and was gathered in a loose bun on her neck. Her eyelids drooped over gray eyes, and she wore an ankle-length dress of some dreamy, lilac-colored fabric. For one frantic moment Lilly wished she had worn her shoes that morning.

"Yes?" Mrs. Riley said quietly. Her accent betrayed immediately that she was not from Kentucky.

"I heard you wanted a maid."

"I do. Are you applying for a job?"

"Yes, ma'am."

"Come in, then. It's too hot to stand outside talking." She drew the door open wider, and Lilly stepped cautiously into the kitchen with its gleaming floor, white painted ceiling, and warm red counter tops. The coolness of the linoleum floor seeped into her calloused heels.

"Now tell me your name."

"Lilly Burchett, ma'am."

"How old are you?"

"Fourteen."

"Where do you live?"

"Up Sand Lick. Right at the fork where it divides."

"I've never been up that way." Mrs. Riley made a dismissive gesture, showing long white fingers and finely trimmed nails. "Have you ever done maid work before?"

"No, but I'm willing to learn. I know how to cook and clean."

"Yes," Mrs. Riley said briefly, "in a cabin, I suppose. You do live in a cabin, don't you?"

Lilly heard the touch of sarcasm in her voice, and she recoiled from it as from a whiplash. "Yes, ma'am."

"Never mind," Mrs. Riley went on. "I might be able to teach you." Her eyes dropped to Lilly's bare feet, and she studied them for a moment. "Do you own shoes?"

"Yes."

"Why don't you wear them?"

Lilly ducked her head and let her hair fall down in front of her shoulders. Her feet, so wide and brown, did look odd on Mrs. Riley's linoleum floor. "I-we-always go barefoot in the summer," she stammered. "Why wear out our shoes when it's warm enough to go without them?"

"Oh, I see."

Mrs. Riley kept examining her up and down, while Lilly grew more and more uncomfortable. "Do you have something for me to do?" she asked at last.

"I believe I'll try you out and see how you do. Start with the breakfast dishes. I was feeling too ill this morning to wash them." She sat down at the table and rested her head on one slender hand, her soft skirt sweeping the floor around her chair.

Lilly turned to the red counter and saw two spoons, two bowls, two glasses, and one little kettle, surrounded by a litter of bread crumbs. "Where shall I go to get water?" she asked. She couldn't see a bucket either, and hoped Mrs. Riley would remember that detail.

"Go? Oh, don't go anywhere. See that little silver knob by the sink? Turn that, and you'll have all the cold water you need. You can just scrub them with cold water this morning."

Cautiously Lilly turned the knob and a waterfall of pure water cascaded down into the sink. "Put the stopper in and let the sink fill with water," Mrs. Riley told her.

"The stopper?"

Mrs. Riley sighed. "All right then. I'll have to show you what I mean." She got up and walked over to the sink. Lilly caught herself staring at the easy, graceful way she moved, like water over the stones under the bridge.

Mrs. Riley stood close beside her, close enough that Lilly could have reached out and touched the dreamy soft dress. "Now watch. I don't want to have to show you this more than once." She slipped the plug into place herself and then said, "Reach under the sink and get out the soap."

Lilly opened the cupboard door and saw only a tub filled with pink crystals, a far cry from the white shapeless lumps they used for everything from washing dishes to washing their hair. "This?" she asked doubtfully.

"Don't you even know what soap is? No wonder. . ." Although she left the rest of her statement unsaid, Lilly winced under the whiplash again, knowing instinctively that she was thinking of dirty faces and dirty clothes on children like Patty and Sonny. But why should she care, she asked herself, what fine ladies like Mrs. Riley thought?

"Our soap doesn't look like that," she explained, keeping her voice even with an effort.

"Put in a scoop," Mrs. Riley went on composedly. "I suppose you can wash dishes?"

"Yes, ma'am." Lilly plunged her hands into the water and began swishing the dishrag around the glasses.

"Be sure you get them clean," Mrs. Riley said, the sharpness in her voice dulled only by weariness.

"Yes, ma'am."

When the dishes were done, Mrs. Riley told her to pull the plug and let the sink empty itself of water. "It runs into the creek," she explained. "I'll show you around the house next." She crossed the kitchen to a beautifully paneled door and opened it briefly, giving Lilly only a glimpse of a heavy table, long wine-red drapes, and a glimmering chandelier. "This is the dining room. Mr. Riley and I never use it unless we have important company. That isn't often—here." The soft lines around her mouth hardened into momentary bitterness.

"If I hire you," she said, "you will stay out of this room. We have much china and crystal, and I handle it myself."

"Yes, ma'am." Still awed by the patterned wallpaper and linoleum floors in the kitchen, Lilly had no desire to set foot in the dining room. She followed Mrs. Riley to the second door leading out of the kitchen. This opened into a hall with outside doors at either end.

"We don't use the front door much," Mrs. Riley said. "Across from the dining room is the parlor. That stays closed as well. We mostly live in the back of the house and upstairs." She stepped across the hall to the only open doorway. "This is my sitting room, where I spend most of my time."

It was a softly appointed room, with delicate feminine touches. It had a pale sofa and chairs, covered in pastel vines and flowers, a lush rug the color of early sunrise, a painting of a forgotten villa in an emerald countryside, and a fireplace with a screen in front of it. Creamy curtains softened the sunlight so that it lay gently across the flower-patterned walls, and the waxed wooden floor. The harmonious blending of color and light gave Lilly an unexpected thrill of pleasure. A single book and a bit of knitted lace with the needles still in it lay beside the sofa.

"And now let's go upstairs," Mrs. Riley went on. They climbed a torturously narrow and steep set of stairs. "There are wider stairs at the front of the house, but you won't be using those."

They came up out of the dark stairs right by a tiny, round window. Across a large open area on their right, another door stood open. Lilly's heart leaped suddenly into her throat. In that room were books—ten, twenty, maybe thirty times as many books as they had in the whole Sand Lick school. For a moment she forgot to follow Mrs. Riley out into the open area and almost missed her next words.

"Mr. Riley and I have our bedroom at the front of the house. The guest bedroom is there as well. The bathroom is here on the right. Have you ever seen an indoor bathroom?"

"No, ma'am."

"I thought not." Mrs. Riley showed Lilly how the toilet, sink, and bathtub worked. "We only have cold running water. For a hot bath, the water needs to be heated in the kitchen and carried up. That would be another of your jobs. And then there's the library, over there behind our bedroom."

She put her hand to her temple, as if she was too tired to think anymore, and her shoulders sagged. "I need to lie down again; I'm feeling so fatigued. Under the sink in the kitchen you'll find some rags. I want you to work at dusting the library. Be sure you don't misplace anything. Take the rug outside too, and beat it out. Do not disturb me; I must have some quiet. I'll come and check on you after a while."

Lilly couldn't believe that this, out of all the possible jobs in the house, should have been handed to her. She followed Mrs. Riley back downstairs, treading silently on each wooden step. The door to the sitting room clicked closed. Lilly pushed back her hair from her face and took a deep breath.

She found the rags without a problem, wetted one, and wrung it out until it was almost dry again. Then she fairly ran up the narrow stairs. At the library door, she stopped running and tiptoed in, reverently. Here too, heavy drapes kept out the heat and sunshine, leaving it dim and cool and smelling thickly of old leather and glued bindings.

She stopped just inside the door, staring. There were even more books than her first glimpse had shown her. Shelves full of them from floor to ceiling. More books than she had ever dared imagine. Mrs. Riley couldn't expect her to move all of them and dust the shelves. Although it would be fun to touch so many books, it would take her the rest of the day. She picked up several lying by themselves on a table and held them gently while she dusted the dark wood where they had been.

She decided to run her rag very carefully just along the edges of the shelves. This would give her a chance to read the titles too, she realized exultantly. After bundling up the rug and carrying it downstairs, she found a stool in a corner and started with the high shelves. She whispered each title as she came to it, caressing them, and stumbling over unfamiliar words. She found half a dozen books with the name Shakespeare on the back. "I didn't know he wrote so many," she murmured.

She worked her way around the room, doing the top shelves from the stool. Then she put the stool back in the corner and tackled the lower shelves, the window sill, the mantlepiece above the fireplace, and all the wooden parts on the reading chairs. She saved Mr. Riley's desk until last. It was the only thing in the room she didn't like. It looked and felt too much like him.

Out in the back yard, she found a sturdy stick and whacked vigorously at the rug several dozen times. It was hard, sweaty work to haul it back up the narrow stairs, but Lilly managed it. She repositioned it in the middle of the room, the chairs placed exactly where they had been before. She panted for a few moments from the exertion, then reached down and ran her hand lightly over the deep burgundy padding on one chair, feeling the strength of the fabric, and the firmness of the wood below. She wanted to sit in it, but repressed the desire.

Her eyes went back to the books. Would Mrs. Riley care very much if she would open a book, just one, and see what words it held? She stepped softly to the books on the table and touched the top one. It had a plain blue cover with silver words, "Letters of Adam Cuttler." The colors together looked like a midnight sky flooded with stars.

She was still standing there, with her hand on the book, when Mrs. Riley said, "Lilly."

She snatched her hand back swiftly, as if the whiplash she had felt before had come down cruelly across her fingers. Her face flushed a deep crimson.

But Mrs. Riley didn't sound angry. "Are you done in here?"

"Yes, ma'am."

She stepped into the room and moved gracefully around it, wiping her long fingers on the shelves, straightening a couple books, and finally sinking into one of the chairs. "Sit down," she said, motioning to another.

Lilly had wanted to sit there before. Now she perched reluctantly on the edge of the chair, pulling her pink skirt down to hide her bare feet. For a while she kept her eyes on her skirt. But when Mrs. Riley didn't say anything further, she finally looked up and found the lady studying her keenly. Lilly sensed a subtle difference in her gray eyes. Before she had thought they were cold as metal. Now they reminded her more of the sides of her own cabin in a drowsy afternoon's sunlight.

"You let me get my morning nap," Mrs. Riley said. "Thank you. And you did a good job with this room. I would like to hire you. Can you come every Monday, Wednesday, and Saturday?"

"I think so, ma'am."

"How does ten cents a day sound for wages?"

"It sounds fine, ma'am." Lilly felt a little breathless, unable to believe that she was sitting in a library, talking to a lady, and agreeing to a job.

Mrs. Riley's voice softened from its business-like tone. "What do you think of this library, Lilly?"

"I think it's grand." Lilly's eyes shone.

"You know how to read, don't you?"

"Oh, yes."

"Are you still in school?"

"No. Not since March."

Mrs. Riley looked around the library with a smile of satisfaction in her eyes. The smile moved to her mouth and transformed her face from long and plain to soft and enchanting. "I love this library," she murmured. "Books are my friends. They've kept me company for many long hours. I'm glad you like them too. And now—it's time for lunch."

Mrs. Riley sat at the kitchen table and directed Lilly step by step in preparing a simple lunch of cold sliced chicken on top of wheat bread, along with sugared strawberries and lemonade. Then she said, "Mr. Riley is coming home for lunch today. I think he would prefer that we have the kitchen to ourselves. Why don't you take a sandwich and some lemonade and eat outside."

"Yes, ma'am," Lilly said willingly. Popular mine gossip credited Mr. Riley with being the most hard-hearted, ruthless man this side of the Mississippi; and Lilly had no desire to sit in the same room with him, even for a meal. She had expected Mrs. Riley to be like him, and had thought she was, at first. But after the brief conversation in the library, she felt puzzled.

"And Lilly?"

Lilly turned toward her.

"There's no need for you to call me ma'am, every other time you open your mouth."

Lilly had no problem finding a shady spot a few paces from the kitchen door. The woods crept down nearly to the back of the house. Mr. Riley owned the only car in town, and within minutes he roared up the hill. He parked in front of the house, but went in the back; and Lilly saw him for a few seconds before he slammed the kitchen door.

She finished her sandwich and leaned back against the oak tree, drawing her knees up under her chin and letting her eyes fall half shut in order to dream. She could still feel the excitement of the library in her fingertips, an excitement much like the one she felt when she had a blank piece of paper and a pencil in her hand.

"Wonder what Jesse would think of that library," she whispered. But she didn't wonder, really. He would look thoughtful and say, "Why would one person need so many books? Why would they even want them? We don't have so many, and we make out fine."

Lilly was aware suddenly of a hunger that no chicken sandwich and lemonade could satisfy. She wanted to know what was between all the covers of those hundreds of books. She wanted to defy Mr. Ferguson's assertions that she would know nothing but raising children and hoeing corn. The longing rose up in her so strong that she could feel it in her throat. She swallowed hard.

Mrs. Riley had her clean the kitchen that afternoon, and then make supper. She wrote letters from the kitchen table, stopping often to tell Lilly what to do. "The potatoes and onions are in the shed in the back yard. Bring in a jar of kraut while you're out there too." Or, "Don't you know what sauté means, Lilly?" Or, "You don't seem familiar with keeping an even fire in the stove. What do you cook on at home?"

At last Lilly had a roast, surrounded by potatoes and covered with an onion sauce, simmering in the oven. She had adjusted the dampers according to Mrs. Riley's instructions and added a log of slow-burning hickory.

Mrs. Riley's eyes swept around the freshly cleaned kitchen. "I believe that's all for today. I'll be looking for you on Wednesday."

"I'll be here early," Lilly promised.

As she left the house and walked down the hill, heat seemed to come up and meet her in a wave. The thunderstorm had come and gone in the afternoon and left only steaminess behind it. She heard the whistle blow to signal the end of the work day at the mine and knew she would have to hurry to get ahead of the rush of men on their way home.

When she neared the bridge, she had the road to herself. She ran the last few yards and slid down the creek bank. While she stood with her hand on her chest, catching her breath, a horse clopped by over her head. "That was close," she muttered.

She stood on tiptoes and reached far back over the rocky bank to where she had hidden her treasures. They were still there, untouched and undamaged, although the paper had gone soft with dampness. She wanted to start the story of the miner's wife with twins, and she had her first sentences ready and memorized. She took the top sheet of paper and began writing. When she had filled half a page, she stood up with a regretful sigh. It was hard to know how much time to allow herself. Ma didn't know when to expect her back, but she would hear plenty if she got home after dark.

On up the road, Mrs. Keeton was again sweeping in front of her store. Men might gather to loiter later in the evening, but for now most of them had gone home to their suppers. "Come on up," she called. "I've been waiting for you. You've took so long, I thought I missed you. Did she hire you?"

"Yes, she did."

"To do what?"

"Cook and clean, I think. She didn't tell me everything I would need to do."

"Every day?"

"No. Monday's and Wednesday's and Saturday's."

"Is the house as fine as everyone says it is?"

"It's fine all right."

"Did you see the bathroom?"

"Yes."

Elzinnie stopped and rubbed one knotted hand over the other. "Why can't she take care of her own house, do you reckon?"

"I don't know. She looked tired and tuckered out, but I don't know what she's sick with."

Elzinnie rubbed her hands together again, lingeringly, a wondering look in her eyes. "Must be nice to hire a maid to do your work when you're tuckered out. Well, I expect your ma's waiting for you for supper. I think Jesse's there too. I saw him ride past a spell ago."

Must have been him that rode over the bridge, Lilly thought. What would he think if he knew that she had been right under his feet? And what if he knew why?

He was waiting in the yard, lounging against one of the apple trees. For some reason, the sight of him irritated her. She was uncommonly tired, and she wanted nothing more than to go off by herself and think. Perhaps it had been the change from her normal world to a new one and now back again. She noticed like never before how small the cabin was, and the way it seemed to grow like a gray toadstool from the earth around it. She hardly even gave Jesse a greeting.

"I was down to the mill," he told her. "Thought I'd stop by on the way back home." He looked at her appraisingly. "Heard you were in town yourself."

"I suppose Ma told you why?"

"She did. Have you got the job?"

"Yes, I do."

Maybelle hollered from the doorway, "Supper, Lilly. And Ma says you can bring your beau in with you."

Lilly was too tired to care about Maybelle's use of the word, or about the pleasured way Jesse smiled when he heard it. "Want to eat with us?" she queried simply.

"I'd be glad to."

Ma was as full of questions as Mrs. Keeton, and instead of eating first and talking later, she started right away. "Did she hire you on the spot?"

"No, Ma. She wanted me to do some work first."

"What work?" Vince drawled, not taking his attention from the corn-bread and beans on his plate.

"I washed the breakfast dishes and cleaned the library."

"What's a library?" Bobby wondered.

"A room with a lot of books." Lilly shot a sideways look at Jesse.

"Nothing else?" he asked.

"Some chairs and a table. And Mr. Riley's desk. It's a room for reading."

"So that's how the mister spends his evenings," Pa spat. "Reading! Worth-less trash!"

"I think Mrs. Riley spends more time there than he does," Lilly countered cautiously.

Vince kicked Lilly under the table. "Don't mess with him," he half-whis-pered, half-mouthed. "He's mad that he didn't know you were going."

The normal meal-time silence descended after that, as everyone focused on filling their stomachs. Ma had more questions while they were doing dishes, and she seemed proud that her daughter had landed this job. "Pa will get used to the idea," she said.

"Why doesn't he like it?"

"He doesn't trust Mr. Riley. He'd rather have you at home."

"Mrs. Riley is different from Mr. Riley."

"Does she look down on us?" Ma asked sharply. "Does she make you feel cheap?"

"She. . . did, a little. I think I'll wear my shoes next time I go."

"No, you won't."

"Why not?

"You have nothing to be ashamed of, going barefoot."

"I think she would rather—"

"I'm glad you got the job," Ma interrupted her, "but you'll get this straight before you go again. You are a woman who can hold her head up, without being like Mrs. Riley. Our family owns our land, we're not in debt to anyone, and we've never been in trouble with the law. You don't have to follow Mrs. Riley's ways to feel right good about being a woman."

She and Jesse only walked as far as the top of the furthest cornfield that evening. They sat down within sight of the sandstone slabs that marked five graves, two of Mammaw's infants, two of Ma's infants, and one uncle killed in the war. And they talked at length about Mrs. Riley's house. The longer Jesse stayed, the more Lilly relaxed, and the more she liked having him there. She told him everything, except her feelings in the library, and the comment Mrs. Riley had made about books being her friends.

Jesse was easy to talk to, she reflected, as she watched him ride off amid the lightning bugs. His thoughts came slowly to the surface, but he made a comfortable place in the silence for her own thoughts. She had thrilled to the beauty of the Riley house, but perhaps she was only a homespun hill girl after all. She felt more rested after an hour in Jesse's company than after a day with Mrs. Riley.

Chapter five

That feeling of strangeness in working for Mrs. Riley dimmed in the next few weeks. Lilly grew accustomed to turning a knob for water, dragging heavy rugs up and down stairs, and cooking multitudes of things beyond cornbread, beans, and fried potatoes. But her favorite job was still dusting the library. Before long, Mrs. Riley took to coming and sitting down in the same room. Sometimes she would talk, sometimes she would read quietly, and sometimes she would simply watch Lilly handling the books and arranging them carefully.

One day she asked casually, "Would you like me to read to you while you work?"

"Oh, yes."

Mrs. Riley selected a book from a shelf close to her chair and crossed her legs. Her first words made magic in the library, and Lilly hardly knew what she did from that point on. Mrs. Riley read with more expression than Miss Sparks, with more understanding and empathy than Mr. Ferguson. The words rolled like liquid silver beads from her tongue, strung out upon a silk cord, filling the room with their richness.

When Lilly had finished dusting, she stood raptly just behind Mrs. Riley, listening with her heart even more than with her ears.

Finally Mrs. Riley laid the book down on her knee. "Finished, are you?"

"Yes. I guess you'd better stop reading so I can get back to work."

"Come around in front of me where I can see you." Mrs. Riley laughed softly. "I've never had a listener like you. Haven't you heard stories before, Lilly?"

"Not many." Lilly had forgotten who she was and where she was. But the spell was broken, and she knew again now. She was simply Lilly Burchett, still barefoot, and still wearing pink calico.

"Sit down," Mrs. Riley said shortly. "It's obvious you love them. I think you should hear another. We have time." She pointed her book to the chair beside her.

"Please. . ." Lilly shifted her weight from one foot to another. "I'm not used to sitting on such fine chairs. I think I would enjoy the story more if I could just sit on the floor."

"All right. Sit on the floor. I don't care."

Lilly sat down beside Mrs. Riley's chair, crossing her legs under her. Almost unawares, she inched closer to the chair, absently playing with the ends of her hair, closing her eyes so that she could truly slip from the library into the castles and moors of England.

Much too soon, Mrs. Riley stopped reading. Silence, golden with the story just told, descended in the library. Lilly kept her eyes shut, trying to delay the moment of coming back to Kentucky. While she sat still, a hand came down lightly on her hair, lifting and stroking the long brown strands with slender fingers.

A shiver shot through Lilly. She opened her eyes slowly. With Mrs. Riley's hand on her hair, she didn't feel like a fourteen-year-old woman who might be married within six months. She felt like a little girl.

She shook herself and stood up, saying with unaccustomed stiffness. "Thanks for the stories, Mrs. Riley."

"You're welcome, Lilly. You're a good listener."

Lilly looked at her to ask what she should do next and was shocked to see tears in Mrs. Riley's gray eyes. She glanced away quickly, uncomfortable.

"Time to make supper," Mrs. Riley said. "Why don't you go down and start peeling potatoes. I'll come soon and tell you what else I want you to do."

Lilly went blindly down the back steps and mechanically began peeling potatoes. What was wrong with Mrs. Riley? For that matter, what was wrong with herself? Why this longing and yearning so tangible that it made a lump in her throat?

The readings continued after that, and increased in frequency. After a while, Mrs. Riley would sometimes tell Lilly, "You've worked hard this morning, and I don't have much more work for you this afternoon. I laid a book out on the table in the library. Go up and read while I lie down for a nap. All you have to do until I get up is answer the door if someone comes."

Week after week slipped away in this fashion. Besides the reading, Lilly often stole ten minutes at a time to write under the bridge. When she finished the story about the miner's wife, she decided that she now knew enough about fine ladies, fine houses, and fine manners to disregard Mr. Ferguson's instructions. So she started a story of a princess. Before that one reached completion, a sudden inspiration for a children's story came to her.

Much of July had crept by, and she knew that Mr. Ferguson would soon be back. With a flushed feeling of happiness in knowing that she would please him, she began writing this one on a clean sheet of paper. She wrote smaller and smaller, since her precious hoard of paper had dwindled to nearly nothing.

Of course she kept all this secret, never breathing a word of it to Jesse, Pa or Ma, Vince or Maybelle. She only finished each story, wrote "Lilly Burchett, Sand Lick, Kentucky" at the end, and tied them in a roll with string.

Ma noticed a difference in her that summer, but attributed it to Jesse. "Not wedding plans in the air, are there?" she asked more than once, slyly.

"No, Ma," Lilly always said simply, and fell to wondering how soon Jesse might ask her if she gave him the right kind of encouragement.

The summer had started out dry, and then turned unusually wet. The cornfields closest to the creeks stopped growing at knee-high and turned a sick yellow. Sometimes water stood between the rows. The corn made a feeble attempt to tassel and grow ears, and then gave up. The only harvest would come from the high fields on the sides of the ridges.

Jesse looked discouraged whenever he talked about their farm. Most of their fields lay low, on coveted creek banks. This year that boded ill. "We just won't have much of a crop a'tall," he would say darkly, and give her a look that told her plainly his desire to marry after harvest. But he never spoke it, and Lilly knew he was afraid to. She felt sorry for him, but clumsy when she tried to comfort him. For she was relieved on her own account. Mr. Ferguson wouldn't come back and find that he had prophesied truly.

For Beulah it was different. She met Lilly by chance at the store one day and took her by the arm. "Let me walk up towards your place a ways," she whispered confidentially. "I want to talk."

She started abruptly the minute they left the porch. "Are you and Jesse getting married this fall?"

"No."

"Wilson and me are."

"When?" This wasn't really a surprise.

"October. November at the latest." Beulah lifted one eyebrow, saucily. "*We* don't have to wait on a good corn crop. Wilson says the future for Kentucky is in the mines."

"You trying to make me jealous? You can have your Wilson and get married this fall. I don't care."

"I'd take my Wilson over your Jesse."

"I wouldn't."

"Why not?"

"Wilson's got a temper." She could have added that he was weak-spined, lazier than Jesse, and a mite loose with his money.

"Jesse is a mule," Beulah retorted. "No dash."

The words stung slightly. "He's dependable," she said. "But you needn't call him mine. We've not promised."

"Everyone knows you will, sooner or later."

"Maybe. Maybe not." The moment Lilly had said this, she wanted to bite her tongue. Beulah was quite capable of having fun with this statement. It could go anywhere. It might get back to Jesse, and he didn't deserve to be hurt like that. She fumbled at fixing it up. "I mean, I like him a lot. But a body never knows what might happen."

Beulah laughed at her. "I know what you're doing. You're getting high-toned notions from working for that there Mrs. Riley."

"I like Jesse," Lilly repeated weakly. "Forget what I said. I didn't mean it the way it sounded."

"I might forget it and I might not." Beulah grinned wickedly.

After supper that evening, Lilly joined the rest of her family on the porch. Uncle Harris and his family had come from up the holler, and she should have enjoyed herself. But she felt unaccountably restless; more so when

Vince said, "Haven't seen Jesse around in a while. Where is he?"

"Too discouraged to come courting," Uncle Harris suggested. "His farm is worst of anyone's."

"Jesse'll take it like a man," Ma predicted.

At last Lilly excused herself and climbed to the point of the ridge where the five gravestones were. From there she could clearly see the fork in Sand Lick and hear its heavy surging, turbid with all the water that had poured into it in the last weeks. Above the sound of water came the hum of mosquitoes, the skirl of crickets, and the intermittent grumbling of frogs. The high whinnying sound of a screech owl trembled through the air.

Lilly sat there, still, until Uncle Harris's had gone home. By then rain had begun to fall again gently. She dashed for the house, but not in time to beat the downpour. Shivering in her wet dress, she went inside.

Pa was abed, snoring. "That you, Lilly?" Ma whispered.

"Yes."

"Is it raining?"

"Yes."

"Be sure the door is tight shut."

Up in the loft, Lilly climbed shivering into bed beside Patty. It seemed only moments later that Ma was calling frantically from the foot of the stairs. "Lilly! Vince! Get the others awake and come down right away."

"What's wrong, Ma?"

Her voice rose another pitch. "Get on down here!"

The loft was completely black. Lilly shook Patty and reached across her to grab Maybelle's shoulder. "What's going on?" Maybelle complained.

"I don't know. But we have to go."

None of the six took time to dress. They simply tumbled out of the loft the way they were, in night shirts and dresses. Gradually Lilly became aware of a thunderous roar behind all the noise of creaking stairs and Sonny's crying. "What is it, Ma?" she asked again.

"Sand Lick is flooding," Ma said tightly. "Upper and Lower."

Usually the slight knoll where their house stood protected them from floods, even at the merging of the two branches. Lilly didn't fully understand the seriousness of the situation until T.J. screamed, "There's water on the floor."

"Out on the porch, children." Ma swatted at them. "Go on. Pa's there. Follow him."

In the light of Pa's swinging lantern, Lilly saw muddy water everywhere. He grabbed up Patty. "Stay close behind me," he shouted. "We're gonna make a run for it through the cornfield."

Lilly grabbed Maybelle's hand on one side and T.J.'s on the other. Water lapped at her ankles when she leaped from the porch, and in the next step it was above her ankles. She splashed wildly, trying to follow Pa's bobbing lantern. He was heading straight for the ridge, disregarding rows of corn and thick mounds of squash. They were strung out in a line behind him now. Then T.J. fell in the mud and water.

Lilly bent down. "Heave him on my back, Maybelle. Hang on, T.J. I can't hang onto you."

T.J. was crying. He wrapped his arms around Lilly's shoulders, and his legs around her stomach in a death grip. "Run, Maybelle. Run!" Pa's lantern was away out ahead of them, and the water was rising at a tremendous rate, soaking the hems of their nightdresses. They ran, and slipped, and ran again, through water, and then through heavy, slimy mud. They crossed the highest cornfield, and the ground rose almost vertically to the ridge. Lilly grabbed for handholds and got only rain-soaked soil that came away from the hillside in bunches. She slid down a few inches and tasted grit in her mouth.

"Here, Lilly," came Vince's voice out of the darkness just above her. "I've got a good grip on a tree. Grab my hand."

She reached up blindly and felt his hand coming down. "You got T.J.?" he asked.

"He's on my back."

Vince hauled her up and then reached for Maybelle. Another five minutes and they were all together again, clustered around Pa and the lantern. Ma counted twice to make certain they were all there.

"What happened, Pa?" Vince asked. "How did it come up so sudden-like?"

"It's been raining off and on for weeks." Pa wiped his wet arm across his wet face in a useless gesture. "Creeks are already running full, and the ground's got all the water it can hold. And then tonight it begun to pour. Fact is, it's still pouring."

It was, though Lilly had hardly noticed.

"All that water ain't got nowhere to go. Made a bad flood fast."

Lilly could hear but not see the vicious thundering of water out of control below her on both sides. And she could well imagine it ripping through their cabin, tearing at the furniture and the log walls. Was the old structure strong enough to stand that?

"I'm cold," T.J. whimpered on Lilly's back.

"Have patience," Lilly soothed, trying to still her own shivering. "We can't go home."

"Where will we go?" Bobby cried. "I'm cold too."

Pa looked at Ma. "Think we can find old Rob's cabin in the dark?"

"Hester Sue is closer."

"We can't get to her place from the ridge top."

"Then we've got no choice but old Rob's."

Shriveled Rob Ferguson lived with his wife Sally, still higher above them. Everyone called him old Rob, and folks hardly saw him unless they were crossing into the next valley. Some said that old Rob had committed a crime in his younger days and was hiding out from the law. No one doubted that he made moonshine in an isolated cove, and some of the men knew it for certain.

The ordinary path to his cabin went up Lower Sand Lick, cut up to the ridge, and followed it for half a mile. The ordinary path was out of the question now. Pa thought for a moment, muttering to himself and turning this way and that. "I think I can find it," he announced. "Let's go."

A weary half hour later they came out in the tiny clearing that surrounded old Rob's cabin, all of them muddy, soaked to the skin, and well-scratched by briars.

"Hallo, Rob," Pa shouted, and a faint echo "Rob" circled back through the wetness.

After several minutes, during which they crowded onto the tiny porch and huddled close to the door, a light appeared inside the window. "Who's there?" came Rob's thin high voice.

"Bernie Burchett and his family."

Rob opened the door and held up the lantern to see them all. He was bent nearly double and peered up at them by crooking his neck backwards. "Why this coming in the middle of the night, neighbor? Something wrong?"

"Flood down in the valley," Pa answered briefly.

"Bad?"

"Worst I've seen."

"In your house?"

"We ran for our lives."

"Never heard it raining," old Rob said. And then he seemed to notice for the first time just what condition his visitors had arrived in. "Sally, I say, these folks is cold. Let's start up a fire." He swung his lantern up toward Pa and looked him over again. "I've had visitors in the night before. I'm just mighty thankful you didn't come with guns." He chuckled soundlessly.

His wife stood beside the bed at the other side of the room, blinking owlishly at them. Now she trotted briskly forward and began laying sticks across the still warm coals from the supper fire. Her night robe swished around her ankles, and her nightcap was twisted rakishly over her gray hair.

The Burchett family stood dripping on the cabin floor, in front of the fire, turning themselves about to get the heat on all sides. T.J. had cried most of the way up the mountain, and Lilly hadn't dared to put him down until they were inside Rob's cabin. Now as she bent to let him slide off, her muscles screamed in protest.

"We'll just bed down here on the floor," Pa said gruffly. "You can go back to sleep. We hated to bother you folks, but we didn't know where else to go."

Old Rob poked the fire and added another log. "Settle in. You're welcome to the floor space."

Lilly had never tried sleeping in a one-room cabin with her whole family and two old folks besides. She had nothing but her arms for a pillow and nothing but her wet clothes for blankets. It took only a few minutes until Pa was snoring. T.J. and Sonny cuddled up close to each other, and Ma lay down protectively near them. Lilly squirmed into an out-of-sight corner behind the table, with Maybelle and Patty on either side of her.

When morning came it showed how truly deplorable they all looked. Lilly woke up when old Sally went to use the outhouse. The pale beginning of light crept in through the two windows and showed bodies sprawled every which way across the floor. Lilly's night dress had dried hard while she slept, but the brown mud stains remained. Patty had bits of sticks and pine needles in her hair, and Maybelle had ripped her night dress right down the back.

And none of them had clothing to change into. She cringed at the thought of walking around in her nightdress, made simply by cutting and hemming holes in a hundred-pound flour sack.

For breakfast Sally made soda biscuits while Ma browned bacon and fried eggs. Rob brought in a dish of honey and set it in the middle of the table to eat with the biscuits.

"Guess the first thing to do is go and see if the house is still standing," Pa said. He dragged a finger across one red-rimmed eye.

"I'll go with you," Vince said immediately.

Ma turned from the fire, her cheeks flushed pink. "Bring back clothes for all of us."

"If there's a cabin," Pa answered flatly. "We'll go right after breakfast and come back as soon as we can."

The morning dragged. Eventually the sun came out and burned away the rain clouds. A fresh wind frolicked in the pines, as if in apology for last night's damage. Pa and Vince returned after several hours, muddy to their knees and disheveled.

No one dared to ask, but Pa answered quickly anyway. "The house is still standing." He threw a haphazardly wrapped bundle of clothes toward Ma, while holding one hand at shoulder level. "But the water was this high inside it. I couldn't find any of your dresses. Can you wear Lilly's?"

Ma took the pink calico, since it was the bigger of the two, and stuffed herself into it without a word. Lilly put on her smaller everyday homespun.

"Let's go," Pa said gruffly. "We've got a mess to clean up at home."

They tramped back the way they had come, straight down the side of the ridge. When they emerged from the trees, they could see at once how high the water had risen, for it had left a tide of mud and desolation half way up the slope. Away below them, the creek was mostly in its banks again, but still running swollen and brown.

Ma made it to the door of the cabin first. A low moan escaped her. Lilly looked over her shoulder. Filthy oozing mud lay several inches deep over the floor, with the beds and chairs all washed up against the front wall, and everything, including the books, swept cleanly from the fireboard. In the eating room, the long table had been turned on its side, and in the kitchen, pots and pans and bowls were piled in jumbled heaps. The bag of cornmeal had turned over, and the precious golden meal mixed with dirt and a sock from someone else's cabin.

Ma sagged for only a moment, hanging onto the doorway for support. Then she pulled herself together. "Thank God the house didn't go," she said resolutely. "We can clean up mud."

And so she, Lilly, and the younger ones began immediately, while Pa and Vince went to check on their neighbors. Lilly scooped at the deepest areas in the front room with the water bucket while Ma found a shovel and started at one side. "All you little ones get in and scoop it together with your hands to make it easier for Lilly," she ordered.

"I'll keep Sonny happy," Maybelle offered.

"No. Tie him on Lilly's back and get to work."

Maybelle found a long strip of cloth, dirty only on one end, and hefted the chunky Sonny onto Lilly's back. Lilly knotted the fabric securely around her waist. Already trickles of sweat ran down her neck and face, and Sonny's unhappy wiggling only added to her discomfort. She would fill the bucket with mud, send one of the children to empty it while she straightened her back, and then bend to fill it again.

After a while she decided to use a hoe to scrape it together, and sent Bobby out to see if one might still be standing against the back of the cabin. He came back much later, the hoe he held smeared from top to bottom with mud. "It was down close to the creek," he reported. "I didn't see the others anywhere."

Lilly tried to wipe off some of the mud, looked down at her dress, and realized it didn't matter anymore how much muddier she got. "All right," she directed, "you can take turns holding the bucket, and I'll scoop the mud into it with the hoe." By this time Sonny had fallen asleep, and he hung limply on her back. Ma worked in a grim silence, shoveling fast.

Pa appeared suddenly in the doorway. "Borrowed a shovel," he said briefly, and got to work beside Ma.

"Are Mammaw and Pappaw fine?"

"Yeah. They're cleaning up too," Pa answered while throwing mud out the window. "I left Vince up there to help them."

"And the others?"

Pa talked in rhythm with the moving of his shovel. "Clara's best off. They lived far enough back. No water in their house. Harris's have mud. Like this. Goldie and Sandy's house went."

"Did they save anything?"

"No."

"They'll come here tonight, won't they?"

"I told them they should."

"What about down the other way?"

"Lots of houses gone. It got worse after the forks."

"What about the Keeton's? Is the store okay?"

"Still standing. But they'll be hard put to restock. There's not much good left, folks are saying."

"Did Okla and Elzinnie get out? Okla can't walk."

"One of their neighbors hauled him up the ridge on his back. They're staying up there for now."

"And the Greer's?"

"Silas wanted to make a run for it, but Silva wouldn't let him. Didn't think he could. They climbed up into their loft."

"Their house is so small. I'd think it'd be gone."

"The water took it around half way and left it sit again. That's all."

"Anybody killed?"

"Only our preacher, that they know of yet."

"Brother Holbrook?"

"Who else?"

"Why didn't he get out?"

Pa stopped to catch his breath. "He lives by himself. You know he's nigh deaf. His neighbors hollered and tried to rouse him, but he must not've heard. They found his body wedged between some old logs. It's not fit to be viewed. The funeral's going to be tomorrow."

"Can we cross the creek all right?"

"We'll do it someway. The bridge is gone, but Jaybird said he'd fell a tree across to make do for now."

Lilly felt a sudden numbness in her arms, and a weakness in her knees.

"The bridge?" she repeated. "What bridge?"

"The high bridge over Sand Lick. It was a hundred years old. I'm surprised it didn't go before this."

He said it calmly, because to him the bridge meant nothing. To Lilly it meant private flights of fancy, a hidden life of stories that belonged only to her. She was suddenly aware of how tired she was, how sweaty and dirty, how discouraged.

Goldie, Sandy, and their five children arrived in time for supper. No one talked. They ate boiled potatoes and green beans with a sense of weary urgency and went back to scooping mud, not quitting until darkness had plastered itself starless across the hills.

Then while the others washed up and prepared to all bed down in the loft, Lilly slipped away. She was still wearing her mud-streaked dress and glad of it as she slipped and slid down the trail. She went as far as where the bridge had stood. The creek still tore through its banks, maddened by the flood of the night before. On its white froth, it carried broken tree branches and clumps of weeds. Several of the old pilings, snapped off jaggedly, poked above the surface. But the bridge was gone.

Lilly felt a wild desire to go and search for her stories, the pencil stubs still remaining, and the sketchy attempt at a diary. Then she laughed bitterly at her own folly. Of course they were gone too, never to be seen again.

A chill had descended with the evening, and she hugged her arms around herself, absently rubbing at her sore muscles. They would build a new bridge; she had heard Pa and Jaybird and Dan discussing it already. And Jaybird's log lay across the creek to serve until they had time to make the real one. But no new structure with yellow lumber could take the place of the old one for Lilly.

She stood there a long time, unmindful of the night, unmindful of the whippoorwills that called plaintively, unmindful of the fact that Ma would be wondering where she was. She remembered that the next day was Saturday, and wondered if she should try to let Mrs. Riley know she couldn't come. Maybe she should tell her she wouldn't come again, ever. The books in Mrs. Riley's house and the stories under the bridge had gone together in such a way that she couldn't think of one without thinking of the other. Since she had lost one, it seemed that she should also lose the other.

At length she heard a man approaching from across the creek and turned to go.

"Hey, Lilly," he called softly, and she realized it was Jesse. "Going somewhere?"

"No."

He came confidently across the log toward her. "Can I walk you back to your cabin?"

She only nodded.

He looked down at her gently and took her hand. She did not meet his gaze. As they walked back up the hill, he told her quietly that the water had only come to their front door, but that the corn fields were totally ruined now. He asked her if she would be going to Brother Holbrook's funeral the next day, and when she said she would, he offered to let Mrs. Riley know about her absence.

He said no tender words, but Lilly could feel them just below the surface. She let them comfort her. Had he spoken, proposed to her then, she would have told him yes. For it seemed that the loss of the bridge had cast her lot with the mountain farms, and the men who worked them, even if they had never heard of Shakespeare.

Part 2

Chapter six

It wasn't until the following Wednesday that Lilly saw Mrs. Riley again. By then good men up and down Sand Lick had laid Brother Holbrook to rest in the cemetery. The women had cried and hugged each other, feeling without saying it, how thankful they were that all their families remained intact.

The walls in the Burchett cabin had been scrubbed, the bedding washed again and again, and the chairs and cooking utensils returned to their proper places. Pa and Ma now slept in one of the front room beds, and Uncle Sandy and Aunt Goldie in the other. Cousins filled all four beds in the loft.

School started as soon as the creek dropped low enough for children to cross it. On Wednesday morning Lilly walked down with a group of them on her way to town. She now wore her best dress, a navy with white trim, because the mud stains hadn't come out of her pink one. She felt odd and out of place and much older than the children she walked with. In the thin morning shadow of some roadside trees, she stopped just long enough for her gaze to run over the sagging schoolhouse and the frolicking students. They were all barefoot, some of them wearing tattered shirts and dresses, their faces and arms and legs brown as acorns. Some of them didn't want to be there, but some of them loved books as she had. Nostalgia rushed over her, and she went on in a hurry.

Quietly she let herself in the kitchen door at the Riley house and drew water for washing up the few breakfast dishes. She had nearly finished when Mrs. Riley appeared. She glided in noiselessly and stood at Lilly's elbow before Lilly was aware of her.

"It's good to see you again, Lilly," she murmured, smoothing a hand across a pale forehead. "I've been feeling worse the last couple days. I think it's the heat."

"I'm sorry, Mrs. Riley."

Mrs. Riley smiled briefly. "And here I am complaining about myself when I should be asking after you and your family. The flood was bad up your way, I hear."

"Yes, it was, ma'am. But our house is still standing. We're thankful."

"Was the water in your house?"

"Yes, ma'am."

"You wouldn't have needed to come today. I would understand."

"No, ma'am. That's all right. We've mostly cleaned up already." Lilly finished wiping the counter, wrung out her dishcloth and laid it precisely on the edge of the sink. She found herself avoiding Mrs. Riley's eyes. Any easiness and camaraderie in their relationship had washed away with the bridge. Mrs. Riley's books and library were part of the old life. Lilly had grown suddenly into a new life these last few days—a life that included hard things like floods and good men like Jesse, but no easy opulence like what was found here, and no unrealistic dreams.

A thread of silence wove its way between the two. Mrs. Riley made no immediate move to break it as she studied Lilly in bewilderment. What mysterious thing had the flood done to her sensitive maid? She would have liked to probe, but knew Lilly would not let her. So at last she said simply, "There's laundry to do. I didn't feel well enough to do it on Monday. You can start the cleaning too. But don't work too hard. When you dust the library, take a few minutes to sit down and read the book I have lying out for you."

"Thank you, ma'am. But I've missed two days. I'm sure there must be a heap of work."

"Not so much that you can't read for a bit."

"I think I'd rather just work today." *Keep me busy* . . .

"Well, as you like, of course," Mrs. Riley said with a sudden sharpness. "I wasn't expecting this. What has gotten into you, girl?"

Lilly flushed painfully. Mrs. Riley hadn't hurt her with this kind of sarcasm since the first day when she made snide remarks about barefoot girls and log cabins. She bit her tongue and said nothing. She couldn't explain that the thought of sitting down with a book was torture since she knew she could no longer write her own stories. She couldn't tell Mrs. Riley that she kept herself from thinking about such things to hold off the sharpness of the loss, and that reading would only make her more vulnerable. She hardly understood this herself. So she only said, quite humbly, "I'm sorry. I'll start with the laundry right away."

When she had washed everything and hung it out to dry, she found Mrs. Riley in her sitting room. She was gazing out the window with a faraway look on her face, her hands dropped onto an unfinished piece of lace. "Shall I start the cleaning or make lunch?" Lilly asked quietly.

Mrs. Riley roused herself with a sigh. "I'm not hungry yet, and Mr. Riley won't be home today. Why don't you start cleaning here." She laid aside the lace and took a book from the table near her, in a gesture by now so familiar that it stabbed Lilly. "How about a story while you work?"

"Yes, if you'd like," Lilly answered, keeping her voice low and her back turned.

"I'm not doing it for my own pleasure. If you don't want me to, I won't."

"Just do—whatever you want, ma'am." Lilly moved from one piece of furniture to another, unconsciously adopting Mrs. Riley's grace, as she always did in her presence.

Mrs. Riley opened the book, turned a few pages, and sat silently with it in her lap. Lilly had expected her to go ahead with the reading, and she stole a cautious look in her direction.

Mrs. Riley gave her a faint, puzzled smile. "You do good work," she said suddenly. "Have I ever thanked you?"

After a few more minutes, she read one short story, perhaps with a bit less enthusiasm than usual. Or perhaps the difference was only in Lilly.

Chapter seven

A lean winter lay ahead for the people who lived along Sand Lick and up other nearby hollers. Even the ones who worked in the mines depended heavily on fields and gardens for food. Ma, Lilly, and Vince salvaged all the corn they could from the upper fields and dug through layers of mud to find unharmed potatoes. "We'll be sparing of the corn," Ma said, "for there's others need it just as bad as we do. We can eat lots of fried taters this winter."

Bobby, Maybelle, and T.J. were the Burchett scholars from their house, along with the cousins Jeremiah, Frances, and Polly. Reports came home from school about Mr. Ferguson—that his hair was as red as ever, and his temper as sharp. On the second day of school, he had reportedly rapped a second grader once on the head because she said she had forgotten how to read.

A month into the school year, Maybelle came home with a note for Lilly, meticulously folded into fourths. "Mr. Ferguson said for me to give you this." She winked slyly.

Ma slid the cornbread into the nest of ashes she had prepared for it and straightened up with her hands on her hips. "That Mr. Ferguson ain't courting you, is he?"

"Oh, no, Ma."

"Then why's he sending you notes?"

"I think it's got to do with something we talked about last spring. In school."

Ma looked at her suspiciously. "What's so important that he's got to bring it up again six months later?"

"Ma, I haven't even read the note yet."

"Then read it now."

Lilly hesitated, but saw no way out. She unfolded the plain, unlined paper, shielding it from Maybelle. Ma couldn't read anyway.

The note said briefly, "Guess you were serious about not coming back to school. Gossip tells me that you're not married—yet. I also hear you're working for Mrs. Riley. Stop in at the schoolhouse on your way to or from. I want to know what happened to the children's story."

"What is it?" Ma asked.

"He asked me to do something for him when he left. He's wondering if I got it done."

"Do something for him? And you say he's not courting you?"

"No, Ma," Lilly answered desperately. "It's nothing personal. It's about school."

Maybelle sat at the table, idly swinging her leg back and forth and enjoying the whole altercation. "Yeah, Ma, he was always talking to Lilly after school last spring."

Ma whirled from Lilly to Maybelle. "And why didn't you tell us anything of this then?"

Maybelle shrugged. "I didn't know it was important."

"I don't trust that red-headed school teacher. He'd pretend he's talking about lessons and take Lilly right out from under our noses. Jesse courts in a normal, above-board fashion. I like—"

"Listen, Ma," Lilly pleaded. "This was related to school. Honest. And besides, I didn't do what he wanted me to." She didn't add that she had been half done, and only the flood had kept her from finishing.

Lilly kept the note in her pocket and promised herself that she would stop in after work the next day.

In the morning Mrs. Riley greeted her with flushed cheeks and a sparkle in her eyes. "We're getting company. A dear friend of mine, someone I haven't seen for years. They're coming all the way from Louisville." She opened the doors and windows of the dining room and parlor and had Lilly sweep and dust, and re-sweep and re-dust. She was no longer a slowly-moving, languid lady; but one touched with a bit of frenzy, half of delight, half of dread. "We get so few visitors," she said. "I fear I've forgotten how to be a proper hostess. And Amy is so sophisticated. What *will* she think of my house?"

Lilly, looking just then into a glass-fronted cabinet holding silver and china and crystal, was speechless. Were there really people in the world who would think this mansion humble?

When she reached the schoolhouse that evening, and walked in unannounced, she was more tired than usual. She sagged into a desk.

Mr. Ferguson looked up at her, his green eyes cordial under his mop of hair. "Got my note?"

"Yes, sir."

"Did you bring the story with you?"

"I don't got one."

"You didn't forget." He said it as though he knew.

"No." Lilly traced the initials carved into the wooden desk top. J.W. Jesse Wright, perhaps? Or maybe his brother Jim. "I started it, but I lost it."

"How could you lose it? Why didn't you start again? You had all the paper I gave you."

"I lost that too. Most of it was full anyhow."

"So you did write this summer."

"Yes."

"How could you lose it?"

"You know the flood. . ." She wouldn't tell him any more than that. He could think what he pleased.

"I know about the flood. So it's all gone?"

"Yes, sir."

"If I give you more paper, will you write it again?"

"No, I can't." In spite of her words, in spite of her decision that her stories were back in her girlhood, a wild hope flared inside her for a moment.

"Why not?"

"I'm too busy." It was a pale excuse, since she really was no busier than she had been all summer when she regularly stole ten-minute slots of time to write. "I have a job," she added. "Maybe you heard that too. Mrs. Riley depends on me a lot."

"And courting keeps you busy in the evenings," Mr. Ferguson added coldly. "I warned you about that last spring. I'm not saying it again."

Thank you, Lilly thought.

"My sister gave me some more paper," Mr. Ferguson tried again.

"No. I'm done writing." The new bridge hadn't gone up yet, and Lilly knew she dared not store paper and pencils at home, especially with the house still over-full.

Mr. Ferguson stood up and leaned over the desk. He suddenly seemed very tall, very strong, and very—that something else again that Lilly couldn't name. "Lilly Burchett, how many times do I have to tell you that you're a fool?"

"This is the last time," she said coolly, standing up too. "I won't be stopping in here anymore. I couldn't even if I would keep writing. Ma thought you were trying to court me when you sent that note up the other day. She would be upset if she knew I stopped in here once. But once is all it'll be. Good-bye, Mr. Ferguson." She turned toward the door.

Mr. Ferguson's voice rose. "Court you?" he shouted after her. "I've never thought of it. Courting and getting married; that's all you folks can think of."

Lilly shut the door firmly behind herself and started for home again. She ran lightly across the log that spanned the creek, setting her jaw and trying not to think of what used to be there.

Behind her in the schoolhouse, Jim Ferguson strode to the window and watched her out of sight. She was so young. And yet she had changed over the summer. Mrs. Price, his landlady at the boarding house, had dropped a comment or two about her while catching him up on community gossip. "She'd be marrying this winter if the crops had come in fine," she said. "Jesse Wright makes a good match for her, to my way of thinking."

Was it Jesse that had created this change in her, given her this hint of regal coldness? He didn't think so. Her job with Mrs. Riley then? "Be careful, girl," Jim muttered to the empty schoolyard. "I want to see you make something of yourself, but I'm not sure if I like the way you're doing it."

When Pa came home from the mine the next day, he carried a note from Mrs. Riley. "Our company is coming sooner than we first thought," she had written. "I don't feel up to all the serving and entertaining by myself. Please come down Friday night by four o'clock. I will need you to stay overnight and spend Saturday here as well. You may go back home for Sunday."

Maybelle was incredulous when she heard this. "You'll sleep there?"

"I guess I'll do whatever she tells me to do." Lilly felt a tremor of mixed fear and excitement.

"Who are the visitors?" Aunt Goldie asked, without taking her eyes from the corn she was cleaning.

"Mr. and Mrs. Barker. They're old friends of the Rileys."

"Do they have a family?"

"I don't know. Mrs. Riley only told me that they're from Louisville."

Ma came to the kitchen doorway, her hands dripping water. "You'll serve and wait on the table?"

"I don't know. Probably."

Ma looked displeased. "Cooking and cleaning because Mrs. Riley is poorly is one thing. Waiting on the table like a common servant is another."

"I am a servant there."

"No, you're not," Ma said emphatically. "You are a woman who has a job."

"What dress will you wear?" Maybelle asked, to divert the conversation.

"My best one, of course. I haven't any other."

On Friday afternoon, she met the school children coming up the hill. "My, don't you look fine," Eula said. "Heard the Rileys are getting company. Is that where you're going?"

"Yes."

"The company coming tonight?"

"Yes."

"Reckon you'll see them?"

Lilly laughed. "Don't be silly. If I'm in the same house with them, of course I'll see them."

Several more people stopped her on the way into town, wanting to know any details she could impart about Mr. Riley's company. No one had any concrete ideas about why the Barkers were making this trip. The men guessed that something might be changing in mine management, and were equally divided as to whether that would be good or bad. Someone had caught wind that Mr. Barker was interested in education, and the school children quaked in their seats for fear he would come and ask for recitations. The women gossiped over the news eagerly, wondering what clothes Mrs. Barker would wear, and if she was young or old.

Lilly found Mrs. Riley distractedly going from room to room, straightening a doily, counting her stack of china plates, checking the ham in the oven. "I've been waiting for you," she said. "I'm glad you're here. I need you to bring hot water up to the bathroom so I can bathe."

Lilly dipped two buckets of water from the warmer beside the stove and emptied them into the shining bathtub upstairs. She opened the faucet and let cold water run in and mingle with the hot as Mrs. Riley had taught her. Mrs. Riley came in herself and added a sprinkle of powder that smelled rich and sweet.

"Thank you, Lilly," she said. "Now just run downstairs and keep an eye on everything while I bathe and dress. The dinner rolls are ready to bake. Watch them closely that they don't burn. And check that no leaves blew into the hall."

In the immaculate kitchen, Lilly very carefully slipped the pan of fluffy rolls into the oven. They had cleaned everything on Wednesday, but Mrs. Riley must have touched it up again. She peeped into the dining room and saw the table set for four with plates in three sizes stacked one atop the other. The chandelier sat on a side table, waiting to be lit just before the guests arrived.

She walked the length of the hall and stood by the front door, scrutinizing the glass for smudges. Everything sparkled. Finally she pulled up a stool and sat down in the kitchen to wait for the rolls to brown.

About the time the mine whistle blew, Mrs. Riley reappeared in the kitchen. She wore a creamy satin dress, with long sleeves ending in lace cuffs, a tight waist, and a floor-length hem. She had put on the air of a gracious hostess with the dress; and now she moved gracefully, talked softly, and smiled easily.

"I'm so excited about this visit, Lilly." She touched one finger to the top of a perfect golden roll. "I haven't seen Amy for so many years." She glided to the window in the dining room, from where she could see the train station, and after a moment glided back to the kitchen.

"Did you bring your clothes to stay the night?"

"Yes, ma'am. I left them just outside the kitchen door."

"Bring them inside. I planned that you would sleep in the bedroom right at the head of the back stairs."

"I could bed down in the kitchen," Lilly protested.

"Of course not, Lilly. I know I make you work hard. But I won't have you sleeping in my kitchen. What if Mr. Barker would come down for something in the night and stumble over you? He'd think we keep slaves."

From the back porch, Lilly retrieved her tiny, tightly-knotted bundle, which contained only her comb and night dress. She had bathed and put on fresh clothing before she came.

"Where's your dress for tomorrow?" Mrs. Riley asked.

"I'll wear this dress again, ma'am," Lilly answered in surprise.

"Where's your other one? The pink one you used to have? It was a cheap dress, but the color looked very becoming on you."

"That one's not fit to wear anymore. It got stains on it when we were cleaning up from the flood."

"And you have no others?"

"Only my homespun. That one's worse."

"I don't like the idea of you wearing the same dress in front of the Barkers for two days in a row," Mrs. Riley fretted. "I wonder if you could wear one of my old dresses."

Lilly shifted her bundle from one hand to the other, uncomfortably. She had never suspected that wearing her good dress for one evening and the next day would make such a problem.

"Well, take your stuff up to the bedroom for now."

Lilly ran up the back stairs and pushed open the narrow door to her left. It was a tiny room, compared to the others in the house, and probably intended for a servant. But it still had a white quilt on the cot, a heavy dresser with a mirror, long dusky-blue curtains at the windows, and a rug in shades of blue and white. She dropped her bundle inconspicuously in the corner.

Mr. Riley came home with the guests soon after five thirty. When they finished the first joyous greetings, Mrs. Riley showed them their bedroom and the bathroom next door. She told them that supper would be served at six-thirty, and that if they liked, they were welcome to relax and freshen up before that.

Lilly could hear their voices from the kitchen, but she didn't see Mr. and

Mrs. Barker until supper time. While she was slicing the ham and melting butter for the mashed potatoes, they all came into the dining room, and Lilly stopped working momentarily. She had never seen a woman like Mrs. Barker. And yet she found it hard to describe what made her different. Maybe it was the intense green of her dress, or the way she let some of her hair rim her face instead of gathering it all into her bun, or the decided clicking from her heels wherever she went.

As for Mr. Barker, Lilly decided at once that she didn't like him. He was big everywhere—big chested, big-stomached, big-headed, and big-voiced. He and Mr. Riley monopolized the conversation at the table.

Lilly waited on the four of them, feeling unsure of herself. But eventually, when she realized that they were interested only in the food and each other, she became more confident. The meal started with soup and the dinner rolls, and progressed slowly to ham, mashed potatoes, creamed peas and carrots, coleslaw, and finally pies and coffee. Eating this meal seemed to be the main thing planned for the evening; it took so long. Lilly had plenty of time between the courses to grab bites of ham in the kitchen.

Finally they pushed back their chairs and retired to the parlor. Lilly knew without being told that it was her job to clean up the table, wash all those plates and glasses and china cups, and tidy the kitchen. She held her breath every time she lifted a delicate plate from her hot water to the drain board, afraid that she might smash it against the counter or the floor. She had barely finished when Mrs. Riley came out to the kitchen.

"Is there water hot for baths?" she asked.

"I refilled the reservoir."

"Good. Our guests are tired and would like to go to bed. Take three buckets of water up to the bathroom so they can bathe."

As Lilly turned to fetch the buckets, she caught Mrs. Riley watching her intently, a slight smile on her face, obviously thinking of something besides hot water.

"Lilly, dear," she said.

"Yes, ma'am?" Lilly tried not show how startled she was at the "dear."

"Our visitors liked my maid, and they wanted to know more about you. Mr. Barker is especially interested in you. He'd like to talk to you tomorrow."

Lilly stiffened. Speechless, she filled the first bucket, then the second.

"He's a kind man, Lilly."

"I'm sure of it, ma'am," she said in a low voice, although she was sure of nothing of the kind.

She slept poorly that night, partly because of the uncomfortably high, soft mattress, and partly because of the pending interview. Early the next morning, Mrs. Riley knocked on her door and came in with three dresses draped over her arm. "Let's see if one of these will fit you," she said.

One was the color of wine, one the color of dogwood leaves in the spring, and one the color of sourwood honey. "These are old dresses," Mrs. Riley explained when she saw the wonder in Lilly's eyes. "They're some of my shorter ones, so they might fit you. Try the green first; I think it would look especially good with your brown hair."

Lilly felt like she slipped out of her own life and into the life of a princess in one of her stories when she put the smooth green gown on. It nearly swept the floor and was cut in a completely different way than her other dresses. She shut the buttons up along the back and felt it brushing softly against her ankles.

Mrs. Riley turned her around and examined her from all sides. "Not a perfect fit," she said, "but really quite good on you. I want you to wear it today."

She left without taking the other dresses with her, and Lilly lifted them carefully and fingered them. She wanted to try them on too, but the sun was already edging up into the sky, and she needed to hurry down to make breakfast.

Mr. and Mrs. Barker didn't appear until nine o'clock. Lilly knew that at home the morning chores would be finished, breakfast eaten, Pa and Vince in the fields, and Ma and Maybelle cleaning and cooking for Sunday. Did rich people always sleep so late into the day?

That morning the table talk centered mainly around the town and hills surrounding it. Mr. Riley gave his estimate on the richness of coal veins in the area, and Mr. Barker asked if most of the miners came from nearby.

"Some move in," Mr. Riley answered. "The boarding house is always full, and we've got a nice lot of company houses. But most of the miners come from the hills. The men here want the jobs."

"So there are quite a few people living up these creeks?"

"More than you would imagine."

"Do they have good houses?"

"Cabins, mostly. A few newer houses."

"Large cabins?"

"Not so large as you would expect from the size of their families." His voice held the same fine edge of sarcasm that Lilly had felt from Mrs. Riley on her first day of work. He gestured toward Lilly. "You'll have to ask her about that. I haven't seen many of the cabins myself."

As if Mr. Barker had needed this opening, he really looked at Lilly for the first time. "How many children are there in your family, Lilly?"

"Seven, sir."

"Are you the oldest?"

"Yes."

"Is your father a farmer?"

"No. Pa works in the mines."

"I see." Mr. Barker buttered another biscuit and broke it in half. He took most of one piece in a single bite.

Lilly realized suddenly that she felt no sarcasm from Mr. Barker. Everything he said came out frankly. He meant exactly the words he had uttered, and nothing more.

After breakfast the ladies went to Mrs. Riley's sitting room, and Lilly could hear the soft murmur of feminine voices. Heavy masculine tread climbed the front stairs, probably on the way to the library.

Alone in the kitchen, Lilly carefully washed the china again and set it neatly on the table in preparation for the next meal. Then, unsure what to do next, she went to the door and stared out unseeingly into the back yard, finding it hard to control her trepidation about Mr. Barker when she had nothing with which to occupy her hands.

After a time, both sets of footsteps came back down the front stairs. At the door of the sitting room, Mr. Riley said, "My dear, I need to go up to the mine office at least for a few hours."

And Mr. Barker added, "I'm going along down. I want to scout around town and see what there is to see. We'll be back for lunch."

Chapter eight

At the boarding house, Jim Ferguson had just walked through the kitchen and told his landlady that he was headed to the post office.

Plump Mrs. Price, her arms elbow deep in a bowl of dough, stopped kneading and panted for a few moments. "Going to be here for lunch?"

"Yes," he said briefly. "No one's hiring me out to help with harvest this year. Not much to harvest."

He went out, across the porch and down half a dozen shallow steps to the street. He threw back his shoulders and stuck his hands in his pockets.

A deep throaty voice spoke unexpectedly from behind him. "I'm looking for Mr. Ferguson."

He turned around to see a large man, obviously well-fed, dressed in smart city pants and a shirt starched to perfection. "That's me."

The man caught up to him and took his hand in a firm grip. "I'm Ellis Barker."

"Jim Ferguson, sir."

"I hear you're the schoolteacher."

"That's right."

"I'm interested in education. It's a hobby of mine. I'd appreciate if you could show me the school here."

"It's not much to see," Jim said, a hint of bitterness creeping into his voice. "Not after what you're used to."

"I want to see it all the same."

"Come along then. I have a postcard to drop off at the post office. It'll be on our way to the school."

They talked little as they left the town behind and crossed the railroad tracks. Jim had walked this way every day now for three school years, and he liked the trail. But with Mr. Barker beside him, he saw it anew—how narrow and rutted and steep it was.

"Lots of people live beyond here in the hills?" Mr. Barker asked.

"Yes, lots. More than half of my students come from out that way."

"Are they intelligent students?"

"Some of them."

"Willing to learn?"

"Some of them," Jim said again.

He felt acutely ill-at-ease by the time he stood in front of the log schoolhouse and opened the door for Mr. Barker. He knew he had inferior books, never enough time, and students who skipped classes when the creek rose or the fields needed worked. But just now he wished he had somehow managed to do better in spite of these drawbacks.

Mr. Barker walked around the perimeter of the room, looking out each window. He sat down in one of the student's desks and then in Jim's chair, and examined the books. "I don't see a single new book," he said.

"No, sir. These folks pass them down from parents to children."

"They must take care of them well."

"They respect books."

"How many years of schooling do these children complete on average?"

Jim shifted and looked away from Mr. Barker. "It depends. Some of them have to stay home and work. Some of them stop as soon as they can."

"But you have some who really want to learn?"

Jim looked steadily at the rich, cultured man sitting across from him. He felt a slow burning of vexation. "You think that all the mountain people are ignorant and like to be so, don't you?"

"No, I don't," Mr. Barker answered, speaking quietly. "I know about Lilly."

"Lilly?"

"Lilly Burchett. I really hunted you up because I wanted to ask you about her."

"She don't go to school here anymore. She's a maid for Mrs. Riley."

"I know. I saw her there last night."

"What do you want to know about her?" Jim's anger seeped away, replaced by frustration, the frustration he always felt when he thought of Lilly, the frustration of wanting to do more than he could.

"I suppose you were aware of her writing talent?"

"Yes." But how did Mr. Barker know of it?

"Did you push her to write at school?"

"She didn't need no pushing."

Mr. Barker smiled slightly. "Was she a good student otherwise?"

"Not so good on math."

"I didn't mean that exactly. Did she try hard? Did she put herself into what you gave her to do?"

"Most times. Unless she was dreaming of a story."

"Could she benefit from high school?"

"We don't have none close hereabouts."

"I meant away from here."

"Sure, she could benefit. If you could get her there."

"I have a plan for getting her there. Let that with me. But before I put that plan in place with Lilly, I want to know if you think she has potential."

"Yes, sir. Wasted potential as long as she stays here." Although Lilly baffled Jim in some ways, he had guessed at her deep dreams, perhaps because they mirrored his own ungranted ones. For a brief moment three emotions waged war in his mind—jealousy for the chance coming to Lilly, pride which found it hard to admit that his efforts were not enough, and gratitude to Mr. Barker for doing what he could not. Gratitude won, although he still wasn't able to look Mr. Barker directly in the eye as he added, "If you can help her, it would be a wonderful thing. I've tried, but I can't do much."

"I understand that," Mr. Barker said, with neither scorn nor pity. "I believe you've given her a good start."

The two men shook hands again before they left the schoolhouse. "Thank you," Jim said with quiet dignity, although he still didn't know exactly what Mr. Barker had in mind, or even how he had found out about Lilly. "This will be a good thing for Lilly."

Late that afternoon, Mr. Riley came into the kitchen. "Lilly," he said, with a slight sharpness that reminded her she was only a servant.

"Yes, sir?"

"Mr. Barker is up in the library. He wants to talk to you."

"Yes, sir."

Lilly pressed her suddenly clammy hands together and bit the inside of her bottom lip. At the top of the narrow back stairs, she saw that the library door had been left open, and she paused just outside it, not sure if she should go straight in or not.

Mr. Barker had taken one of the chairs in front of the cold fireplace and slouched comfortably down in it. He didn't seem quite so big that way, and a bit of the fear went out of Lilly. He looked up and saw her there. "Come in," he rumbled. "Sit down here across from me."

She sat on the edge of the chair, and as always when she wasn't sure of herself, let her hair hang so that it hid the sides of her face. "Let's get introduced," he said casually. "My full name is Ellis T. Barker, and you are Lilly Burchett, right?"

"Yes, sir."

"You already told me there are seven children in your family. My wife and I have two children. Their names are Lillian and Blair. Lillian is married and lives close to us in Louisville. Blair is attending university in Ohio. Tell me more about your family."

"Pa's name is Bernie Burchett, and my ma is Patty. I have four brothers and two sisters."

"What are their names?" Mr. Barker seemed to be only making unimportant conversation as he fiddled with a brown envelope in his lap.

"Vince, Maybelle, Bobby, T.J., Patty, and Sonny."

Abruptly Mr. Barker changed the subject. "I hear you had a bad flood up this way not so long ago."

She nodded.

"Was your family affected? Did you lose your house?"

"Our house stayed, but it had water in it."

Mr. Barker fiddled with the envelope again, opened it slowly. He drew out several sheets of paper, with crinkled edges and blurred brown splatters. He held them out toward her. "Have you ever seen these before?"

The papers were covered with smudged pencil writing. Her own writing. Instinctively Lilly reached out her hand to snatch them, then stopped herself. Dried mud completely obliterated some of the words, but others stood out clearly. Partway up the paper, one phrase jumped out at her, ". . . 'twas a long white gown that shimmered in the moonlight . . ."

"Yes," she said hoarsely, "they're mine."

"And you lost them in the flood?"

"Yes, sir." Her voice had fallen to a whisper.

Mr. Barker kept his hand securely on the papers while he leaned back in his chair. "Now let me tell you a story. My wife and I are from Louisville, but this summer we spent a couple weeks of vacation time with friends in Jackson. Have you ever been there?"

"No."

"Fine place. Well, our friends have a river running not far from their house, and while we were there, it flooded a little. Not much. Folks said it came from all the rain higher up in the mountains. One fine Saturday I took my fishing line and tackle box and went down to the river to catch some bluegill and bass. Nothing like a fine pan of fresh fish when you're hungry."

Lilly curled her fingers into her palms, wishing desperately that he would get on with his story and stop rambling about fish and the town of Jackson.

"And while I was out there—" he fingered the papers on his lap "—I saw something odd beside me on the bank. It was paper, and there's nothing so odd about that, but it was rolled and tied with a string."

Lilly wondered if he was intentionally making the story take a long time. "Go on," she begged.

"So I investigated. And I found this."

"How did you know they were mine?"

"Well, miss, that was simple. You signed your name and address at the bottom of each story. I couldn't read anything on the first few sheets, but inside the roll further they hadn't been so ruined by mud and water. I could read some of them quite clearly after I let them dry." He held out another sheet for her to see.

Lilly pressed the fingertips on her left hand, one by one. They were ice cold. She began on her right hand.

"So I read what I could," Mr. Barker continued candidly. "I saw 'Sand Lick, Kentucky,' and I said to Amy, 'Don't you have a friend living there?' We decided to mosey on over here before heading back to Louisville and see if we could find a Lilly Burchett. Turns out it was even easier than we thought it would be. Strange set of coincidences, wouldn't you say?"

Lilly thought it strange that he had come all the way down from Jackson to bring back her few stories, and stranger still that he did not hand them over when he had found her. "Can I have them back, sir?" she asked respectfully.

"Yes, after we've talked some more. I haven't quite had my say yet. How many grades did you finish in school?"

"Seven."

"How old are you?"

"Fourteen."

"I hear that girls get married young around here. Are you planning on getting married soon?"

That hateful question again. "No," she answered slowly. "Not yet."

He looked at her keenly. "I'd like you to hold off on getting married for a good long while." He said it like a gentleman, but it reminded her of Mr. Ferguson. Her guards went up, and she wondered instantly what right he had to be telling her when she should get married.

He laughed softly, rumblingly. "Surprised you by that comment, didn't I?" She flushed.

He changed tacks and waved at the books surrounding them on all sides. "You love books, don't you?"

"Yes, sir." She hadn't let herself think much about books since the flood. But now she sat in the library, with her own stories so close to her again. She took a deep breath.

"You don't have a library like this in your cabin, do you?"

"Oh, no. We had two books—before the flood."

"Would you like to have access to more?"

Would she? She had thought those things were in her past, forever behind her. She had thought her life would run parallel with Jesse's over the mountains and between the corn rows in the meager Kentucky fields. She even thought the longings she used to feel in Mrs. Riley's house had died. Suddenly she wasn't so sure they had. Still she said hesitantly, "I'm just a mountain girl, Mr. Barker."

"Yes, you are. And yet. . ."

Lilly's eyes strayed to the table, and she wondered how long it had been since Mrs. Riley had said, "I laid out a book for you to read. Go and take a break."

"And yet. . ." Mr. Barker repeated meditatively, "I think you could be so much more, if you had a chance. I'm here to give you a chance."

"A chance for what?"

"I want you to go to school longer, Lilly."

"No one goes to school anymore when they're fourteen."

"Oh, I don't mean here. I want to take you home with me and send you to high school. I want you to be exposed to better teachers and more books. Lots more books. I seriously think that, with the right training and exposure, you will be writing your own books in several more years. I'd like you to get that training."

The coldness went out of Lilly; and astonishment, disbelief, and pleasure washed hotly through her. She opened her mouth, but he held up his hand for her to wait.

"I know the first thing you will say is that your parents can't afford to send you on for more schooling. But I see promise in your work, and I'm a rich enough man to pay the expenses myself. If I'm right in what I think, and you become a rich and famous author someday, you can pay me back then. If not. . . I'll take it as an investor's loss. My wife and I live in a large house, even larger than this one. But only my wife and I and our two servants live there, except when Blair is home from university. We'll have a room fixed up for you in no time. In fact, I'd like to do this as fast as we can, so that you can enter the classes at the high school before the other students get very far into their year. If you think you can be ready that soon, we'll take you back with us when we go in a couple days. If not, we'll leave and come back for you in a week or so."

He had it all planned in a methodical, business-like way. Lilly's thoughts followed everything he said, and went far beyond as well. She thought of fine dresses and dainty hats, city life that never stayed still, a large high school filled with strangers. And she thought of libraries open to her all the time, and someday books with her name on the cover. The thrills and dreams that she thought she had laid aside forever shot through her with tingling intensity.

"You will agree to that, won't you, Lilly?"

Reality confronted her then, sudden and stark. "Pa and Ma will rather I live at home until I get married," she said.

"Let's leave them out of the picture for right now." Mr. Barker sat up and leaned forward, suddenly seeming bigger again. "Would *you* like to go?"

She was on the point of saying yes, before uncertainty crowded in. "I'm not sure, Mr. Barker," she stammered. "I think so, maybe. I don't know anything about city life or living with fine folks. I don't think I've learned enough to go to a high school, either."

He answered her last objection first. "You would take an entrance exam first thing. That would show the areas you are weak in, and you could get some tutoring for a few weeks until you would be ready to fit in with the other students. As for city life and living with fine folks—you will learn fast. So you really do want to go."

She stayed silent, still unable to think clearly.

"And now, let's talk about what your parents will say. You said they would rather you stay here. Why is that?"

"None of us have ever done something like this," Lilly said, hanging her head.

Somehow she knew Mr. Barker would laugh, and he did. "If no one ever did what their fathers hadn't done, it would be a sad world. Someone in your family had to decide to come to Kentucky, or you wouldn't be here. Have you ever thought of that?"

"It's so far," she ventured next.

"When you come by train, it's no more than five or six hours."

No more than five or six hours! When she had never been out of Harlan County!

"Any more things they will bring up?" Mr. Barker asked kindly enough.

"Ma will think it's more proper that I stay home and get married and raise a family. And Pa will think the city is dangerous. They'll say I'm too young to be so far from home."

"And yet you're not too young to get married?"

"I wouldn't be so far from home then," Lilly pointed out.

"That is, if you marry a boy from the hills."

"They're the only ones I know," Lilly retorted defensively.

"M-m-m." He laced his fingers together and gazed thoughtfully at the pattern in the drapes. "What if I give them my word that I'll look out for you and make sure you're taken care of?"

"But sir, they don't know you."

"I can fix that. I'm planning to come out on Monday and talk to them. Since you've told me what they'll say, I can prepare in advance for what I'll say. That will be a great help."

Lilly gasped. "You'll come talk to my pa and ma?"

"Yes, young lady. Do you have a problem with that?"

A man like Mr. Barker had never set foot inside their cabin. Lilly tried to imagine the ruckus that would inevitably take place. First a flurry of excitement and welcome, with tethered curiosity behind it. Then a row when Pa and Ma found out what he wanted. Uncle Sandy and Aunt Goldie would see it all too. And if he thought a short talk with her family would be enough for them to get to know him, he was sadly mistaken. She tried to protest. "Our cabin isn't a good place for a talk."

Mr. Barker shrugged. "I want to see where you live. When is a good time to come?"

Lilly thought for a moment, turning over bad and worse options. Then she said, "Pa leaves for the mine early. If you want to talk to him, you'd better come in the evening."

"Evening it will be then. I want both of your parents there. I'm sure I can persuade them."

It seemed like he was done talking at last, for he fell silent and stared out the window. She stood up to tip-toe out, and he awoke suddenly. "Here, take your stories with you." He slid them back into the envelope and handed them to her.

When Lilly went down the narrow back stairs, they suddenly felt grand.

In the kitchen, the floor was more vivid and beautiful than she remembered, and the sink infused with extra luster. "If I go with Mr. Barker," she murmured to herself, "I'll live all the time in a house like this." But although she stood running her hand over the counter top, something much larger and finer than the carpets and furnishings tugged at her. Books . . . a library . . . plenty of time to read . . . perhaps a desk furnished with paper and pencils . . .

The hunger had awakened in Lilly again, stirred by the sight of her stories, sharpened by Mr. Barker's offer. She wondered at herself for ever thinking it was dead.

Chapter nine

She went home that evening almost gaily, Mr. Barker's words singing themselves in her mind, "I'm sure I can persuade your parents." She decided she would say nothing about it to anyone. He would stun them by coming in suddenly, and maybe he would extract permission when they hardly knew what they were doing.

So she told them every detail she could remember about Mrs. Barker, about the furnishings of the bedroom where she had slept, and even about the pale green cast-off dress from Mrs. Riley. About Mr. Barker, she kept silent.

On Sunday evening Jesse came for a walk. As never before in his presence, Lilly found it hard to relax. She knew she was keeping something from him, something that might hurt him. They walked down to see how progress was coming on the new bridge. "If the men have a few more days to work on it, it should be done," Jesse predicted. "It's a lot better and sturdier than the old bridge."

When she didn't offer any comment, he asked, "What about Sandy's house? Will it be done soon?"

"Soon, I think. Maybe next week."

Sunday dragged to a close and Monday came. Lilly walked to the Riley house and, at Mrs. Riley's bidding, changed into the creamy tan dress. She did her usual Monday chores of washing and cooking, while the two ladies talked constantly in the sitting room. Mrs. Riley looked more alert and happy than she had for a long time. Maybe her sickness had been mostly loneliness. /depressed

Mr. Barker spent much of his day at the mine with Mr. Riley. But he came back just as Lilly was ready to head home. "I'll come with you," he announced. "You can show me the way."

Lilly hated this idea. She knew that eyes up and down the street, and out of every cabin window, would watch the spectacle of her walking home with Mr. Barker. But she dared not protest.

"Don't wait on me for supper," he said to Mr. Riley. "If you've eaten before I get back, I can easily grab a bite from the leftovers. I've been thinking about this business all day, and I want to get it done before dark. Are you ready to go now, Lilly?"

"I still need to change my dress. This one isn't mine."

"Leave it on," Mrs. Riley disagreed. "I don't mind if you wear it home tonight. Besides, if Mr. Barker is ready to do something, it's not a good idea to make him wait."

Mr. Barker laughed good-naturedly. "Guess you're right there, ma'am."

So, with Mr. Barker escorting her, she started for home in a borrowed dress, feeling ridiculously fancified and self-conscious. She saw Mrs. Keeton staring from the window behind the counter in the store. At the Greers' Silas sat on the porch, and he called to his wife so that she could come out of the cabin and gawk as well. They met Mr. Ferguson, and he tipped his hat deferentially to them.

When the cabin came into sight, Lilly said, "Let me run ahead and tell them you're coming. Just keep to this road. That's our cabin right up there."

She flew past T.J., Patty, and Frances who had stopped playing to stare at the approaching stranger, and up the two steps to the front porch. She walked in the open door into the eating room. "Ma, someone's coming to talk to you and Pa."

"Pa's in the front room with Sandy. You'd better tell them. I don't think they've washed up yet." Ma came to the kitchen doorway, and her voice rose suddenly in horror. "What dress do you have on?"

"Sh, Ma. It's one Mrs. Riley wanted me to wear today, and I didn't have time to change before I came home. Don't worry about that. Mr. Barker—"

Before she had time to finish, he was in the doorway behind her, smiling and taking off his hat. Aunt Goldie pulled her little children close to her, and Ma froze, drawing back slightly into the kitchen. It only took her a moment, though, to collect herself. She came forward cordially. "Howdy, stranger."

Mr. Barker shook hands with her. "Pleased to meet you. My name is Ellis Barker. Are you Mrs. Bernie Burchett?"

"Bernie's my man," Ma answered.

"Is he here?"

"He's out back washing. Set down and rest yourself."

Mr. Barker sat down easily on one of the chairs and put his hat on his knee. He tried to make friends with the children in the room until Pa and Uncle Sandy came in, freshly washed. Then he stood up again and held his hand out toward Pa. "I'm Ellis Barker. Mr. Burchett, I believe?"

"Yes, sir." Pa was as tall as Mr. Barker, but beside this big man, he looked like sinew strung upon bone. Pa fit easily into the contours of this cabin. Mr. Barker didn't.

"I'm sorry to intrude," he said. "When I asked your daughter if I could come, I didn't realize you would have visitors."

"These folks ain't visitors," Pa answered. "It's my sister Goldie and her family. Their house was washed away in the flood. They're working at rebuilding."

"I heard about the flood."

An uncomfortable silence fell. Ma's look, directed at Lilly, said, "What are you doing bringing high-toned strangers into our cabin? Nothing but bad can come of this."

Mr. Barker made some polite conversation, but seemed in no hurry to get the point of his visit. So finally Pa said, "Sit down and eat with us, Mr. Barker."

"We ain't got fine food," Ma added, "but you're welcome to it."

"It would be my pleasure to eat with you," Mr. Barker replied heartily.

With Uncle Sandy's family in the cabin, only the adults and the little children sat at the table for meals. The others reached in and helped themselves and then went to the porch to eat. This time Lilly joined the ones at the table.

When the bowls of beans and fried potatoes and the golden chunk of cornbread came around the table, Mr. Barker helped himself like a man who wasn't afraid to eat what was set before him. At first he stayed quiet like the rest of them, but presently he began to talk again—about the weather, the field work, coal mining, and the new bridge. He didn't seem to notice that everyone else would have rather been giving their full attention to eating than to talking. But they answered him politely all the same.

Eventually he worked the discussion around to Pa's family and said, "I don't know if you realize that Lilly has extraordinary talent."

Pa laid down his spoon. Pleasure flickered in his eyes, and was gone, replaced by wariness.

Ma asked with outright suspicion, "What talent?"

"I'm talking about her way with words."

"She don't talk no better than the rest of us," Pa countered.

"Oh, I didn't exactly mean the way she talks, Mr. Burchett," Mr. Barker returned. "It's her writing that I meant."

"Lilly don't do no writing," Ma said sharply. But she softened her words by adding, "Here, take some more cornbread."

"Thank you, ma'am. Your cornbread is the best." He smoothed butter over the crispy crust, taking his time, obviously choosing his next words carefully. "You're right. She's not doing any currently. And she has done very little. However, I came across some of her past work."

"How did you find it?" Ma looked startled and unhappy.

He smiled easily. "Let's just say it was a lucky accident."

"Don't believe in luck," Pa said with an edge to his voice.

"Call it an act of God, then," Mr. Barker agreed pleasantly. "How it happened doesn't matter. I've read a little of her work, and I think she has a talent that needs to be developed."

"We're poor folks," Ma told him. "We don't have time to be writing trash, developing talents, whatever you call it. And we don't have the money for paper, neither."

"Just so. I understand that, and I have a suggestion to make."

A very brief pause.

"I would like to provide for Lilly's schooling."

Pa straightened in his chair. "I provide for my own family."

"But I see potential in Lilly that you may not be able to provide for her here. She would need to go away for the schooling I'm thinking of."

"Away where?"

"I would like to take her to the city with me and my wife. To Louisville. We would be glad to provide a home for her while she's going through high school."

"High school?" Ma repeated in disbelief. "None of us have ever done nothing like that before."

"There's always a time to try new things, ma'am," Mr. Barker said evenly.

"Cities aren't a safe place to live, seems to me," Pa added.

No one was eating anymore. Mr. Barker pushed his plate away from him and rested his elbows on the table in a gesture he would never have used in Mr. Riley's house. "Accidents do happen in the city," he answered. "But if I correctly understood the things I heard today, they also happen in the hills. Coal mine collapses, floods, things like that."

"She's too young to go so far away."

"She's getting married soon," Ma declared with finality, and sat back with her arms folded. Her eyes telegraphed a message to Lilly, but Lilly only sat numb and speechless.

"She is? I understood from the young lady herself that she has no immediate plans."

Ma's eyes darkened. "She will be marrying Jesse Wright as soon as he has enough money."

"Ma," Lilly said faintly, aware of a myriad of eyes suddenly on her, "we've not promised."

"You will as soon as he has enough money. You've been going together and everyone knows it."

"Even if they do promise to marry," Mr. Barker said, "engagements can be held for several years." In spite of the calmness of his voice, Lilly now detected a dangerous flash in his eyes. "This community has suffered a serious loss from the flood, and it may be a couple years before it's back on its feet. The young man might not be able to afford to get married for some time. Until then, Lilly may as well be going to school."

"What good will it do her when she gets married?"

"Education will benefit her whether she is married or not. With an education, she could marry and live right here on Sand Lick but still succeed in the world of writers. Successful writers make a great deal of money."

That bald mention of money did it. Pa stood up slowly and put one hand on the back of his chair. "We're mountain people, Mr. Barker," he said, and Lilly could hear his unspoken "no." "Your offer is kind. We appreciate it. But we don't hold with our young ones going off so far from home. They belong here until they get married and start families of their own."

"You'll deny Lilly this chance?" Mr. Barker's voice rose, and Lilly wondered if he would stoop to losing his temper with strangers.

"The chance to get married and raise a good family and get to heaven at the last is good enough for her or anybody," Ma said coldly.

"I wish I knew how to change your minds. You're making a terrible mistake."

"A terrible mistake?" Pa asked. "I don't know how to talk so pretty [*fancy*] as you, Mr. Barker." His words no longer hung slow and easy in the room, but knifed through the air. "I don't know if I've quite made you see what I mean. But I know how to say no and stick to it. I'm saying no right now."

Mr. Barker stared at him for a long moment, then pulled himself away from his anger. "I understand it when I'm beaten. I'll not pressure you. But may I go outside and talk privately with Lilly for a few minutes?"

Ma's eyes flashed. She didn't have Pa's dignity, but she knew how to speak her mind. "Oh, no. You've done enough messing with my girl. I know your kind. You'll take her outside and persuade her to run away to the city without us giving her leave. She will stay right there in her chair until you're good and gone."

Without a word, his eyebrows drawn low over his eyes, Mr. Barker stood up, slid his chair back into place at the table, and walked quickly toward the door. The children outside, listening breathlessly, parted like the Red Sea to let him through.

Lilly hadn't known that sixteen people could be so quiet as they waited for him to go down the steps, across the yard, and down the trail. Then Bobby called cheerfully, "He's good and gone."

Only then did Pa look at Lilly. "Get upstairs right now," he said angrily, "and take off that brown abomination of a dress. Then you've got some confessing to do."

Lilly ran up the stairs from the front room, wishing she could slip off all her shame and disappointment with the dress. She got to the window in time to see Mr. Barker disappearing around the copse of spruce trees, his head held high, his back straight. She had a terrible moment of imagining the words he would use to describe this evening when he rejoined his wife and friends.

Pa and Ma got the whole story out of her by prying and prodding, all except for the exact spot where she had hidden her stories. She knew if she had been any younger, a whipping would have been forthcoming for her secrecy. As it was, Pa hung around the kitchen and glowered, instead of joining Uncle Sandy in the front room, while Ma rattled pots and pans in an alarming way. All the younger children had made themselves scarce, to Lilly's intense relief.

"It's the will of God for you to stay in the hills like we've always done," Ma declared. She gave a quick swipe with her rag to the table and her hand connected smartly with Lilly's arm on the upswing. Lilly was sure it was intentional.

"How do you know what the will of God is?" she asked hotly.

"You claim to know more of the will of God than your ma?" Pa retorted. "You that's not been baptized a year?"

Lilly went to bed that night bruised in a way she couldn't explain. She had been scared and uncertain while Mr. Barker was there, and furious after he left, but now she felt only hurt. Maybelle whispered to her in the dark. "I wonder what it would be like to live in a city. Do you reckon you would have liked it?"

"Be quiet and go to sleep," Lilly hissed back.

And across town, in another hillside house, the Barkers and the Rileys sat in the parlor, lights on, voices low. "I don't understand it," Mr. Barker said again.

"It's the ignorance of these folks," Mr. Riley told him flatly.

"They are ignorant," Mr. Barker agreed. "I can't see why they don't want something better."

"Pure inertia."

"But why?"

"I think they've become fatalistic," Mrs. Barker put in. "The hard life here has made them that way."

"Some of them are ambitious," Mrs. Riley said softly. "Some of them have dreams."

"But if they're never allowed to follow their dreams, how much good will it do them?" Mr. Barker asked. "Their dreams will die sooner or later."

"Even for girls like Lilly?"

He gave her a hard look. "Yes," he said. "I saw their cabin. I know what kind of life Lilly will lead here."

"Is it so bad at her home?"

"No. It's clean and neat. Her family looks healthy. But it's poor all the same. She'll never get beyond that. And she wants to, herself. I would like to tell her father what I thought of him. He's a beast."

Mr. Riley had been smoking lazily. "You didn't tell him that, did you?"

"No."

"Well, good. My reputation is never too stable here, and I'd hate for word to get out that my visitor called one of the workers a beast." After a moment, he added, still more lazily, "Whether it's true or not."

Mrs. Riley got up and restlessly adjusted some pillows behind her back. "Maybe it's best. If Lilly went to Louisville, I would miss her—" her voice dropped as if she was unsure of her own feelings "—like a daughter."

"She's your maid," Mr. Riley said, without turning to look at his wife. "Nothing more."

But Mrs. Barker laid a sympathetic hand on her arm. "You must get so lonely here."

"I do. Lilly gives me a little companionship, when she lets herself open up. I don't understand her, but I love her."

Pa made sure that the Barkers had returned to Louisville before he allowed Lilly to go back and help Mrs. Riley. Lilly told him that they planned to leave on Tuesday, but that wasn't enough for him. He had to stop in at the train station and personally ask the station master if they had left.

"I suppose they're good enough people in a way," he said, "but I don't trust him none. A perfect stranger wanting to take our daughter away." His anger had gone, but his resolute decision stayed.

Lilly wanted to go back to the Rileys' desperately, and dreaded it just as desperately. She found Mrs. Riley worn out from the visit. "I felt so good while they were here," she confided. "But now I'm afraid I may have worked too hard. I think it will be a few weeks until I feel like myself again. You won't mind if we don't have any readings for a while, will you?"

"No, I won't mind," she said, relieved. Best, since things had happened this way, to put everything behind her.

Mrs. Riley laid a hand on her shoulder. "You act so much like a woman, and yet you're so young."

"Fourteen is a woman grown," Lilly disagreed, and knew she was much closer to being a woman than she had been several months before, because she now knew more of loss and disappointment.

"So young," Mrs. Riley repeated in a murmur, as though she hadn't heard Lilly, "with your whole life in front of you, really. I'm sorry you're not going to Louisville."

Lilly had steeled herself for this moment, and she said with studied calm, "I'm a woman of the mountains, Mrs. Riley. I don't know how I would make it in the city."

"I thought you wanted to go."

"I thought it would be a grand adventure."

"Is that all?" Mrs. Riley asked searchingly.

Under her penetrating gaze, Lilly dropped her eyes. She did not want Mrs. Riley feeling sorry for her, and she had fully intended to give the impression that she had changed her mind. Now she found herself saying, "I . . . Yes, I wanted to go. But I can't. I'd rather not talk about it."

Mrs. Riley was extra kind all that day. But every time Lilly saw her warm gray eyes on her, she winced and turned away, feeling as if Mrs. Riley had rubbed salt across a fresh wound.

Mr. Ferguson called to her from the door of the schoolhouse as she went by that evening. "Lilly. Hey, Lilly."

She stopped unwillingly. "You're not usually at school this late."

"I've been waiting on you."

"I thought I told you that—"

"Once isn't going to kill me or anyone else."

She deliberately turned to go on, ignoring him. He came across the yard then and caught at her sleeve. "You *will* talk to me, Lilly."

"Then let's go inside," she muttered. "I'd rather not let everyone see us."

He marched her inside like a first grader and sat her down on the bench at the back of the schoolroom. But he stayed standing, towering over her, his hands thrust deep into his pockets, tiny pinpricks of light in his green eyes. "Do you realize that you've just thrown away a splendid chance, maybe the only chance you will ever have to make a name for yourself, to get out and be someone?"

Lilly could have expected this. The younger children had listened to Mr. Barker's offer and told their friends, who had gone home and told their parents. By supper time on Tuesday, most everyone for five miles around Sand Lick knew what had happened in the Burchett cabin. Mrs. Greer had left Silas alone for once and come up to the cabin herself, wanting the story straight. The whole Burchett clan had hashed it out and come to the unanimous conclusion that Louisville was a powerful long way for one of their kin to go, and with strangers, besides. Mrs. Keeton had called to her on the way to town that morning, wanting her to stop in and talk. And now this.

Mr. Ferguson went on rapid-fire, his words splatting out against the desks, the floor, and the rough-hewn wall. "Mr. Barker came and talked to me Saturday morning. He wanted to know what kind of student you were, how much writing you did, that kind of thing. He's a good man, and he really wanted to help you. I wished a chance like that would come along for me. But I was glad for you, and proud that someday I could say you were my student. And then you go and throw it all away, because of your stubbornness, or pride, or something else, I don't know what."

Lilly wondered what version of the tale he had heard. Evidently not one that laid the blame on Pa or Ma. Fine. Let him abuse her with his tongue. She was too tired to care anymore. She simply sat and watched his feet pacing restlessly back and forth.

"How could you refuse? I've heard of this Mr. Barker before. Some folks say he's a millionaire. And he loves books, Lilly. You would have had access to one of the best personal libraries in the state of Kentucky. Do you hear me? Are you listening?"

"I hear you, Mr. Ferguson. You made me come in here, so I'm listening until you're done. Are you done yet?"

"No, I'm not done," he said coldly. "But if you won't listen to me, then go."

"So you think I should change my mind? And then what would I do? Take the next train and chase after him?"

"No. Tell me, and I'll write him a letter."

Lilly brushed back her hair and looked up at Mr. Ferguson directly, in surprise.

He stopped walking back and forth and finally sat down next to her on the bench. "He asked me to tell you that. He talked to me again before he left, and said you couldn't come now. But if it ever works out, his offer still stands, and we can send him a letter. He left his address with me."

Thankfulness to Mr. Barker for sparing the details came up in her throat and choked her. No matter what Mr. Ferguson now thought of her, this simple act somehow lessened her shame. She stood up resolutely. "I'll remember his offer, if I ever—change my mind." She didn't want Mr. Ferguson to suspect what had really happened, but she couldn't keep from saying the last words bitterly. "And since you've told me what you called me in here for, I'll be on my way."

"Do you want the address?"

"No. You keep it."

He didn't try to stop her, only said with biting sarcasm, "I still have that stack of paper, if you want it."

He couldn't have known how much those last words stung.

She walked laggingly away from the schoolhouse, scuffing her bare feet over the rough spots in the road. She kept her eyes down, and so she was almost on the bridge before she saw it. Then she stopped short in surprise. The men had finished it that day, and it proudly spanned the creek, gleaming yellow in the setting sun, almost as yellow as the trees that hung over the creek and waved at their reflections in the water.

Lilly hesitated only the briefest of moments to make sure no one else was within sight before she slipped underneath. The creek had gone down where it belonged, and she stood on the bank, with her toes just touching the water, as she used to do so long ago. The timbers above her were new and untried, but they protected her from prying eyes just as the old weathered ones had done. There she could quit pretending that it had been her decision, as she had with Mr. Ferguson; she could quit pretending that she was content to be a mountain girl, as she had with Mrs. Riley. Her family pride and loyalty would keep her from telling exactly what went on in the cabin that night, but pretending was hard.

Suddenly she was crying, soundlessly, painfully, one tear after another dropping onto her navy dress front. She clenched and unclenched her hands. She thought of the books in Mrs. Riley's library, especially the fine leather-covered ones. She thought of the joy of creating a new world simply by moving her pencil across the paper. She thought of classes that would teach her to do this more effectively. These hopes had come back to her for only a few days, tantalizing her, and then been snatched away again without mercy.

The tears came faster, and she made no move to stop them or wipe them away, knowing instinctively that they would carry away with them some of the first sharpness of the pain. The red and gold trees above her, and the bronzed ferns beside her wavered through her tears, swelled and diminished.

She thought again of Ma saying, "It's the will of God for you to stay in the hills like we've always done."

How did Ma know? How could anyone know what the will of God was? Lilly knew that she herself didn't come close to understanding God, and she simply didn't see how Ma could be so sure of God's will for her daughter's life.

"Oh, God, can You make me that sure?" she begged. "Maybe if I really knew it was Your will, I would be willing to stay."

At home, the family had eaten supper without her. "There's some beans and boiled taters left," Ma said, and although she watched Lilly closely, she didn't ask where she had been for so long.

Chapter ten

Fall lost her pretty dresses and put on the drabber browns and grays of winter. There were sorghum boilings and corn shuckings in the evenings, with plenty of singing and merrymaking in spite of the scant harvest. "The less we have," Pappaw said drily, "the louder we sing so that we forget."

Uncle Sandy finished his house, and neighbors came from miles around for a housewarming party. Wilson and Beulah went to the county seat one day and were married, since her family couldn't afford a meal for all the friends and relatives. Jaybird took sick, and died quietly in his sleep. And then one day, strangers came, bringing two little girls. They said their names were Lexie and Mexie, and they had belonged to Uncle Buell before he got himself killed in the war. Now his wife had died in Knott county, and someone needed to care for the girls. Pappaw and Mammaw opened their home, although they had never seen these grandchildren before.

And so the seasons of life, the beginnings and endings, came and went.

Lilly still walked into town three days a week to help Mrs. Riley. Only after several months had passed did Mrs. Riley suggest one day that she resume the reading aloud. The suggestion caught Lilly off guard, but she realized almost as quickly that she would be able to listen to stories again without the painful throb at her heart and the sick feeling in her stomach. "I'd like that," she answered quietly.

Mrs. Riley's face broke into one of her rare smiles, and her eyes shone.

And Lilly still stopped at the bridge, slipping beneath it nearly every time she had an empty road on the way home. She didn't do anything there, and she had to wrap her arms around herself to stay warm these days. But she simply let herself be still, let herself listen, let herself watch the play of scattered sunlight over the water. Something as big as the mountains, as gentle as rippling water, and as luminous as the moon seemed to come very close to her when she stood that way. She hardly knew what it was, and yet when she felt it closest, her heart always reached out to God. She never thought of what she was doing as praying, because prayer seemed to be something a preacher did in church on Sunday's, a lifting up of the voice and begging for answers from the skies. All she knew was that she felt quieter after she climbed back onto the road.

Jesse came at least once a week to call on her during those months. He never mentioned marriage, but Lilly knew he was thinking along that line, as soon as he could afford it. Her life seemed mapped out for her.

In December winter came and soon slipped into an unbroken rhythm—a rhythm of snow and wind and ice, followed by melting days of sunshine and puddles. Lilly slogged through snow or mud to get to the Riley house. One morning, when wind had burned her face the whole way, and she was shivering inside her double layer of coat and sweater, she met Mr. Riley at the kitchen door.

He was never home at this time, and she knew instantly from the look on his face that the reason was not a good one. "What's wrong?" she asked in alarm.

"My wife is sick," he said gruffly. "I stayed until you came so she wouldn't be alone."

"What is it?" Lilly wondered. She stepped inside the kitchen and gratefully unwrapped herself in the warmth.

"Don't know. I sent for the doctor." Instead of looking hard and cold, Mr. Riley looked haggard. "Nurse her the best you can, Lilly. I'll be back at lunch, and if you need me before then, send someone to find me."

"Yes, sir." She warmed her hands by the stove for a few minutes, and then went upstairs to Mr. and Mrs. Riley's bedroom. Mr. Riley had a roaring fire going in the fireplace, and slender Mrs. Riley lay on her side in bed, only a narrow ridge under the bedclothes. Lilly tip-toed up near her and saw that she appeared to be sleeping. Mr. Riley had given her no instructions. She didn't even know whether Mrs. Riley was sick to her stomach, or took with a fever. She felt her hand and discovered it was hot. At the light touch, Mrs. Riley stirred restlessly.

"Lie still," Lilly soothed. She wished she could pull down some dried herbs from the kitchen walls at home and make a tea with them, but knew she dared not leave now. She pushed the embers together in the fireplace and decided to go for another scoop of coal while Mrs. Riley was still asleep.

Mrs. Riley tossed and turned as the slow minutes crept away. Lilly kept the fire going, laid cold cloths on her forehead, and went again and again to the window, hoping to see Dr. Damron coming.

When he came in at last, he moved quietly around the sickroom as he took Mrs. Riley's pulse, felt her forehead, slipped a thermometer into her mouth, listened to her breathing, and mixed some white and blue powders from his bag. Lilly watched him anxiously.

"It's influenza," he said at last. "Mix a pinch of this medicine into water and have her drink it every two hours. That should help bring the fever down. Not much else we can do."

He stood beside the bed, looking down at his patient for a long moment. "Has she been bleeding out of her mouth or nose?"

"I don't think so," Lilly said, startled.

"Well, that's good. How long have you been here?"

"Just an hour or two."

"I believe I'd better stop at the office and talk to Mr. Riley too."

When Mr. Riley came home at lunch, he ran straight upstairs. "How is she?" he demanded.

Lilly had just laid a cool cloth on Mrs. Riley's forehead, and she stepped back from the bed, saying, "I can't see much difference."

"Did the doctor give you anything for her?"

"Some powder. He said to mix it in water."

Mr. Riley crossed the room in three strides, took up the little glass with the mixed powders and stared vengefully into it. "That's all?"

"Yes, sir."

After Mr. Riley sat down by his wife, she ventured, "I'd like to go home and get some herbs that Ma has. They always work for us."

"It's snowing and blowing bad," Mr. Riley said doubtfully.

"I know the way," Lilly answered, "and I'll hurry."

"Go then. I'll stay until you get back."

It took Lilly forty-five minutes of running, sliding, stumbling, and falling to go home, get the herbs, and come back again. Ma thought that Lilly had come to stay because of the weather, and when she found out the real reason, she fussed and scolded and said that no rich lady was worth the trip through the blizzard back to town. "They got the doctor, didn't they?"

"Yes, but he only gave her some powders. I don't think they'll do much good."

"If you must go then, wrap yourself up in my shawl over your coat."

She had the white road to herself on the way back, a road fringed with drooping trees and wind-lashed weeds. She checked often to make sure the precious herbs were still in her pocket.

Mrs. Riley was awake and talking when she arrived. When Lilly heard her voice, she feared it was delirium. But her words made sense. "Is it cold outside? I can feel the cold seeping into the room."

"Yes, dear." Mr. Riley laid a hand on her arm with unaccustomed gentleness. "It's snowing up a blizzard out there."

Lilly hesitated in the doorway. "I'm back, Mr. Riley," she said softly.

Mrs. Riley shifted position on the pillow and smiled at her. "Were you here this morning, Lilly?"

"Yes, ma'am."

"I thought so. But everything from this morning is hazy in my mind. I feel better now."

"The doctor was here too," Mr. Riley told her. "He called it influenza."

Mrs. Riley grabbed suddenly at his arm. "Not the influenza that everyone—"

"Hush, dear. He doesn't know. He couldn't tell." Then, slowly, as if the whole truth had to be dragged from him, he added, "But there are several other cases of it. He thinks it could be."

"No," Mrs. Riley moaned. "I hoped we were isolated enough here."

"Hush," Mr. Riley said more sternly.

Mrs. Riley pulled herself up on one elbow. "Lilly, go home right now," she begged. "I must not give this to you."

"I can't," Lilly answered, while fear gnawed at her stomach, fear all the worse because she didn't understand what Mrs. Riley was talking about. "It's snowing harder than ever now. I brought my things to stay the night."

Mrs. Riley shut her eyes and moaned again.

"And I brought some things to make a tea for you," Lilly said. "Ma says these herbs knock a fever in a jiffy every time."

"Go down and make some now," Mr. Riley answered tightly.

Lilly dipped some water from the reservoir and heated it in a kettle on the stove. Meanwhile she ground up the roots and mixed them with the dried leaves. Mr. Riley came and stood in the doorway, popping his knuckles and watching her.

"Mrs. Riley wasn't delirious, was she?" Lilly queried at last.

"No."

Usually Lilly didn't talk to him unless she absolutely had to, but watching him with his wife had made him seem suddenly more human. So she asked, "What influenza was she talking about?"

"Have you heard of the soldier's sickness?"

"Mrs. Riley was never a soldier."

Mr. Riley smiled without a trace of humor or happiness. "It's called that because soldiers are bringing it back from the war. But others get it too. Out there—" he waved his hand in a gesture that included the whole world beyond the mountains "—people are dying like flies from it. I hoped we would be sheltered here."

"How did she get it?" Lilly asked, her hands stilled on the counter, her eyes wide, and her heart thumping strangely.

"Who knows," he answered gruffly. "Somebody passing through, maybe. Or someone she met if she walked down to the town."

He put on his coat slowly, opened the door unwillingly, and looked out into a world of swirling white. "I must be off to the mine. I think I'll call the men out and send them home. This weather is terrible. I'll be back before long."

When he had almost shut the door behind him, he opened it again. "I can send your pa around by the house to walk you home too." Snow swirled in past his shoulders and lay in little white furrows on the floor.

"No," Lilly answered shortly. "I'll stay here."

She finished the tea and carried it up to Mrs. Riley. "I would like to hear some poetry," Mrs. Riley said quietly after her first sip, so quietly that Lilly had to bend low to catch the words. "Will you read to me, Lilly?"

"Of course, ma'am."

"Go over to the library then and get something. Wordsworth. Tennyson. I don't care which."

The door to the library had been shut, and no fire started in the fireplace. Lilly shivered when she opened the door. The long rows of books stared at her out of the dimness, silent, holding their treasures patiently between their covers until someone had time to dig them out. Lilly knew where Mrs. Riley kept her poetry collection, and she selected a book of Wordsworth's poems, handsomely bound in burgundy leather.

She had never read out loud except at school, and she tried to make her voice match Mrs. Riley's—smooth and undulating, pausing at the right spots, and letting the beautiful symmetry of the words fill up the quiet. After two or three poems, she saw that Mrs. Riley had fallen asleep. She sat for several more long minutes, fingering the thick cream-colored paper with its gilt edging, running her hand over the embossing on the cover. Only the heavy ticking of the clock on the bureau, Mrs. Riley's light breathing, and the lighter hiss of snow against the windowpane broke the silence.

Toward bedtime Mrs. Riley's fever climbed again. Nothing, not even another cup of tea, brought it down this time. She began coughing harshly too. Mr. Riley made several starts to go and get his horse to fetch the doctor. Then he always stopped himself and said, "But what more can he do than he's already done," and fell to pacing up and down the landing at the top of the stairs.

Lilly watched him from the bedroom doorway. "Is there something else I should be doing?" she asked when his course brought him near her.

"You're a better nurse than I am," he snapped. "Do what you think is best. Call me if you need me. I'll be close by."

They stayed that way for much of the night. The old clock on the bureau ticked away the hours, and Mr. Riley's footsteps intermittently tapped out the minutes. Sometimes he would stop his restless walking and go down to the sitting room or the kitchen. Sometimes he brought up another bucket of coal. Once when Lilly was on her way to the kitchen for a fresh pan of cool water to dip the rags in, she saw him in the library, without a lamp, staring fixedly at the window drapes.

At three o'clock he came suddenly into the bedroom. "Go and get some sleep, Lilly," he said shortly. "Mrs. Riley will need you again tomorrow. I'll stay with her."

He hadn't told her where to go. She walked downstairs and stood in the doorway of the sitting room, her shoulders dragged down by weariness and dread. Coals glowed red in the fireplace. She added a few more and curled up close by, her legs drawn in tight against herself. She had eaten a little supper, all that her stomach could handle. Now she felt hungry and sick at the same time. She closed her eyes, only to see images of the candle light on Mrs. Riley's pale face, the fierceness that brooded in Mr. Riley's eyes, and the sheen of the burgundy covered book that still lay on the bedside stand. She opened her eyes and stared up into the shadowy dimness of the high-ceilinged room. "Please, God, please don't let Mrs. Riley die."

She woke up the next morning and was aware instantly that the sun was up, and the snow had stopped. She pulled aside the curtain at the sitting room window and looked out into a world of dead white. Cold nipped at her fingers and toes. She added more coal to the fireplace, slipped quickly into her shoes and hurried upstairs.

The dead whiteness had seeped into Mr. and Mrs. Riley's room as well. Mrs. Riley lay white among the white sheets, so still that Lilly thought for a breathless moment that she had died. Then she saw the gentle rise of her chest, and her lips parted in the act of breathing. Mr. Riley slumped in a chair beside her, his head with its heavy shock of gray and brown hair down on his chest. He started suddenly awake when Lilly neared him.

"Is it—morning?" he asked, stumbling to his feet.

"Yes, it's morning. I'll go down and make breakfast."

He sank onto the chair again. "Thanks."

She had to stir up the fire in the kitchen stove and wait for it to get hot enough to fry eggs and bacon. While she waited, she measured out enough of her herbs to make one more cup of tea. She ate her own breakfast in the kitchen, after taking Mr. Riley's up to him in the bedroom. He came down very soon, most of the food untouched. "She's sleeping now," he said shortly. "I hope it's a good sleep. I'm going to the mine, but I'll be back once I make sure things are under control there."

Lilly threw the leftover bacon and eggs out the back door for any prowling neighborhood dogs to find and washed up the breakfast dishes with a faint hope in her heart. But when she went up to the bedroom again, she saw that Mrs. Riley's sleep was not the good one her husband had hoped for. She was lying face up, panting with each breath, her eyes half open, her skin pallid and damp.

Lilly smoothed the hair away from her forehead. "Mrs. Riley."

She moaned and tried to rouse herself.

"Just lie still. Would you like some tea? I have a hot cup." Gently Lilly propped her up on the pillows and held a spoonful to her mouth. Mrs. Riley opened her lips and swallowed convulsively. She drank a dozen spoonfuls that way before the amber liquid started dribbling back out of her mouth. Lilly wiped it away and stood looking down at her, the cup still in her hands.

When Mr. Riley came back, he said brusquely, "All right, Lilly, you've been here long enough. Time for you to go home. Your family will worry."

"But who will take care of Mrs. Riley and make your meals?"

"I'll take care of her myself. If I need help, there are other women close by."

Reluctantly Lilly went. She knew that Ma would want her to come home, and the hard light in Mr. Riley's eyes really left her no choice. By the time she got as far as the store, wading through the drifted snow, she was exhausted.

She would go inside here and warm up for just a few minutes, she decided. Maybe Mrs. Keeton had news of who else was sick. But the store was cold and empty. "Mrs. Keeton," Lilly called in alarm.

"Lilly," a tired man's voice answered her from the back room. "Is that you?"

"Yes."

"Thank God you've come."

Without further invitation she pushed open the door to the Keeton dwelling behind the store. "What's wrong? Where's Elzinnie?"

"She's bad off," her husband answered. He was lying on the bare board floor, blanketless, his clothing rumpled. But he was by the stove, and had the coal bucket within his reach.

"Are you okay?" Lilly asked. He looked so sprawled out there, and she noticed clotted blood on his elbows, telling plainly how he, with legs that didn't work, had made it from the bed to the stove.

"It's not me," he answered impatiently, "it's my wife. Can't you do something for her?"

On the bed, the quilts were over Elzinnie's face. When Lilly drew them back, she saw blood all over the pillow and the sheet. She felt a wave of nausea. "What's wrong with her?"

"I don't know." Okla had one arm flung out over the floor, the fingers of that hand knotted into a tight, frantic, helpless fist. "I don't know. All's I can do is keep the fire going so she don't freeze."

"Has she been sleeping all day?"

"Off and on. When she's awake she's out of her head. And I haven't got but one or two coals left. Can you bring in some more?"

Glad of a job to do outside, Lilly took the bucket. Just beyond the door, she could control her stomach no longer. She retched and heaved, leaning limply against the outside wall, wishing she could throw up her empty stomach along with all her anxiety. Then she resolutely went on and filled the bucket with coal. She set it within Okla's reach. "I'm on my way home from Mr. Riley's place," she said. "Mrs. Riley is sick too. But I'll find someone who can come and help you."

"I'd be everlasting grateful."

"Don't you need a blanket? That floor must be cold."

"No. Leave them all on her."

Finding someone who could stay with Elzinnie was harder than she had imagined. Silva Greer couldn't, and there was only a scattering of houses for the next hundred yards up the trail. At one of them, tow-headed Corinna Blair said, "Ma's sick herself."

At the next one, Floetta Ratliff, Jemsey's mother, came to the door, but when Lilly told her what she wanted, she looked terrified. "What's wrong with her?"

"I don't know. Okla said when she was awake, she was out of her head. And there was blood on her pillow. I never saw such a sickness."

Floetta clutched at the door frame, and the color drained from her. "Blood? That's one of the signs of this bad sickness. People bleed from their ears and nose." Then a kind of hardness came into her eyes. "Of course I'll go right away. Someone has to look after them, and it might as well be me."

At home Ma had news for her, disturbing news. "Beulah has it. And Mexie. Sandy too."

"Oh, no, Ma."

"It spreads fast," she said grimly, "and it's bad."

"Elzinnie Keeton has it."

"Is someone with them?"

"I told Floetta, and she's going."

"She's a good woman. She'll do all she can."

It was almost lunchtime, and after they ate hot fried mush, Ma sent Lilly to bed. When Lilly tried to protest about going to bed in the middle of the day, Ma said, "Listen, Lilly, I can see by your eyes that you didn't get no sleep last night to speak of. Now stop being so fool-headed and go."

Lilly burrowed under the double layer of feather ticks in the loft bed, curling herself into a ball to stay warm. She shivered for a while, but finally drifted into a restless sleep, peppered with dreams. She awoke to hear banging on the door downstairs. She lay perfectly still, watching her clouds of breath as they steamed above her head, and listening to Ma grumbling mildly as she went to the door.

"Hello. What'd you want?"

A thin high treble, panting from exertion, answered her. "I've come for Lilly. Is she home?"

"She's sleeping."

"I've gotta talk to her."

Lilly scrambled out of bed and down the ladder. "I'm awake." She saw a young boy in the doorway, someone she had seen playing in the street that summer, likely the son of a new miner.

"You're Lilly?"

"Yes."

"Mr. Riley sent for you."

"Why?"

"He said Mrs. Riley was asking for you. That's all I know. He told me to run as fast as I could."

Ma had pulled him into the cabin, and he stood there sweating, big drops of moisture rolling out from under his cap and down his cheeks. He must have run all the way up the hill.

"I'm coming," Lilly answered briefly.

"Lilly. . ." Ma took one look at her face and put up her hands in resignation.

Lilly dressed quickly for the outdoors. The boy had already gone, but when she left the cabin she caught sight of his slight figure down at the fork. She ran after him and overtook him by the bridge. She thought about asking him for more information, and then decided against it. Instead she raced past him, her legs strong again after her nap, the wind tearing coldly through her chest. She gasped huge lungfuls of it, disregarding the burning inside her. A sweat had broken out on her by the time she stood in the Rileys' kitchen.

No one was in sight. She listened for footsteps, voices, anything, and when nothing but silence greeted her, she slipped out of her coat and boots and tip-toed up the back stairs.

When she stood in the bedroom doorway, she made a beautiful picture of life, in contrast to the scene inside. Mr. Riley looked up and saw her there. Her cheeks shone vivid pink from the cold, and her brown hair lay in soft ringlets where the wind had shaped it against the edges of her scarf. He felt a sudden anger toward this fresh-faced young girl.

Lilly didn't see immediately why she had been called. The doctor and Mr. Riley stood beside the bed. Mrs. Riley lay under the blankets, very still and white, but with her eyes open. She smiled gently when she saw Lilly. "You must have run to get here so quickly, dear."

Mr. Riley moved away from them and stood with his hands behind his back, staring out the window. Lilly took his place at the bedside. "What is it, Mrs. Riley? Why did you want me?"

"My life is running out, Lilly."

"No, Mrs. Riley!" Lilly felt a cold, sharper than the air she had breathed, clutch at her lungs and force everything else out.

"Yes, dear. I can feel it happening."

"The fever has broken," the doctor muttered. "There might be hope yet."

She smiled slightly again. "This body has been ill and weak for a long time. It doesn't have the strength to withstand this fever, and is simply giving up. I'm just glad I'm able to think rationally."

Lilly hardly realized what she was doing when she sank down on the floor beside Mrs. Riley's bed.

Mrs. Riley reached out a thin white hand and dropped it lightly on her head as if to bestow a blessing. "I wanted to talk to you, Lilly." She paused to take several shallow breaths, and her hand trembled. "I needed to tell you this. I know what really happened at your place when Mr. Barker visited your family. He told us as soon as he came back."

Lilly stared at the pattern of the rug on the floor. Mrs. Riley's words fell as softly as snow in the room. "I think it was noble and brave of you, the way you acted afterward."

Another pause, longer this time. "Lilly, you love books like I do." Mrs. Riley's hand slid off her head and onto her shoulder. "When I'm gone, I want you to choose several from my library for your very own. Look at me, Lilly."

Lilly looked into her gray eyes, familiar warm gray eyes that now held a strange distance, a distance that hinted of things beyond the realm of human sight. "You have been a good maid, and so much more than a maid to me."

"Mrs. Riley, I—"

"You never realized this, but you filled a place in my heart that has been empty for a long time." Her smile this time was unbearably sweet.

Lilly stayed in the room until she died, because Mrs. Riley wanted her to. Perhaps an hour passed, perhaps more—in the presence of death and immortality, time has no meaning. When she drew her last breath, Mr. Riley was holding her hand, almost as ashen-faced as she. The doctor had withdrawn discreetly from the room, and Lilly was sitting on a low stool at the foot of the bed, with her face turned away. She didn't want to watch, but she knew exactly when it happened. The gasping, uneven breathing stopped; the restless tossing of arms and legs stilled. Lilly covered her own eyes with cold hands, and when she next looked, Mr. Riley had already pulled the sheet up over his wife's face.

She went out as the doctor came in and walked down to the kitchen, numbly. She noticed in a vacant sort of way that the stove needed more coal, and she replenished it from the bucket. The doctor found her sitting in a chair when he came down. He looked at her sympathetically. "There won't be a funeral," he said.

"No funeral?" she repeated blankly.

"We have an epidemic on our hands," he explained grimly. "Until it's over, we can't have any public gatherings of any sort."

Lilly went home in a cold gray twilight. The road seemed long and rough, her feet unused to walking it, her mind somewhere outside her body.

Chapter eleven

After that, the flu spread as rapidly as gossip at Mrs. Keeton's store. Five weeks of death passed over the valley and the hills that surrounded it, leaving it forever altered and scarred. Mrs. Riley's was the first death bed that Lilly watched beside, but certainly not the last.

In the Burchett family, Patty died first. Lilly was sleeping when it happened, and awoke to hear dull hammer blows outside. It was still too dark in the loft to get up, but dawn might be creeping over the mountains in the east. For a moment she wondered stupidly why Pa was doing carpenter work so early in the morning. Then as she came fully awake, she realized those were the same noises they had heard from neighbors on other mornings and evenings when sound carried like bells through the crystal air. Whenever they heard that repeated thudding, Ma always looked more sad and said, "I wonder who it is this time." Neighbors never visited neighbors now. They only buried their dead and sat by their sick.

Shivering uncontrollably, Lilly lifted the unbleached curtain at the tiny window. Outside, she could just make out Pa pounding rough pine boards into a box shape. She knew without going downstairs that it was for Patty, unless Maybelle or T.J. had taken a sudden turn for the worse during the night.

Pa and Vince dug a grave the best they could in the frozen soil and buried Patty not far from the house. It was too hard for the two of them to drag the coffin up to the knoll to join the other five graves. Ma and Lilly stood inside the window and watched, not daring to leave the sick ones alone. Ma held

Sonny close and wept a few tears, the stoic tears of a woman who has loved and lost again and again.

She didn't scold anymore, and it seemed that she never slept. When Lilly offered to take a night with the sick ones, Ma always said quietly but firmly, "No. I'm their ma, and I will tend them." She had more wrinkles, and more gray in her knot of hair, but more kindness in her voice, and more gentleness in her hands.

Lilly stood close beside her now and had a sudden impulse to reach out and put a hand on her shoulder as Mrs. Riley had done so easily. But they were mountain people and didn't show love and sympathy that way. She only swallowed again and again, trying to dissolve the painful knot where her throat should have been.

The only time she went further from the house than the barn or outhouse was the time Ma sent her to Hester Sue's cabin. By then the snow had melted, and the streams were muddy and full and frantic. "It's a hard road this time of year," Ma said, with pleading in her voice, "but she knows everything about what grows in the hills. Maybe she'll have something that will help."

Lilly was already reaching for her coat. "Of course I'll go, Ma."

She fought her way up the upper fork of Sand Lick, crossing an ice-crusted log bridge at one place, and simply walking through water above her knees when there was no bridge. From the creek trail, the path to Hester Sue's cabin twisted up the side of the hill and stopped right at her steps. There were eight of them, because Hester Sue's cabin jutted out from a nearly vertical hillside.

It was tiny, but snug and solid and warm. Hester Sue opened the door with a look of astonishment on her leathered features. "Don't nobody come see me this time of year. But you're right welcome. Sit down and rest. You're wet. I'll build up the fire."

Like her cabin, Hester Sue herself was tiny, a full-blooded Cherokee Indian woman who had escaped from a band being herded west and had carved out a life for herself alone. With quick energy, she heaped wood on the already blazing fire and knelt down to pull off Lilly's soaked shoes and socks.

"I can—" Lilly began.

"Now you sit still. I know what it's like to come up here in January. I know just how high the creek is by the wet on your dress. And you're not going home until you've dried out and eaten something."

Lilly flexed her bare toes in front of the heat, feeling for a brief moment that the flu was something far away from her. Then Hester Sue asked, "What's wrong down your way? I know you wouldn't come if it wasn't bad."

"You've not heard of the flu?"

"I've not heard of no flu."

"Everyone's down with it. We're not having church, nor school. The store is closed, and the men aren't going to the mines."

"Tell me what it's like. How do folks act that get it?"

So while she made coffee and hoe cakes, Lilly told her. She told her of the fevers, the coughs and deep labored breathing, and the worst symptom of all—the occasional bleeding from ears and nose.

Hester Sue seemed to be giving all her attention to her food over the fire, but she looked more and more serious the longer Lilly talked. "I'll send some things with you," she said, "but I've never heard of a sickness like this one."

She made Lilly drink the coffee scalding hot and eat the hoe cakes fresh from the coals. "You've got to warm up your innards. And stay by that fire until you're so hot you think you'll bust into flames."

That happened quickly, and she backed away cautiously. It took longer for her heavy dress to completely dry, but it also took some time for Hester Sue to go through her herbs, mumbling to herself all the while. At last she announced, "Horse mint, wintergreen, hornbean bark, and pine top. Boil those together and make a strong tea. That's the best I've got."

"Thank you," Lilly said gratefully.

Hester Sue came out on her porch to watch her off. "Be careful," she warned, "but hurry home. I smell a rain coming."

Lilly was shivering again, more at the thought of the creek crossings ahead of her than from the actual chill in the air. And what if she should slip and drown the precious herbs in the creek?

But she arrived safely, and Ma made batch after batch of tea for the next days, giving it without much faith to all the sick ones. Lilly got the fever herself and wrestled through two nights and a full day of delirium. When she awoke from it, feeling limp and exhausted, it was to feel Ma stroking the hair back from her face and saying softly, "Thank God I still have my Lilly girl. The fever has broke and you'll recover."

She was awake the night Vince died, because by then Ma was too sick to care for anyone else. Pa went out again as soon as it was faintly light and nailed together another coffin, even though he was weak-kneed with fever himself. This time he and Bobby dug the grave and filled it back in again. This time Lilly stood at the window with Maybelle, and when Maybelle cried, she put her arm around her. This time she cried as Ma had the other time, a few tears that did nothing to ease the ache inside her.

Ma understood through the haze of her own illness what was going on and tried to get up, mumbling something about going to find her Vince.

"No, Ma. No." Lilly finally sat on the edge of the bed and pressed her hand firmly down on Ma's shoulder. "Stay in bed. You're too sick to get up."

"Not too sick to look after my children," Ma mumbled almost incoherently. "Let me get up, Lilly."

"No!" Lilly cried. "Stay in bed, or you will die yourself."

The moment she had said it, she looked up and saw Maybelle's face, still pinched from her bout with fever, now white, wide-eyed, and terrified. As soon as Lilly was sure that Ma would stay in bed, she followed Maybelle into the eating room, where the table was always empty these days. Maybelle sat in one of the chairs, her head down on her arms in front of her.

Lilly touched her.

"She won't, will she?" Maybelle asked haggardly.

"No, Maybelle, she won't. She's too tough."

"How do you know?"

"I. . ." Lilly walked to the window and back again. She didn't know; she only hoped that the brave words spoken aloud would somehow make the thing itself real.

After that the days and nights blurred into an endless cycle of brewing tea, wringing out cool rags, cooking thin corn gruel, chopping wood, drawing water, keeping the delirious sufferers in bed by sheer force, if nothing else.

Pa took to his bed after burying Vince, and for a few hours, Lilly was afraid the work and cold had made his sickness the worst of all. But for him it turned the following night, the same night that Sonny came down with it.

Maybelle made tea and cooked corn and kept the fire roaring in the fireplace. She worked so hard that late one evening Lilly found her slumped over in a faint, worn out from her own sickness. Bobby chopped wood for them like a man, nearly always silent, his face grave, his eyes shadowed. T.J. got over his fever, but he didn't recover his childish bounce. He lay beside the fireplace, silently, hour after hour. Lilly was so busy running between the sick beds that she almost forgot him, until the time she saw Bobby holding him on his lap and rocking him back and forth. "Poor little boys," she muttered, and the tears almost came then.

Ma died at daybreak one morning, just as the east turned from pale gray to faint rose. She had become lucid again in her final minutes, long enough to say a few quiet words to Pa, to touch Lilly's hand and whisper, "You've been a good daughter, Lilly. You'll take care of the other children, won't you?"

Almost before Lilly could answer, she was gone, slipped out with the night into the great beyond.

A third hole joined the other fresh graves. Only Sonny was still sick, and Lilly held his hot little body tightly against her own as she watched Pa and Bobby fill in this grave. Life as she knew it descended into the gashed earth with the coffin, and she grabbed for the windowsill in front of her. T.J. understood only that his ma had been carried outside in a box, and he suddenly had enough energy to scream relentlessly.

The screams filled the cabin, and Lilly heard them but hadn't the strength of will to do anything about them. Pa and Bobby had taken shovels by now and begun throwing the clods back on top of the coffin. Pa stopped after every other shovelful and wiped his coat sleeve across his eyes. Lilly had never seen him crying before.

"Make T.J. stop crying," Maybelle suddenly shouted viciously.

Lilly handed Sonny to her and scooped up T.J., a six-year-old small for his age and made thinner by his fight with illness. "T.J., stop hollering so," she whispered into his matted hair, smelling the odors of dirt and ashes there.

He turned around and clung to her like a baby. "Ma. I want Ma."

No words came to Lilly, so she said none. She only held him tighter, sat down on the bed where Ma had so recently lain, and rocked him back and forth. They were still sitting that way, Lilly with T.J., and Maybelle with

Sonny, when Pa and Bobby came back in. Bobby went straight to the fire and lay down in front of it, turning his face away from everyone. Pa sank down heavily on a chair without taking his coat off. Lilly realized suddenly that the six of them there in the front room, together and yet alone in their sorrow, were all that remained of their lively family of nine. She held tighter to T.J., and he responded by throwing his arms around her neck in a squeeze so hard it almost choked her. She felt powerless to give him the love and care he so desperately needed.

The sickness left them at last, with only Bobby untouched. Pa erected stone slabs by the graves, but Lilly avoided looking that direction.

The community came to life again. Neighbors stopped in and shared sympathy and stories. Mr. Ferguson started a fire in the school stove again and opened the doors for the students who were left. The men went back to work in the mines. But Mrs. Keeton's store stayed closed, because she now lay under the ground behind it, and her husband had moved in with the Ratliff family.

After a time, Jeb Cantrell came over the mountain and had a memorial service for all those who had died. The living from miles around attended it, but many of them came thin and pale, ghostly shadows in body and spirit of what they had been before.

Jeb preached for a long time, mentioning many of the dead by name, and causing his congregation to weep openly, again and again. Then he wound up his three hour sermon by beseeching anyone who wasn't right with God to get right at once, lest He send a worse punishment upon them. Pa straightened up stiffly on his bench at that, and glared toward the front of the church.

Barely were they out of sight of the church on the way home when he growled, "The nerve of the man, to hint that this plague was a punishment of God. A punishment for what? Surely not the sins of my good wife."

Lilly had neither the heart nor the will to enter into a discussion with him. Besides, she did think—and wondered at herself for thinking it—that God could have done a fairer job of punishing the guilty and sparing the righteous. What sins had Patty, for instance, done?

Not a week later, Pa brought a message back from work. "Mr. Riley told me you're to stop in there when you're in town. Something about some books. He said you would know what he meant." Pa peered closely at Lilly.

"Oh, yes," she answered. "I know. I'll go tomorrow."

Normally Pa would have asked her what was going on, but he kept most of his words to himself these days. He only sat down at the table and asked, "Supper ready?"

"Yes, Pa." She set a steaming cornbread in front of him and brought some potatoes baked in the ashes.

She decided to get at the business as soon as the children came home from school the next afternoon. Maybelle begged to go along, but Lilly was adamant. "No, I'm going alone. Tend Sonny and start supper. I'll hurry."

"What are you going for?"

"You'll see when I get back."

She flew light-footed down the path, across the bridge, past the school and church, and into the town itself. Out of long habit, she let herself in by the Rileys' kitchen door without knocking. The remnants of an untold number of meals littered the counter, and dishes were piled high by the sink. If it hadn't been for Sonny and Maybelle and the boys at home, she would have washed things up for him.

She knew by the chill in the room that the fire had gone out. All was dim and very still, waiting for memories to come alive. Lilly walked silently up the steep back stairs, across the landing, and into the library. This room felt like it hadn't seen a fire since Mrs. Riley died, and perhaps it hadn't. The heavy drapes kept out the light, so that Lilly wished she had brought a lamp along up. Instead of going back for one, she pulled the drapes aside and looped them up out the way.

Two books lay on the table, one of them the book of poetry that she had read to Mrs. Riley the day before she died. Lilly ran her hand once more over the burgundy cover, the gilt-edged pages, and the book became hers. Choosing the other one took longer, but she settled at last on a collection of stories. Spying a pencil and paper on Mr. Riley's desk, she wrote a quick note. "I chose my books today. Thank you. Lilly Burchett."

Then she turned to leave the room and found that she couldn't just yet. Something invisible held her there. She ran her eyes over the rows of books, longingly. She thought of the days when Mrs. Riley's voice had carried her far away from the hills of Kentucky into other wonderful worlds, and she wished she could go back to those days. No way of escape seemed open for her now. She felt herself clinging to this room and the memories it evoked, much like T.J. had clung to her the day Ma died. Just before she got to the point of tears, she turned and ran.

When she stepped outside, clutching her books close inside her coat, she discovered that a fine driving rain had begun to fall. She stopped running, but continued to walk fast, all the way to the bridge. It had been months since she had slipped below it, but she needed it now. She slid between lank stems of dead grass and accidentally stuck her shoe into a slushy puddle. When she reached the creek where it murmured sadly over the rocks, she stood still, her arms folded across her chest, the books held close to her heart.

Usually she felt a deep peace when she stood this way under the bridge, but this time she felt only loss, an unreasoning sense of betrayal, and a pain too deep for tears. Ma, Vince, Patty, and Mrs. Riley, all gone. Pa gone too, it sometimes seemed. Four motherless children looking to her for love and care.

This life was too hard. Lilly wished frantically that she had gone with Mr. Barker, that she had run away, stood up to Pa, something, so that she would now be gone from the mountains. No one could endure life here. "I will get out," Lilly whispered between clenched teeth. "The next time I have a chance, no matter what it is, I'll take it. I can't live here."

Part 3

Chapter twelve

The whole Burchett family changed after feeling the hand of death. Maybelle worked harder and enjoyed it less. T.J. clung to Lilly like a two- or three-year-old. Bobby never laughed, and his smile was only a thin shadow of what it had been before. Pa came home every evening, ate supper silently, and went straight to bed. Lilly saw all these changes in her family, but she could not see the changes in herself. Others, however, noticed a new hardness, mixed with a gentle protectiveness for T.J. and Sonny.

Not that anyone saw her much. Since Mrs. Keeton's store was closed, Pa brought all their essentials from the commissary in town. Neighbors stopped in occasionally, and Lilly treated them with aloof politeness. But as the long winter dragged to a close, she mostly stayed secluded at home. The two books from Mrs. Riley's library provided her only release, and she read them often on the evenings when Jesse didn't come for a walk.

He talked hesitatingly of marriage, just once, in February.

"I can't consider it yet," she told him. "I have to look after the children."

"I thought as much," he said gently. "They need you. But maybe, when they're older, or when your pa marries again. . . I'm willing to wait."

She looked away from his frank eyes, the eyes that had searched hers so often in the past ten months. "I don't know, Jesse. I don't know when that will be, and I'd rather not promise anything just yet."

"I understand," he answered simply.

Underneath the uncertainty of her reply lay her resolve to leave the mountains, firm as a cast-iron frying pan, polished by the long weeks of hard work and sadness. She knew that Jesse had no part in that goal, but she put off telling him, hoping that time would give her kinder words with which to do it.

He was silent for a few minutes, and she worried that she had hurt him even now. But when he spoke, his voice was easy, relaxed. "Heard today that Mrs. Keeton's store is opening again."

"Who will run it?"

"Her son is coming from Lexington."

"Is he bringing his wife with him?"

"Why, sure."

Mr. and Mrs. Keeton had only one living child, this son who had gone off to the war, found a girl, married, and settled in Lexington. They had never come back to visit. "Folks here always thought she was too proud to visit the mountains," Lilly said slowly. "Where will they live?"

"They're going to fix up the old house, just up the way from the store. They can live there and take care of Mr. Keeton too."

"Do you think they'll be happy there?"

"Of course. It's a fine house yet, though no one has lived in it for nigh on ten years."

Lilly reached out to a roadside bush, snapped off a twig, ran her fingers up its smooth straightness. Jesse didn't understand. Would this young Mrs. Keeton, Charlotte, be able to live in a cabin at all? Would she fret and chafe and long for her friends in Lexington? Would she associate with the other women on Sand Lick?

Unconsciously, Lilly had drawn a picture of Charlotte Keeton as a younger version of Mrs. Riley, tall, delicate, quiet, and softly feminine. She was shocked out of this picture the first time she went to the store and actually saw her. Charlotte, her husband Joe, and old Mr. Keeton were all behind the counter, the two men sitting, Charlotte standing.

Both men looked alike, their eyelids drooping over tired eyes, their arms seeming long and gangly in their stillness. Against this background, Charlotte stood out like a ginseng berry in a damp green woods. Her hair hung loose, instead of being fastened up in a bun, and it swayed with her constant movements. She had scarlet lips and teeth that shone white when she talked.

She was talking now, with her head tipped invitingly to one side. But she broke off suddenly when she saw Lilly. "Oh, hello! What can I get for you?" Her voice didn't purr softly like Mrs. Riley's, or drawl gently like Jesse's. It vibrated with suppressed energy.

"I need some matches, ma'am."

Charlotte spun on one heel and reached for them from the shelf. None of the men moved, just looked at Lilly steadily. "Anything else?" Charlotte asked.

"Not today."

"And who are you, anyway?"

Lilly stepped up to the long, rough counter and reached out for her matches. She saw Charlotte's eyes then, big and baby-blue, innocent-looking. Sunlight from the window brought out reddish tints in her blond hair, and she was smiling.

"I'm Lilly Burchett," she said.

"Married?"

Joe stirred slightly. "Hush, Charlotte. You needn't ask personal questions of someone you don't know."

She tossed her head. "And how will I get to know her?" She pushed the matches across the counter with soft pink hands, hands that had little dimpled fingers. "I like the looks of this girl. I think we might be friends."

"I'm not married," Lilly said, blushing.

"Have a boyfriend?"

"Yes. His name is Jesse Wright."

"Oh, that's swell. What's he like?"

Okla Keeton cocked one eyebrow at Lilly, but she hardly noticed. She fumbled for words, unable to think. "He's tall. He has dark hair."

"Does he work in the mine?"

"No, he's a farmer."

"Where do you live?"

"Just up the hill from here. At the fork of Sand Lick."

At last Joe spoke up, slowly. "Heard your ma died. I was sorry to hear it. She was a good woman."

Suddenly Lilly felt the familiar choking in her throat. She was still aware of Charlotte's gaze on her, but Joe's words had brought her back to reality. "You lost your ma too," she said. "We all miss her."

His eyes shifted away from her. "Yes," he answered.

Lilly left with her matches, but her mind stayed in the store. This woman, full of vitality and restless energy, had carried something strange and new with her into the reaches of Sand Lick. She exuded the world outside, a world that Lilly had determined would be hers. At the same time, her brashness frightened Lilly just a little.

Jesse didn't like her at all. "It ain't right the way she dresses," he declared with contempt.

They sat on chairs on the porch together, the creek too high to go for a walk. Lilly had Sonny on her lap, and she tickled him in his ribs to make him giggle, delaying her answer. Finally she said, "Other women dress like her, out there."

"She puts something on her lips to make them red."

"Lipstick," Lilly murmured.

"It's a shame to do that. And wrong."

Lilly had been taught this too, and Charlotte's lipstick, along with her short sleeves and the skirt that exposed several inches of her leg above the ankle, made her slightly uncomfortable. At the same time, she liked it. Not knowing what to say, she said nothing.

"I'm not surprised," Jesse added, "that she never came to visit."

"Why do you think Joe picked her? They don't seem a bit alike."

Jesse pondered this for a moment, scratching dirt out from under one fingernail while he thought. "I dunno. But she is kind of—exciting. Maybe he liked that."

This exciting aura that breathed around Charlotte attracted Lilly. Coming from her house, where everyone was still submerged in stale sorrow, it was like being drawn into sunshine to see Charlotte's crimson smile, and hear her thin, high laughter. Sometimes, when she went to the store in the next few weeks, she lingered and chatted.

In March, about the time Lilly and Maybelle were planting out the first of the garden things, and the grass was beginning to green over the raw graves,

Pa started coming home in the evenings and dressing up to go away again.

Lilly understood the signs: men needed wives, and children needed mothers. She only wondered who the woman was, and grieved afresh over Ma, Vince, and Patty. For a while, she stayed home and sent one of the children to the store, feeling the need to hide again.

Maybelle noticed Pa's actions too and asked about them. "Where does Pa go every evening?" she wondered, leaning on her hoe and grubbing dirt up around the lettuce and mustard plants with her toes.

"I think he's planning to get married again," Lilly answered.

"Did he tell you?"

"No. I've just been watching him." Lilly chopped viciously at a pig weed, wishing she could so easily do away with the hurt she saw in Maybelle's eyes.

"Who is it?" Maybelle asked at last.

"I don't know. We'll have to wait until he tells us."

"Do Bobby and T.J. know?"

"I don't think so. Can you. . . We're the oldest, Maybelle. We need to be strong for the little ones."

Sonny toddled over just then and grabbed at Lilly's skirt. She picked him up and hugged him close. "What do you want, little man?"

He grunted his half intelligible word for "drink." "Take him to the house, Maybelle," Lilly suggested, "and get him some water. Bring the bucket out here to the field while you're at it. And make sure the boys are still chopping up that tree. I haven't heard the axes for a while."

She sighed as she watched Maybelle's retreating figure. The girl was so thin, so young, so vulnerable; and Lilly had just gotten done telling her they needed to be strong for the younger ones. She had become accustomed enough to the ache in her own heart that she figured it would always be there. She wondered if Maybelle carried one just like it.

Maybelle came back with the bucket of water in one hand and Sonny on the other hip. "I got the boys working again," she reported. "Here's your drink."

Lilly took the bucket and tipped the wooden rim up to her mouth, while Maybelle stood looking strangely at her. "Lilly," she choked, "does Pa have to get married again?"

"Men need wives," Lilly said gently, although she wanted to shout, *No! No, he doesn't have to get married again.* "And the little boys need a ma."

"Why, Lilly? We're making out fine with you and me to run things."

Her words drove home Lilly's own feelings, but in spite of the wrenching pain, she said steadily, "Maybe a new ma will help us to be a happier family again."

Maybelle sat Sonny down abruptly. "No, Lilly, of course it won't."

The very next day Bobby, T.J., and Maybelle came back from the store with Maybelle grimly silent, and Bobby in tears. It was so odd to see him crying that Lilly immediately became alarmed. "What's wrong, Bobby?"

T.J. set the jug of kerosene on the table, looking troubled.

"What happened, Maybelle?" Lilly asked.

Maybelle shrugged and arched her eyebrows. "He cried the whole way home, but he won't tell me what's wrong."

Lilly threw down the armful of laundry she had just brought in from outside. She took Bobby by the shoulders and tipped his tear-streaked face up to look into hers. He so rarely let anyone have a peek at what was going on in his heart, and she knew she needed to get to the bottom of this before he disappeared inside himself again. "Bobby, what's wrong?" she repeated.

She was struck with the abject misery in his eyes, and the helpless way he hiccupped. "Is it true that we're going to get a new ma?"

Lilly's grip tightened on his shoulders. "Who told you that?" she demanded.

Maybelle's eyes flashed. "I didn't know he heard."

"Heard what?" Lilly asked in desperation.

Maybelle's voice hardened and rose. "Etta was at the store too. She was so pleased with herself, knowing something I didn't know. She said Pa's going over there to visit her aunt."

They flashed a message between themselves, over Bobby's and T.J.'s heads. "Etta's aunt?"

"Caroline," Maybelle answered.

"Is she right?" Lilly asked hoarsely.

"How would I know?" Maybelle put her hands on her hips and stared defiantly at Lilly and Bobby. "I hate Etta."

"Maybelle!"

"I do. She had no call to act like she did. Flinging the news at me just out of spite. But I—" Maybelle hesitated and suddenly looked nearly ready to cry herself, "—I didn't know Bobby heard. I thought he had gone on ahead."

"It is true?" Bobby asked, fear shining out past the lingering tears.

Lilly sat down suddenly and let her hands slide off his shoulders. She knew Etta's Aunt Caroline only from seeing her at church. She was a quiet, unmarried woman, younger than Ma had been, not someone to attract attention in a crowd. And she lived with Etta's family, which gave credibility to the story. If Pa was creeping over there in the evenings, Etta would find out sooner or later.

"Is it true?" Bobby repeated. He had stuffed his hands into his pockets and stood very still in front of Lilly. She had to answer him, and the words came from somewhere outside herself. "I think so, Bobby. Pa would like to get married again. Don't you think it would make it easier for him and for us?"

"Easier?" His eyes seemed to be staring right through her.

T.J. crept close, and Lilly pulled him to her. Maybelle picked up Sonny and went outside with him. It was up to Lilly to explain this, and she tried. "Men need wives, and it's all right for them to get married again when their wife dies, like Ma did. Pa is lonely, like the rest of us. He thinks this will help."

"Will it, Lilly?" Bobby asked with a gravity far beyond his years.

"What do you think?"

His face puckered up again as though he would cry. He looked away from her.

"It's not good for a family to go without a ma for a long time," Lilly went on very quietly. "Pa is trying to do what is good for all of us."

"How soon is it gonna happen?"

"I don't know. I imagine Pa will explain it all to us soon."

A week elapsed before he did so, a week during which Lilly detected a subtle difference in Bobby. When Pa finally opened up the subject, he said simply, "How would you like a new ma, children?"

"We already know about that," Bobby said with fine scorn.

Pa sputtered into the cup he had just picked up and set it down again without taking a drink. "Her name is Caroline."

"We know that too."

"Be quiet, young man, and listen to me. I've been visiting her for six weeks." The children all looked at him, waiting, not shocked as he had expected them to be. He took a bite of beans and chewed it slowly in the silence. Then he said, "She's going to come and visit us here this Sunday. She wants to see my house and my family."

"Will she be here for dinner, Pa?" Lilly asked.

"Yes, she's coming home with us after church."

"How soon will you be married?" Maybelle queried.

Pa coughed nervously now. "I haven't asked her to marry me yet."

In the days that followed, Lilly could feel herself and the rest of her family tensing warily against this unknown. T.J., whom she had thought was adjusting slowly to life without Ma, suddenly became more clingy again. Maybelle declared laconically that she didn't care a hill of beans what the house looked like, or what they had to eat on Sunday, and Lilly snapped at her to help get ready whether she cared or not.

"Maybe if the house looks awful, she'll decide she can't do it and say no when Pa asks her to marry him," Maybelle suggested.

"No," Lilly said, wanting to let loose a whole river of liquid frustration, but controlling herself, "she'll decide we need a new ma bad, and marry Pa quick."

On Saturday evening, after they had bathed, washed their hair, and climbed the steps to the loft, Maybelle's carefully nurtured show of bravado evaporated. She reached across Sonny, who now slept in the girls' bed, and pinched Lilly to see if she was still awake.

Lilly grunted.

"Do you think she'll—like us?" Maybelle faltered.

"I hope so."

"I'm scared, Lilly."

"I am too."

"I don't want a ma I don't even know."

"That's why Pa is bringing her here tomorrow. They're not getting married just yet."

"But they will. You know they will."

Silence. A faint sniffle. The play of moonbeams through the thin curtains. Lilly feared life with a new step-mother too, but she feared other things more. When Jesse heard the news, he would ask her more boldly to be his wife, and she hadn't yet found the gentle words to tell him no. Her dreams had stayed alive against all odds, cherished in quiet moments when she lifted her books from the shelf in the loft, or gazed for a moment beyond the rim of the mountains at sunrise and thought of the world beyond. Seeing Charlotte reminded her that this world was tangible, hers for the taking—someday.

For her dreams were simple dreams no longer, but goals and determinations forged through suffering. She no longer had the quietness that used to come to her under the bridge, but she hardly missed it, knowing instead this fierce longing to leave the mountains. If Caroline came and took over running the house, it would leave her free. Perhaps Pa, his mind taken up with other things, wouldn't mind any longer if she accepted Mr. Barker's offer. When Mr. Ferguson came back in the summer, she would get the address from him. What did it matter that she was now a year older? She fell asleep composing the letter.

When the preacher had pronounced the benediction the next afternoon, Pa walked up to Caroline in full view of all the worshipers and asked her graciously if she would walk home with him. Heads immediately turned and nodded. A momentary silence fell, then men and women alike called out congratulations.

Caroline had dressed in plain gray with a bit of white lace at her neck and wrists. She blushed and smiled, and her thin pale face lit up so that she was almost pretty. Without a word she took Pa's arm, while Pa stood beaming down at her.

"The girls have done up a fine dinner for you," he rumbled. "Ready to go now?"

"Yes, Bernie," she murmured.

The children followed them home, quietly self-conscious, aware that this news would spread on the wings of words until not a soul would remain, from old Rob on the ridge top to Hester Sue in her cabin, that didn't know of Bernie Burchett and his new woman.

The fried chicken dinner with biscuits and string beans was a silent affair, eaten in haste. Caroline kept her eyes on her plate for most of it, which gave Lilly plenty of time to examine her. She noticed the narrow pointed nose, the fine, straight eyebrows over colorless blue eyes, the thin faintly pink lips, the wavy hair that escaped in tendrils from her bun, the long slender fingers. She wasn't hard to look at, taking everything together.

After that, Pa brought her to the cabin every Sunday, and often tramped over to the next holler after work. Although it had seemed so hard on Bobby when he heard, he adjusted to the new situation with surprising ease. Lilly hoped that a new ma would be good for him, to help him forget the horror of the winter just past.

Pale green leaves came out on all the trees, grass grew long beside the creeks, violets and dandelions flung out vivid colors on the green, rain fell softly, winds blew warmly, and the sun shone intensely. It was a time of softness and beauty, of healing.

Chapter thirteen

One evening after Lilly had spent the day scrubbing dirty clothes and starching Sunday shirts and dresses, she took down her book of Wordsworth's poems. Pa had gone away again, and she could hear the children down in the creek. She sat on the edge of the porch, while dusk poured gently around her from a violet sky. The first of summer's insects hummed in the trees.

She opened the book at random and let it lie on her lap. It had opened to one of her favorite poems, and she read it slowly, savoring the words, touching them lightly with her forefinger.

> . . . *The rainbow comes and goes,*
> *And lovely is the rose.* . . .
> *Whither is fled the visionary gleam?*
> *Where is it now, the glory and the dream?*
> *Our birth is but a sleep and a forgetting:*
> *The soul that rises with us, our life's Star,*
> *Hath had elsewhere its setting,*
> *And cometh from afar.* . . .

When she finished the long poem, she leaned her head back against the porch pillar and closed her eyes, the better to slip into another world.

Jesse found her sitting there half an hour later, still gazing into a future full of prismatic dreams. She opened her eyes when she heard his step.

"Alone?" he asked, looking from her to the book in her lap.

"Yes."

"Your pa gone visiting again?"

"Yes."

"I saw the children playing in the creek as I came along."

Lilly started to her feet. "I forgot. I must go call them in. It's too cold for them to be in the water after dark."

"Wait a few minutes, Lilly. I need to talk to you." He sat down beside her on the edge of the porch, stretching out his long legs to the sparse grass that grew in front of the house.

They sat in silence for a few moments. Lilly shut her book caressingly, and stroked it. She thought she knew what was coming, and the feel of the leather and gilded pages gave her confidence.

At length he said, "Your pa is getting married soon, isn't he?"

"He hasn't said so yet."

"You know he is, Lilly."

She dropped her head and closed her hands more tightly around the book. "Yes. I'm sure it's not far away."

"When he gets married, you won't be needed at home anymore. We've planted more corn than last year, and it's growing nicely. It will be a good time to get married. Will you be my wife, Lilly?"

"I'm sorry, Jesse, but I. . ." He was looking at her so intently that she couldn't finish her sentence. Instead she said, "Remember when Mr. Barker was here to visit Mr. Riley?"

"Yes." He sounded puzzled.

"Remember his offer to me?"

Jesse nodded. Everyone knew this. They had talked it over a time or two, and Jesse knew everything that had happened in the cabin that night. But Lilly had left out her deep longings, her disappointment, her anger. Now she was trembling, though the night was warm, trembling with the need to let Jesse know these things. She pressed her knees tightly together. "I really wanted to go," she said. "But Pa and Ma didn't want me to."

He looked at the cherished volume in her lap. "You like books a lot," he answered, trying to understand.

"Yes, Jesse, I like books. I like to read them, and someday I'd want to have a library like Mrs. Riley's. But I want to write books too." She paused to swallow down the lump in her throat. When she spoke again, her voice was resolute, although she knew she was being cruel. "You want to be a farmer and stay in the hills with a cabin, and a wife who will give you a big family. I don't want a life like that. I want to leave the mountains and go see the world. I feel like I'm missing so much. How could we get married when we want such different things in life?" In spite of her need to be decisive, her voice almost broke. "Life here is so hard. I can't stand it. I want to get out."

Jesse reached for her hand, and she pulled it away, sharply.

He sat beside her, silent, one hand cupped over the other. The posture was so familiar, the silence so calming. Lilly took several deep breaths. "I know I'm just a farmer," he said at last, "and I think I'll always be a farmer."

The strength of his humility wounded her in a way she hadn't expected. "I'm sorry, Jesse," she cried. "I like you a lot. But I'm not ready to get married yet. I want. . ." She found suddenly that the huge longing inside her was impossible to translate from heart to speech.

"Yes, Lilly. You've had a rough winter. Life here in the mountains looks hard to you just now. I guess I rushed you."

He didn't understand. Desperation made her harsher. "No. I can't ever marry you, because we don't want the same things. We won't ever want the same things. We don't think the same."

"I thought we did, about many things."

He had shared much with her, but she felt sure he had held back, just as she had held back things about Mrs. Riley, her own fascination with literature, and her longings for a different life. When she didn't answer, he went on, "May I keep coming to see you, if we don't talk about marriage again for a while?"

She wavered, knowing how much she would miss his companionship. But her hands closed convulsively around the book in her lap. "No," she said bluntly. "I'm quite sure I'll never change my mind, so you might as well not."

"Someday. . ." He stood up and looked at her so compellingly that she was forced to glance up. She saw a trace of anger, but mostly pity, in his eyes. "Someday you will discover that you are missing the most important thing about these mountains."

"What's that?" she asked in spite of herself.

His voice took an unaccustomed edge. "You'll have to find it yourself. Good-bye, Lilly."

He went only three steps before he turned again and accused her, "You've been friends with Charlotte. That's why a mountain man isn't good enough for you."

"I hardly know Charlotte," Lilly answered, shocked.

"That woman is trouble," Jesse said flatly. "Be careful. You like her because she's from off. But she's going to hurt you."

"How could she hurt me?"

"Just be careful," Jesse repeated.

Lilly watched him out of sight, without stirring from her spot, analyzing his last words. They seemed unmerited, since she rarely saw Charlotte for more than five or ten minutes at a time. And Charlotte stood more as a symbol of freedom than someone Lilly wanted to imitate. Still, his prediction stirred a faint feeling of unease.

Before long, the children came up from the creek, wet and muddy. "Children," she said sharply, "you're wet, and it's chilly. Go inside and get ready for bed right away."

They all trooped past her merrily, quite unfazed by her scolding. Bangs and thumps and bumps echoed from inside for a few minutes. Several lightly clad figures went for a last run to the outhouse. After his trip, instead of going back up to the loft, T.J. came around to the porch and sat down by Lilly.

"I'm not tired," he whispered, snuggling close.

Without a word, Lilly put her arm around him. The feel of his warm body tight against hers unleashed something inside her, and quick tears sprang to her eyes. When she sniffed lightly, he looked up at her.

His face grew more sober when he saw the tears, but he didn't seem alarmed. In the last months, he had seen so many tears that they seemed a normal part of life to him.

She didn't cry long. When the tears stopped coming, she sat still, feeling a queer emptiness, hoping she had done the right thing, wondering what the great thing was that she was missing about the mountains. T.J. fell asleep, and his head slid down limply into her lap. She watched the moon rise, tipping the pines with silver and making the ripples on Sand Lick things of shimmer and mystery. Off to her right, the stone slabs marking the three graves shone whiter than they ever did under the glare of sunshine. A breath of wind whispered down through the pines above the cabin. The dew fell heavily.

Lilly had the same feeling of timelessness that had come to her when Mrs. Riley died in her bedroom that wintry afternoon. She sat with her arm wrapped around T.J., not feeling either happy or sad, young or old, empty or full.

After quite a while, Pa came up the path, his head thrown back as though he were ready to burst into song. "Still up, Lilly?" he asked.

"Yes, Pa."

"I asked Caroline to marry me," he announced abruptly. "She said she would."

Lilly felt a momentary stab of something between fear and sadness. "When will the wedding be?" she asked quietly.

"In a few weeks. No more than a month."

Lilly moved her bare toes closer together on the wooden step, overlapping them, curling them up against the chill. "Pa?"

He stopped in the act of going into the house and sat down on the creaky wooden chair behind her instead. "What?"

"You won't need me so much at home after the wedding."

"No, guess not."

She was silent so long, framing her next words, that he wondered, "You thinking on getting married too?"

"No, not exactly."

"Then what?"

"Remember Mr. Barker?"

"Reckon I wouldn't forget him right away."

Pa's tone was neutral, not spiked with anger, and Lilly went on. "He told Mr. Ferguson that if I ever changed my mind I could let him know, and his offer would still stand."

"M-m," Pa said.

"I thought maybe I could. . . now that Ma is gone, and you're getting a new wife, I thought maybe I could go now."

"You mean you haven't got that foolishness out of your head yet?"

She winced to hear her dreams and ambitions and goals, the very reason she had told Jesse no, called foolishness.

"Our family has been broke up enough," Pa added more gently. "I don't aim to have no one else leaving."

The moon slipped behind a cloud, and the cabin, porch, pines, and creek disappeared into shadow. "You're a mountain girl, and you'll always be a mountain girl. Read your books if you have to. But none of my girls is going to go off to the city and be made into a highfalutin lady."

How could he be so kind and cruel at the same time?

He went on relentlessly, "Ma always wanted you to get married soon. What about Jesse?"

"He'll not be coming anymore," Lilly said without emotion.

"What do you mean?" Pa stood up suddenly and sent his chair crashing against the side of the cabin.

"Sh-h, Pa." As T.J. stirred, she stroked his hair lightly; and he settled back down with his head in her lap, his long hair lying softly on the book.

Pa paced to one end of the porch and back again. "What do you mean?"

"I told him he didn't need to come back again. We're not alike enough to get married."

"Jesse's the nicest—"

"I like him a lot," Lilly interrupted. "But. . ."

"It's your books, I suppose," Pa spat. "And that Charlotte woman down at the store. Jesse is a good common-sense farmer, who don't hold with reading and education. Guess he's too much like your pa in that way."

Lilly was stung into silence.

"It's your life, girl." Pa shrugged to close the subject. "But if you thought that by turning Jesse down, you could go to the city, you were wrong. Caroline won't need your help when she comes. Maybe you could get a job in town again."

"Yes, Pa, maybe I could."

After he went inside, she half-carried T.J. up the stairs and put him to bed beside Bobby. Then she crept into her own bed and cuddled the sleeping Sonny close. Somehow she couldn't stand to have nothing to hang onto anymore, not when her life was slipping out of her control.

Stories of cruel step-mothers were sprinkled liberally through all the old tales that people told around firesides. Lilly had heard many of them, and she battled raw fear in the weeks that followed. She slept poorly, and wished for Jesse to come, just to have someone to talk things over with in the old familiar way. Her books held no appeal, although she tried to glean scraps of comfort from them now and again. Pa was buoyant, and the children extra quiet.

Word got around that the next time Jeb Cantrell crossed the mountain for preaching, there would be a wedding. Before that, Lilly and Maybelle scrubbed the cabin from top to bottom. Some days, Mammaw and the aunts came to help. They whitewashed the outside as well; and Pa, Bobby, and T.J. built two new chairs for the front porch.

Caroline and Pa took a day off and went to the county seat for the marriage license, a stove to replace the fireplace in the kitchen, and dress goods for the wedding. They came back with soft, pearl gray fabric for Caroline, and some the color of violets for Lilly and Maybelle.

"At least it's pretty," Maybelle whispered in relief.

"I think," Lilly returned cautiously, "that Caroline knows how to dress well."

Caroline sewed their dresses with a flattering pattern of tight waists and flared skirts that reminded Lilly of the days in Mrs. Riley's house. The dresses fit well, and Caroline smiled her satisfaction when she saw them. Lilly felt more shame than satisfaction. She should have sewed the dresses herself instead of letting this woman she hardly knew do it for them.

Just several days before the wedding, Lilly left the little children in Maybelle's care and walked down to Keeton's store, wanting to make sure that Caroline would find a well-stocked kitchen when she moved in. She had still been avoiding the store in the last weeks, remembering what both Pa and Jesse had said about Charlotte. But this job belonged to her.

She heard voices inside and felt relief that she wouldn't be alone with Charlotte. She reached for the door and saw a new sign on it. "Revivals," it said in large uneven letters. "Brother Cox will be holding revivals starting June 17."

Nollie Smith and Sarah Wright, mothers to Beulah and Jesse, stood inside, baskets on their arms, talking and waiting for Charlotte to gather their things when she finished with old Abel. The women nodded to her. "Did you see the notice for revivals?"

"Yes, I did. Who's Pastor Cox?"

"He's from north of here," Nollie answered. "Almost in West Virginia. He's a traveling preacher."

"It's about time we have revivals," Sarah added happily. "It's been a whole year."

"My sister and her man know this Pastor Cox," Nollie went on. "They say he's a right fine preacher. He always gets touched strong by the Spirit."

Old Abel took his new plug of tobacco from Charlotte and turned to shamble toward the door. He winked openly at Lilly. "How's the wedding coming on?" he drawled.

"We'll be ready for it. The cabin's shined up good. It's only two days away, you know."

"Naw. . ." He winked again. "I meant your own."

Lilly blushed in confusion, and old Abel laughed outright. She said quickly, "Oh, I'm not getting married."

"Seems I've been hearing some stories about Jesse."

Lilly cringed. "You might have," she said shortly, aware that Sarah and Nollie had stopped talking, sure that Sarah must know.

"Hasn't got to the marrying stage yet? He'd better hurry up. Some other young buck might get in ahead of him."

Lilly clutched at her basket. In slow motion she saw Sarah turn and face the two of them. She held her head proudly, and her face looked oddly like Jesse's had on the night she had told him no. Her dark eyes seemed enormous in the dimness of the store. "He'd have her if she'd have him," she said viciously.

Abel let out a low cackle of laughter. "Oh, the wind lies that way, does it?"

"This young girl could be planning her own wedding too." Mrs. Wright's voice was loud and defiant, as if she didn't care who knew that her son had been jilted by this girl, as if all the shame of it must slide onto Lilly.

Lilly cowered now. She wanted to yank the door open and run home as fast as she could, but something heavy held her on the plank floor. Behind the counter, Charlotte was quiet, collecting things for Sarah. The moment of silence held, stretching out like a thin banjo string that would cry with the faintest touch.

At last Charlotte said, "There. That's everything for you, Sarah."

Sarah Wright threw it all into her basket helter-skelter, her movements jerky. Then she swept from the store. Old Abel went out after her, placid and uncaring about what he had stirred up.

Charlotte tried hesitantly to make conversation, but without success. When Nollie had left, Lilly said, speaking low, "I need some baking soda, and two pounds of salt. Give me a pound of brown sugar too, and a box of matches."

Charlotte drooped today. The crimson vitality seemed to have gone out of her. She piled all Lilly's things together on the counter and tallied the total on the back of an envelope, her face expressionless. But abruptly she asked, "Is it true? Did you tell Jesse off?"

"Yes."

"Can I know why?"

Charlotte's eyes were kind, and after what she had just endured, Lilly couldn't harden herself to that kindness. "He's just not the type of man for me," she said.

"I could agree with that, since I've seen him." Charlotte laughed briefly. "But don't tell his ma that I said so, of course. Don't marry the wrong man, Lilly."

Lilly stopped in the act of piling her things into her basket. "I don't intend to."

Irrelevantly, it seemed, Charlotte said, "It's been a long while since you were in here."

"We've had things going at home."

"Yes. A wedding coming up. Everyone's talking of it."

"Will you be there?"

"Will I be welcome?"

"I think so." Lilly said it without much conviction. "You live here."

"But I don't belong."

"You just feel that way because you didn't grow up here."

"It's true. You know that the folks here barely tolerate me."

"Some of them, maybe." Was this what bothered Charlotte, put the shadows under her eyes, and took away the restless energy that Lilly had seen at first?

Charlotte gave her a withering look. "You're playing with me. Have you had schooling?"

Lilly could hardly keep up with these wild jumps from subject to subject. "Seven years," she said.

"No high school?"

"No. Where would I go?"

"Ever want to go?"

She thought instantly of Mr. Barker. "I had one chance at it," she said slowly. "Someone from Louisville wanted to send me. But Pa and Ma didn't want me to go."

"Have you ever been away from here?"

"No. No farther than the county seat."

"I don't see how you stand it. These hills will kill me." Charlotte wiped one finger under her eye in a restless gesture. Her lips were not so scarlet as usual, and her cheeks paler. "Don't you ever want to get out?"

"Yes," Lilly answered softly. "Very much."

Charlotte's eyes widened. She stood and leaned across the counter and grabbed at Lilly's hand. "You're telling me the truth? You want to leave too? I thought everyone here was willing to stay. I thought they loved the hills and they hated outsiders, and all that."

"I want to see what's out there."

"Well, so do I. I've seen it for most of my life, but I think I'll die if I can't see it again."

Lilly drew back, embarrassed by her vehemence. And yet this young woman was saying the same things she felt, saying them out loud instead of hiding them in her heart. And perhaps for her it was worse because she had known culture and education and social life. "You won't be here long, will you?" she suggested.

"Joe wants to stay," Charlotte said bitterly. "He says it's his duty to take care of his pa, but I know that what he really wants is just to stay here and grow old in the place where he was born, and eventually to die here and be buried with all his uncles and aunts and grandparents. I want to go back to Lexington. I want it worse than anything I've ever wanted. I don't know why I'm telling you this, except that I can't hold it any longer."

Lilly, abashed by Charlotte's candor, had no ready words of empathy. But she understood just what Charlotte meant, and she felt a tenderness for her that she could not have imagined earlier. "I know," she whispered.

"Joe and I have fought over it," Charlotte went on. "I threatened to go back to Lexington without him."

"You wouldn't, would you?" The idea of severing marriage ties this way was completely foreign to Lilly.

Charlotte's shoulders slumped. "I would. And I might someday. But I'll stick it out a little longer yet. And my brother is coming to keep me company. That will help." She was chattering now, filling up the emptiness of the store, perhaps so that her thoughts wouldn't run away with her. "He's my half-brother, really. His name is Talmadge Preston, and we normally don't get along all that well. But I was desperate, and I sent for him to come and be with me as soon as his uncle lets him off from the planting this spring."

"How soon is that?" Lilly asked.

"I just had a letter from him. He says he'll be here Monday of next week. Come down to the store and meet him." A bit of sparkle returned to Charlotte's eyes. "I think you might like him."

Lilly had more to think about on the way home than she could well process. Sarah's anger, Charlotte's desperation, and the sudden flowering of understanding between Charlotte and herself. Lilly realized suddenly that Pa and Jesse, the ones who most harshly criticized Charlotte, were also the ones who could not comprehend her own longings. The thought warmed her.

Chapter fourteen

The wedding day came too soon, and the whole Burchett family rose before sunrise. Pa left ahead of the rest of them, to go to Caroline's house, immaculately dressed and neatly combed. He looked lean and work-hardened and older perhaps than his years, but handsome too.

She combed Maybelle's hair and rolled her own up into a bun held in place with long pins. In the front room mirror, she examined herself briefly, noting her worried eyes. She ran a comb through the boys' hair and made sure their shirt tails were tucked into clean overalls. For this important service, she demanded that all of them put on socks and freshly shined shoes.

T.J. clung to her wherever she went, and when they started out on the mile walk, he gripped her hand. "Caroline won't be like ma, will she, Lilly?" he asked.

"No, T.J.," she answered absently.

"Do I have to call her ma?"

"No, I don't think so."

"I wouldn't," Maybelle declared, "even if Pa gave me a licking for it."

T.J.'s eyes widened in alarm.

"Hush, Maybelle," Lilly scolded. "You're scaring your little brother, all without reason. Pa wouldn't whip you for that," she added, although she didn't feel too easy on that point herself.

Neighbors brought their own chairs and set them up in uneven rows in the yard, close to the house where Caroline had lived with her sister. Pa and

Caroline took seats in the front row, and the children came in to sit silently behind them. The full heat of summer hadn't yet come, and a cool breeze blew across the assembled crowd. With it wafted the smells of the mountains—wood and coal smoke, dogs and mules and chickens, bacon and shelly beans, branch water, tobacco, and faintly, a hint of perfume. Charlotte must have joined them.

After Jeb Cantrell had married them, and Caroline's friends and family had cried all over her, and then served fried chicken and cornbread, Pa took her home. Caroline came to the Burchett cabin as easily as she had come all the previous Sunday's, except that this time she wore her wedding dress, and this time she came to stay.

The next day at the breakfast table, Lilly announced, "I think I'll go down to town today and look for a job."

No one objected, but T.J. asked wistfully, "Can I go along?"

"Yes, of course you may," Lilly said impulsively. Caroline had already made friends with Sonny before the wedding and had a good start on a relationship with Bobby as well. Maybelle could look out for herself fine, but T.J. needed her in a way that the others didn't. She made him put on a clean shirt before they started out.

"Will you be back for dinner?" Caroline asked quietly.

"I don't know. Don't wait on us."

The day was fresh with promise, and Lilly absorbed it, in spite of the heaviness that seemed to hang around her neck. Her steps lightened as she left the cabin behind and walked between the whispering trees on either side of the path.

"Isn't it a nice morning?" T.J. asked hopefully.

"Yes, it is."

"Where are you going in town?"

"Wherever I need to until I find a job. I think I'll try Mr. Riley first."

"Will you be gone every day if you have a job?"

"I don't know. I'll be home on Sundays, at least. Caroline is there now to make meals and wash your clothes."

"But—"

Lilly interrupted him hastily. "Look there in the grass." She bent down and picked up half of a dainty blue eggshell, hoping to distract him. "There must have been a robin nest here."

He took the shell from her and held it gently in his palm. "I'm going to keep it."

Mrs. Greer was out feeding her chickens and muttering to herself. "Lilly!" she called. "You going to the store?"

"I'm going in to town."

"How soon are you coming back?"

"Maybe not till evening."

"Can you stop in at the store for me on your way back? I'm plumb out of coffee, and Silas needs his coffee." She set down her pan of corn and hobbled out toward the road. "Can't you stop in for a minute? I'm that wore out that just the sight of someone else does me good."

"No," Lilly answered kindly. "I don't have time now. But I'll be glad to stop for your coffee." She saw genuine worry in Silva's eyes.

"Silas is worse this morning. That cough is eating him up. The doctor says it's black lung. He soon won't be able to breathe at all." She swayed toward Lilly, until Lilly could see, close-up, the hard bitterness in her eyes. "I hate those coal mines. I hate the men who hired him. They've ruined him, and they don't care."

"Maybe I should tell the doctor to come out," Lilly suggested.

"No, don't bother yourself. He was out two weeks ago, and he says there's nothing he can do more. What he meant is that I'll have to listen to Silas choke himself to death for the next—" She broke off and rubbed her eyes angrily on her apron. "Well, pick up the coffee for me. And come in and talk on your way home."

In town, Lilly stopped first at the post office to check for mail. There was none. Then she crossed the main street. High above her on the hill sat Mr. Riley's house, white and glaring in the sunshine, still snubbing its nose at all its lowly neighbors. She turned aside and went in at the building marked "Office." Here a man sat on Friday evenings and gave out paychecks through a little window. But at this time of day, the window was shuttered. She pushed open the door and went into a sort of empty hall. Another door stared at her, a door with Mr. Riley's name on it. She could hear him moving in there, shuffling papers, thumping something down, sliding his chair over the floor. She didn't know if it was proper to disturb him at work, but she took her courage in her hand and knocked on the door.

"Yes," he answered shortly. "Mr. Smith?"

"No. It's Lilly Burchett."

He opened the door and peered out at her in amazement. "What are you here for?"

"Please, sir. I'm looking for a job. I thought maybe you would like someone to clean your house and cook for you."

His eyes narrowed. "I live simply since my wife died."

Living simply must have meant a wrinkled shirt, an unshaven face, and a stale breath of cheap wine. His manner had always been hard, but now it was coarse. He needed someone to shine his shoes, fix him a hot cornbread, and set out plates, glasses and silver on the table. Because of her memories of Mrs. Riley, Lilly felt sorry for him.

"I'm making out by myself," he added.

He nearly made her believe that he would have no use for her, and then suddenly hired her for two days a week, Tuesday's and Friday's. Lilly left his office, still holding tight to T.J.'s hand, and pondered her options under the blue sky and sunshine. Two days a week wasn't enough to really get her away from Caroline. She stopped at the one eating house, thinking they might could use a girl several days a week to peel potatoes, wash dishes, or wait on tables. She was turned away before she even set foot inside. "But check at the boarding house," the owner told her. "Hear Mrs. Price is full and looking for help."

The town's boarding house was a cheap, two-story board structure, square and small windowed. Mrs. Price had sold her farm after her husband died, taken the money, and put up this building. She now lived in two back rooms, and rented out the others to a constantly changing set of young men, most of them single, sometimes a married one who might bring his wife. It had two doors that faced the front porch. The one on the left went into the common sitting room, and the one on the right into the kitchen. Lilly knocked on the kitchen door.

"Who's there?" Mrs. Price called. "Don't come in if you're wanting food."

Lilly opened the door and stepped into a massive kitchen. Mrs. Price, standing at the long heavy table and kneading a spongy mass of dough, looked her over coolly. "Who might you be? Not mine workers, I'm think-ing. At least the young one looks too small, and I hadn't heard that they were taking in girls to work."

"No, ma'am. I'm Lilly Burchett, and this is my little brother T.J."

"Burchett? Bernie Burchett's daughter?"

"Yes, ma'am."

"What are you coming into my kitchen for? Come over here where I can see you."

Lilly stepped closer, feeling the heat from the huge stove at one end of the kitchen. Smoked hams and bacon hung from the ceiling, along with bunches of dried herbs. All along the back wall sat tubs and barrels and crates filled with food—potatoes and onions, cornmeal, lard, and sugar.

"I'm looking for work," Lilly said. "My pa just got married, and they don't need me at the house no more."

"What can you do?" Mrs. Price lifted a suspicious eyebrow. "Can you cook for ten or twenty people at a time?"

"I think so."

"The work here is hard," Mrs. Price warned her as she attacked her bread dough with renewed vigor, pounding and pummeling it with strong fingers. "The men have huge appetites after working all day."

"I'm willing to work hard."

"Fact is, I am looking for help."

"How often can you use me?"

"Every day." Mrs. Price grunted. "My house is full. Twelve men, and I'm working myself to death trying to keep up with it all."

"Mr. Riley already hired me for Tuesday's and Friday's."

"I'll take the other four. I'd get you to come on Sunday too, if I could. And you can start today."

"I've got my little brother along."

"Don't matter. He looks quiet enough. Sit him down in the corner and give him a cookie from that bucket. Then get started."

Mrs. Price had not spoken idly when she said that the work was hard. She drove herself so that she barely had a minute to relax, or a chance to grab a bite to eat. Lilly discovered quickly that it would be far different working for her than for Mrs. Riley. On that first day, Mrs. Price had her start cleaning the bedrooms. "They should've been spring cleaned months ago," she complained, "and I haven't had a lick of time."

Lilly finished three of them before Mrs. Price wanted her to peel a couple gallons of potatoes and mix up some biscuit dough for supper. She dismissed her about the time the men came home from the mine, saying she could serve the supper by herself.

T.J. had followed Lilly around from room to room and spent part of his day playing in the back yard by himself. Now Lilly called him to come. "I'll be back on Wednesday," she said to Mrs. Price.

For the first time that day, Mrs. Price smiled. "You know how to work," she admitted. "I think we'll get along fine."

Lilly nearly forgot that she had promised Silva she would stop at the store for coffee. And she entirely forgot that Charlotte's half-brother was due to arrive that day. When she neared the store, she heard an unfamiliar voice coming through the open windows and doors, a deep voice, not one that tripped over its words, but that formed them thoughtfully. " 'I'd brush the summer by,' " it said.

"Is that poetry?" Charlotte asked, a trifle suspicious.

"Yes."

"What's the rest of it?"

"Oh, the rest of it doesn't fit for this occasion at all," the voice said easily, not in the least perturbed. "But the one line did."

"I suppose you'll go quoting poetry all around these mountains?"

"And what if I did?"

"The people here would think you queer."

"I know when to keep my poetry to myself. You underestimate me, Charlotte." There was a hint of laughter in the words now.

Lilly's weariness had vanished, replaced by wonder. She slipped through the door.

The young man behind the counter with Charlotte was blond like her, but tall and slim. He caught himself in the middle of a yawn when he saw Lilly, and came to quick, erect attention, suddenly a gentleman, polite yet aloof. "Good evening, miss," he said.

She was startled by his eyes, the crystalline blueness of them. She had thought Charlotte's blue eyes pretty, but compared to his, they were too soft and weak. "Good evening," she returned hesitantly.

"This is Lilly," Charlotte said with a giggle. "And this is my brother Talmadge. Come to entertain his lonely sister."

"Pleased to meet you," he said with genuine courtesy. "I've heard about you from Charlotte."

She flushed.

"Only good," he assured her, but he looked her over intently, as if trying to decide whether he could believe what he had heard.

"I need some coffee for Mrs. Greer," Lilly said.

Charlotte promptly turned to the sack behind her and measured out a pound. "There you go. Anything else?"

"No, that's all."

"Stay and visit," Charlotte suggested.

"I can't. I'm on my way home for supper."

"Well, we're running home soon for supper ourselves. Joe is cooking tonight."

Lilly tried to conceal her shock, and then almost laughed at the picture of her pa in the kitchen fixing something to eat.

"He's real handy with the food," Charlotte said carelessly. "I can't make cornbread to suit him anyway."

Not sure what to say, Lilly glanced from her to Talmadge. He looked surprised too, and puzzled.

On up the road, she and T.J. crossed the bare brown patch that made do for the Greers' yard and howdy-ed on the porch.

"Come in," Mrs. Greer called. "Come right on in."

The air inside was fetid and close, saturated with the smells of kerosene and tobacco. Silas sat in one corner, wheezing heavily. A small window was open beside him, but it did little to lighten the cheerlessness of the house.

Lilly had often sat on the porch, but rarely come inside. For a moment, what she saw, felt, and smelled sickened her. At the same time, it seemed like such an extension of Silva herself that it should have come as no surprise. "I brought your coffee."

"I didn't know you would be so late."

"I'm sorry. I worked the day in town and I'm just on my way home now."

Silva took the coffee, her lips compressed. "Well, thanks," she said grudgingly.

The others had waited supper for her, and while Caroline dipped the beans from the pot and pulled the cornbread from the oven she told them of her success. Pa smiled slightly, but without comment.

"What did T.J. do all day?" Maybelle asked.

"Played outside and helped me clean."

"Mrs. Price has a huge house," T.J. added, awed.

"What did you do today?" Lilly asked Maybelle.

"Field work." Maybelle shrugged.

They sat down to supper, still uncomfortable all together as a family. Caroline had spread out cornbread, beans, onions, and buttermilk, and it was hearty and satisfying, but not as tasty as Ma's, that was sure.

Mrs. Price's house had seemed full and bustling, somehow, even when the boys were gone. Everything in it was sturdy and received constant hard usage. So it was a distinct shock to open the door and step into Mrs. Riley's cool, silent kitchen the next morning. Its emptiness hit Lilly like a slap in the face. All that remained of Mrs. Riley was this silence, this calmness; and Lilly had not felt it for so long that she shrank from it instinctively. When she recovered her poise, she spied a note on the counter.

"Laundry is in the hall upstairs. Do whatever else you think needs done."

She went softly upstairs and collected the heap of dirty clothes from outside his bedroom door, thankful that he had put it there. She had no desire to go into that room again. After finishing the laundry, she tidied the kitchen and sitting room, dusting, sweeping, beating out rugs, putting misplaced things back in their places. Almost unconsciously as she worked, she found herself moving as silently as she could, a part of the quiet spirit of the house. Before she left, she ironed the dried shirts and trousers, and fixed supper for Mr. Riley.

Outside, a golden luxurious afternoon had come down to kiss the valley, turning the ever present floating particles of coal dust into a soft, almost pretty haze. In spite of her sunbonnet, Lilly could feel the sun warm on her head as she headed through town. Then, when she reached the first trees, they dropped shade over her, a shade as restful as Mrs. Riley's sitting room.

She went along, humming to herself, thinking now and then of a line of poetry. "And by the vision splendid/ Is on his way attended" or "But trailing clouds of glory do we come/ From God who is our home."

She climbed steadily up, crossed the bridge, neared the store. Just before the store was a close-knit grove of slender birches, and as she came up to them, she saw a young man among them. She stepped a little to one side, stealthily, and realized it was Talmadge Preston, leaning against one of the trees, his legs stretched out in front of him, and a book lying face down on his lap.

He saw her at almost the same instant and stood up quickly, while slipping the book behind his back. "Miss Lilly?"

"Yes, sir."

He laughed. "Calling me Talmadge would suit my fancy better than sir. Are you on your way home from town again?"

"Yes."

"Do you work every day?"

"Every day except Sunday." She was answering him, but wondering about the book. She thought she had read "Selected Poetry" on its cover, but she couldn't be sure.

He seemed to know what she was thinking and brought the book back into view, smiling slightly. "You caught me reading. Do you read poetry?"

"Not much. . ." She stopped, abashed, and then decided she had better make herself clearer. "I don't read much of anything. But I have a book of Wordsworth's poems at home."

"You do?" He looked pleased, and his blue eyes flashed bluer as a sudden bit of sunshine came aslant through the birch leaves. "Wordsworth is good."

"I think so too," she answered shyly. "But I haven't read much of anything else."

"Where did you get the poems?"

"Mrs. Riley gave them to me."

"I don't believe I know who she is."

"She was the mine manager's wife. She died in the epidemic."

"Did you know her well?" Talmadge asked, contriving to show that he was interested, but not intrusive.

"I worked for her. I. . . Yes, I knew her pretty well." And then, to her own surprise, she added, "I was there when she died."

She immediately wondered if she had said more than she should have, because Talmadge didn't answer. She glanced at him furtively. He was caressing the book he held, much as Mrs. Riley had done, much as she herself did with her own two books, and his face was sober. But he didn't comment on that, only said, "I wasn't expecting to find much poetry in this community. Not from what my sister had led me to believe."

"Has she been talking about us then?" Lilly remembered the scrap of conversation she had overheard from the store porch.

Talmadge finally looked at her again, frankly. "I didn't mean that she's been talking evil of the people here. But it's been a challenge for her to adjust."

"I know."

"That's why I'm here, I guess."

"How long do you reckon you'll stay?"

"I don't know yet." He grinned ruefully. "My sister runs my life sometimes. I suppose I'll stay until she tells me I can go."

Examining him as he stood at ease among the birches, Lilly could see why Charlotte ran his life. Where she was energetic and resourceful and bold, he was pensive and gentle and even a mite shy. But when he smiled, he looked boyish and young; and there was a quiet dignity about him that she instinctively trusted.

"It's a nice place," he said. "I don't think I'll mind."

"What's so nice about it?" Lilly was wary again. She had heard others rhapsodize about this country, people who had no idea what living here really meant.

"The hills are breathtaking," he answered simply. "And the quiet. I love the quiet."

"It's not quiet in town."

"That's why I stayed up here all day. My sister loves the noise and activity of a place like Lexington. I don't exactly."

"Is that where you live?"

"Thankfully, no. I spend most of my time on the farm with my great-uncle, helping him. Have you lived here all your life?"

"Yes," Lilly answered, ashamed somehow, even though Talmadge had just said he loved the hills. "I've never been out of Harlan County."

"Well, there's nothing wrong with that, as far as I can see. The world is still yours, if you read."

"I don't have much to read, really." Her eyes took on a dreamy look. "Before Mrs. Riley died, she let me read anything in her library. Then she told me to pick two of her books for my own. I picked a book of poems and a book of stories."

"A few poems, a few stories, and the Bible," Talmadge answered. "That's all you need."

"We don't have a Bible anymore. It went in the flood."

"Oh, yes, I've heard of that flood. Wasn't that just last summer? And the epidemic came this winter?"

Lilly nodded to both questions.

"How do you folks keep on going?"

How did they? They pushed into each day, each new season, relentlessly, sometimes ceasing to care, ceasing to think, only surviving as best they could until the good Lord released them. But she couldn't say this to a stranger. "We just do what we have to," she explained, teasing a twig on the ground with one toe.

"I'm sorry. It was a rude question."

She didn't know how to answer him, and thought maybe she had better go. Then he asked, "Have you ever read Emily Dickinson's poetry?"

"No, I don't think so."

"You should. It fits you people."

"What do you mean?"

"Listen. I'll read a poem to you. It's a short one." He flipped several pages in his book, obviously knowing exactly where he wanted to go. Then he began reading in a clear, resonant voice, touched with the sadness that was so much a part of the poem.

> "*Success is counted sweetest,*
> *By those who ne'er succeed.*
> *To comprehend a nectar*
> *Requires sorest need.*

"Not one of all the purple Host
Who took the flag today
Can tell the definition,
So clear, of victory,

"As he, defeated, dying,
On whose forbidden ear
The distant strains of triumph
Break agonized and clear."

It was, unlike Shakespeare, simple language that anyone could understand. And yet this poet had caught the shape of disappointment and put it so poignantly into words that Lilly wanted to cry.

Talmadge closed the book and slipped it into his pocket. "I can see that you understand. Her poetry is lovely, I think."

"I think so too. But it's sad and lonely."

"Not all of it. I'll read you some different pieces another time. That is—" he stopped for a moment "—if you want to hear them."

"Oh, yes." She tried then to break the mood that Talmadge had created, and said lightly, "I need to go. Caroline will wonder where I am."

"I apologize for keeping you so long."

"That's all right. Thank you for the poem." She was tingling as she walked away. Never before had she met a man who loved poetry as she did. Even Mrs. Riley had married a prosaic business man who tolerated her love of books but did not share it. Talmadge was sharply different.

Chapter fifteen

On Wednesday Mrs. Price talked more as she worked. Side by side, they toiled in the endless rows of beans, corn, sweet potatoes, Irish potatoes, turnips, and onions. When the sun rose high enough that the sweat rolled off them, they went inside where it was nearly as warm and cleaned two more bedrooms. By the end of the day Lilly had amassed quite a store of knowledge about the miners who lived at the boarding house. She knew that Larry came from a family of drunkards and sometimes stumbled into his room drunk himself, that Tim had worked in different mines since he was ten and hated it, that Buell loved a red-headed snippet of a girl who had refused him three times, that Ollie had been married and lost his wife and their first child, that Glenn lived at the boarding house for the week, and walked fifteen miles home every weekend.

Mrs. Price took excellent care of all these and the seven others, though she sometimes used her privileges as their housekeeper to give them the rough side of her tongue.

Thursday, Friday, and Saturday followed, days all filled with work either at the boarding house or the fine house on the hill. Lilly only had occasion to stop at the store once, but she and Talmadge said no more than polite greetings to each other. In all her coming and going, she never saw him outside among the birches. She hungered for more of Emily Dickinson's poetry, hungered enough that she would have stopped and asked for it if she had seen him.

Revivals started the next week, and on Monday evening, Lilly hurried home from the boarding house so that she could go to the first service. As soon as she set foot in the house, Maybelle hollered from upstairs, "Are you coming with us? We're almost ready to go."

"I'm coming. Just give me time to change my dress and comb my hair. I can eat a johnny cake on the way."

"Are you wearing your best dress?"

"Of course." By this time Lilly had reached the loft where Maybelle was fussing with the bow at her waist. Lilly reached for her own violet-colored dress and slipped it on. She had a sudden urge to wear it the next time she went to Mr. Riley's house. She would feel then like she truly belonged there.

She shook her brown hair out of its pins and ran a comb quickly through it. Working only by feel, for there was no mirror in the loft, she pinned it back up and tucked in the stray edges. "Are the little boys cleaned up?" she asked. "It's taking you forever to get ready."

"Oh, Caroline can get the boys ready. It's nice to have some time for myself again."

Lilly had looked after the little boys for so long that she found herself automatically going over them when she came down from the loft, tucking shirts more neatly into clean overalls, smoothing their hair, asking them if they had remembered to wash their feet.

"Caroline already went all over us," Bobby said petulantly. "You don't have to do it too."

Lilly opened her mouth in a quick retort, and then caught herself. She only swung up Sonny, who had come over to her, and said, "Let's go then."

She grabbed an extra johnny cake from the table and ate it on the way to the meetinghouse. Once they rounded the last curve, they could see others walking in that direction too. Far ahead of them were a boy and girl, walking side by side and turning now and then to look at each other.

Lilly thought she recognized them, and her heart sank. Just to be sure, she asked Maybelle nonchalantly, "Who's that walking ahead of us?"

Maybelle squinted against the evening light. "Clerise Price and Jesse."

Clerise with Jesse. Lilly knew she had no right to him anymore, and yet seeing him with another girl hurt. Did Clerise understand when he talked of what could be found in the mountains? Lilly felt bitterness pooling inside her. She had turned him down, knowing they didn't care enough about the same things.

But now she was no nearer leaving than she had ever been. Maybe further away, because the hope of Mr. Barker had been taken from her a second time. Nothing was left now but to grow older, sadder, and lonelier every month, feeling the sting of defeat, and going on with life in spite of it. Unable to completely see herself, she didn't realize that she would also be growing more cold, hard, and bitter.

"Why isn't he walking with you?" Bobby demanded.   *not better*

"He hasn't been up to see you for a long time," Maybelle said slowly. "Lilly. . ."

"Hush, Maybelle. We'll talk about it tonight."

Jesse and Clerise walked slowly, but Lilly made sure she stayed well behind them. They sat on a back bench, and Lilly saw them as soon as she stepped inside. Jesse's dark head, Clerise's brown one—side by side, whispering to each other.

Maybelle slipped off to join her friends, and the boys trailed Pa and Caroline into seats. Not seeing anyone she particularly wanted to be with, Lilly sat down beside Eula.

"No beau tonight?" Eula giggled.

"No."

"Did you see who Jesse came with?"

Lilly looked at her coldly. "Yes."

"What happened between you two? I thought there'd be a wedding soon."

Lilly drew herself up, feeling aristocratic in her smart-fitting dress. "That's my own personal business."

Bright spots of color came out on Eula's cheeks. "You are just—" she began, and then was interrupted when someone started a hymn. "You're just jealous," she hissed under the singing.

"If I was jealous, I could have had him first." But Eula's remark hit home. Lilly wasn't jealous of Jesse exactly; she was only jealous of people whose lives came together in an organized, pleasing way. Hers always seemed to be at loose ends.

She found it hard to pay attention that evening. After singing half a dozen songs, Brother Cox preached long and earnestly. He had a powerful voice that filled the room and resounded through the open windows. Several responded to his pleas for repentance.

After the service was over, Lilly and Beulah joined the stream of people leaving the church. "Look," Eula whispered. "Talmadge Preston is here with Charlotte."

Lilly nodded.

"Have you seen him before?"

"Yes." Lilly would not tell her that not only had she seen him, but she had talked to him for ten minutes, talked of things like poetry.

"Isn't he just awfully handsome?"

When Lilly didn't answer, she nudged her arm and giggled. "Are you taken with him?"

"No," Lilly answered impatiently. She saw Pa and Caroline go out the door and noticed that Caroline held a sleeping Sonny.

"He's young too," Eula said, needling Lilly for a reply.

They were outside now, flowing with the stream of people, shaking hands with Brother Cox, being swallowed in the murky shadows. Lanterns bobbed merrily on all sides, and people called to each other. "Walk up the hill with us a spell." "I've got a wagon. Anybody going down my way can ride." "Come back tomorrow night."

A voice spoke at her elbow, low and hesitant. "Miss Lilly?"

Something thudded in her stomach as she looked up and saw Talmadge.

"I don't know how things are done here," he said, "but would it be all right if I walk you home?"

"There's naught wrong with that," she managed.

"I thought—" he grinned suddenly "—that maybe we could talk some more about poetry."

"I'd like that," she answered.

He had no lantern and neither did she. "Think we can find our way in the dark?" he asked.

"Oh, yes. I've done it many times."

A few minutes later, with the crowd behind them, and darkness and silence before them, he asked, "Are you a church member?"

"Yes, since last spring."

"I am too," he said simply.

In spite of his words outside the church, he seemed reluctant to talk about poetry. Instead they discussed their homes and schooling. He told her about Lexington, and she painted a picture of Mr. Ferguson. When they reached the store, he asked, "On up the road from here?"

"Yes, but I don't mind going alone."

"I'll come with you."

They lingered at the foot of the trail below the cabin, still talking. He talked gently most of the time, with a keen perception, and something about him reminded Lilly of Mrs. Riley's grace. "I'll not come up to the porch with you," he said at last, "Your family might not know what to make of it. Want to hear a little poem yet?"

Want to? Of course she did.

"This one's funny," he warned and launched straightaway into it.

> *"I'm nobody! Who are you?*
> *Are you nobody, too?*
> *Then there's a pair of us—don't tell!*
> *They'd banish us, you know.*
>
> *How dreary to be somebody!*
> *How public, like a frog*
> *To tell your name the livelong day*
> *To an admiring bog!"*

Lilly laughed, and so did he. But at the same time she wondered. Was he answering her feelings that she was nobody?

She felt so full and at peace that she almost expected to see Ma sitting at the table with a lamp when she came in the door. Instead it was Caroline, who looked up and smiled, but said nothing. Ma would have scolded her about coming in so late and told her to eat something more; she hadn't eaten enough to keep a dog alive. A sudden longing for Ma washed in a wave across her open heart. Seeing Caroline feeding Sonny took away her appetite.

Pa was lounging in the doorway between the eating room and the front room, watching Caroline, a look on his face that Lilly could not remember him ever giving Ma. She turned abruptly to go upstairs.

"Good night, Lilly," T.J. called.

She turned back and gave him a fierce hug. "Good night, little brother."

In the girls' end of the loft, Maybelle stood by the window, running her fingers through her hair, holding strands of it up to view by the thin moonlight. "Jemsey told me tonight that I've got pretty hair," she said dreamily.

Jemsey! Maybelle! How old was her little sister anyhow? "You and Jemsey are both too young for courting," she said sharply.

"I'm twelve, Lilly. Jesse was coming to see you regularly when you weren't more than two years older than me."

Lilly prepared for bed slowly, while Maybelle went on playing with her hair and staring out the window. "What happened with you and Jesse?" she asked suddenly. "Why doesn't he come to see you anymore? You said we'd talk about it tonight."

Mrs. Riley, Ma, Caroline, Jesse, and Talmadge all mingled in Lilly's mind in a rush of past and present emotions. She wished she could simply get into bed, go to sleep, and banish them all. "I'd rather talk about it another night," she whispered.

"No, you promised."

Lilly stretched out and pulled the quilt up to her chin even though the night was warm. "He asked me to marry him and I said I couldn't."

"What sort of liar are you?"

"Maybelle!"

"I mean, of course you could marry him. Why did you say you couldn't? Jesse's one of the nicest boys I know. That is, of the ones old enough to marry you."

"I just couldn't," Lilly said wearily. "It's hard to explain. It won't make sense to you."

"Try me out and see," Maybelle pleaded.

"I'm tired. Let's get Sonny and put him to bed so we can sleep."

"I think Caroline's going to get him ready and bring him up."

Lilly stiffened. How could a woman so fully take over the care of her family in a week? She supposed it was partly her own fault; she had handed them over by going to town every day. Yet that was the only way to live through it, and she wasn't sorry she had done so.

The next evening Talmadge asked to walk her home again, and the same on the third evening. By now others were taking notice, pairing them up as a couple. Some whistled and made remarks about a good catch. Others, like Silva were dead set against it. "You'll suck sorrow if you go with that boy," she said blackly, hailing Lilly from her porch with the purpose of telling her just this.

Lilly felt herself going stupid and silent in her uncertainty. It didn't feel like Talmadge was courting her, and yet it certainly looked it to everyone else. And Silva's words brought a rush of disgust with them, disgust that Talmadge should be talked about this way.

"You hear me, girl?"

"Yes, ma'am," Lilly said respectfully.

But the evening walks home continued. Talmadge noticed things of beauty that Jesse never had. He saw loveliness in the black of pine and hemlock against the deep blue of a night sky. He plucked weeds idly as they walked along and without seeming to think at all of what he was doing, arranged them into feathery sprays. He stopped on the bridge and listened to the soft trills of Sand Lick with a sigh of satisfaction. "There's nothing like running water to help you think and sort through things," he said.

Almost Lilly told him of her stories, a part of her life she had never fully shared with anyone before. But she didn't know him quite well enough—yet. She would soon, she thought, if they had many more evenings together.

And they did have more evenings. The revivals finished the first week and the second and began on a third. People were being saved, and the lovely weather held, so the evangelist stayed. She stopped in at the store too, on errands for Caroline or Silva, and sometimes Talmadge walked with her a ways. Sometimes when she passed, he was outside the cottage where he lived with Joe, Charlotte, and old Mr. Greer, hoeing in the garden. Then he would stop, lean on his hoe, and ask her how work had been that day, or pass on a trivial bit of gossip that he had picked up in the store.

They talked of so many things in their time together—their homes and families, their school days, their interests, their friends. Talmadge knew how to talk so that what he said would remain in her heart, take root, and grow new ideas. Sometimes she lay awake in bed, marveling at how much she knew of him. Seeing Jesse and Clerise together stung no longer. She could watch them walk to church side by side and smile, knowing that Talmadge would be waiting for her afterward, and that she could share with him in a way she never had with Jesse. And when they would part, she would go to bed, warm and thankful that she had not said yes when Jesse proposed.

Once she asked Talmadge shyly how much longer he would stay, and he said he would need to leave by harvest time on the farm, maybe sooner. "It depends when my uncle sends for me. And of course—" with a grin "—it depends some on my sister." Then he fell silent for a moment and his smile slid away into seriousness and he looked at her with his blue, blue eyes and added, "But I wouldn't mind if I was here all summer. Would you?"

Lilly could only blush crimson.

Maybelle took to calling him her beau before Lilly could figure out if he had any serious intentions. Caroline seemed quietly pleased over the match, and Pa said very little against it. Usually he distrusted anyone who came into the hills from outside, but the knowledge that Talmadge would inherit a farm helped to pacify him. "It's not like he'll be dragging you off to the city," he said.

Talmadge had told her that his father had died, and his mother re-married. Charlotte was younger than him by three years, the first child of the second marriage. Talmadge's father had been a visionary dreamer and Charlotte's a hard-driving businessman. "We never had much money while my father was alive," Talmadge commented wryly. "I think my mother wanted to change that when she married again."

Talmadge's father had left no property, nothing but his name to his only son. A great-uncle, being childless himself, had decided he would pass on his farm to Talmadge when he died. "He wants me there," Talmadge explained, "so he can teach me how to run things while he's still living. I think he's afraid I'll be a poor manager like my father. But I love the farm; it's beautiful. I'll work hard to keep it beautiful when it's mine. I think I'm just a farmer at heart, after all."

"And a dreamer and a lover of poetry too," Lilly reminded him. Jesse telling her he was a farmer, and Talmadge telling her he was a farmer were two very different things, maybe because of where the farms were, but mostly because of the minds inside the farmers.

"Yes, but I'll be bound to that farm as soon as my great-uncle dies. No more gallivanting around like this summer."

"Will he die soon, do you think?"

"He's in good health. But he's in his seventies. He could die anytime."

They reached the bridge just then, and Talmadge stopped to sit on the edge and listen to the water. "Still, my mind is my own, and as long as I have a few books, I can roam free, even if I'm tied in body to the farm."

Lilly remembered the time she had said something just like that to Mr. Ferguson, and thrilled with the thought that they could come up with the same ideas independently of each other. She sat down beside him. "Doesn't your uncle need you this summer?"

He shrugged. "He has other farm hands, and since Charlotte asked for me to visit her, he said he can make out without me for awhile." He went on then, and described the hundred-acre farm, with its white, two-story house, its red barn, its neat tobacco fields, its fine horses. She felt like she would love a farm of that sort too.

"Farmers are good strong folk," she said loyally when he finished.

On another evening, she told him at last about her stories that had washed down the river in the flood. After she started, she felt a sudden fear that he would think her silly for the joy she got from her scribbles. But, since she had started, she confided everything.

"Do you do any writing these days?" he asked meditatively.

"No."

"Why not?"

"I don't have time. Or paper. And I don't think I have what it takes to do really good writing."

He smiled at her again, the smile that gently disagreed with what she had just said. "I'm sure it would take training and practice, of course. But I've been listening to you talk. Anyone who talks like you should be able to write too."

Someone else believed in her dreams! She felt the joy of this in tingles down her back. "Do you know what I long for?" she said.

"I think I can guess. But tell me."

"I'd like a library of my own like Mrs. Riley's. . ."

"And?" Talmadge prompted. He saw the eagerness glowing in her eyes and knew she wasn't finished.

"And enough paper and pencils and time to really write." It had been almost a year since she had felt a firm pencil in her hand, or touched its tip against paper. How could a dream live so long on nothing?

"You should have it," Talmadge said firmly. "And I think that you will sometime, Lilly. Have patience; the good things you deserve will come to you."

This joy lasted for three weeks. Lilly felt the kind of happiness she had thought was gone from her forever. Her determination to leave the mountains was still strong within her, but the understanding she felt from Talmadge softened the sharp edges of it, until it was a thing she could hold in her heart without pain. She hardly realized herself how she was losing the bitterness of the winter and becoming alive and whole again. She only knew that these early days of summer held to her lips a glass of camaraderie, quickly morphing into the wine of love, and she drank full from it.

One Tuesday, Talmadge even sought her out at the Riley house. She came through the back door with a rug to beat, and he was there, leaning against a tree, thoughtfully looking the house over. "Do you need something?" she asked, startled.

"No." He came toward her, smiling. "I've just been exploring around town, and I remembered you worked here today. But if it's not too inconvenient, I would be glad for a drink."

"I'll bring one out."

She filled two cups with water, and they stood in the shade of the porch to drink them. "Do you have to work hard here?" he asked.

"Not so hard as at the boarding house. I like it here."

"You never get lonely?"

"Not often."

"Do you read the books here?"

"I come to work, not read." She hadn't known if she dared to touch the precious volumes in the library.

Casually, he pulled a thin paperback book from his pocket. "I thought if I found you, I could give you this."

"What is it?"

"Poems by Emily Dickinson. Some of her best. I think you'll like it."

She knew by now that while he loved poetry, he was often reticent about it, for people like Charlotte didn't understand his fascination with it. She wished she could make him know how her heart leaped up in gratitude for this gift, but she found no words other than, "Thank you."

"You're welcome."

"Does it have the poem about the frog?"

"Yes, and the one about defeat too."

When he left her, he whistled the whole way down the hill, his whistle at last losing itself in the clanging of machinery close to the mouth of the mine. He stood for a few minutes, hands in his pockets, watching all the frantic action and remembering the reverent look on Lilly's face when she took the book from him. He knew that her pa worked as a facer, chipping the coal away from the seam deep in the bowels of the earth. This occupation fed and clothed the whole Burchett family, but it was a world far removed from his own. Talmadge hated the very sight of the black cavernous opening in the side of the mountain and the thought of working so far away from sunlight and fresh air.

He remembered to stop at the post office and check for mail. The post master had his feet up on the counter, his one cheek distended by a wad of tobacco. "Any mail for the Keeton's?" Talmadge asked. "Or for me?"

The man grunted his answer around his chaw. "Catalog for Charlotte. Letter for you." He flipped both of them toward Talmadge.

"Thanks."

Talmadge ripped open the thin envelope that bore his name and immediately recognized his great uncle's stiff unyielding hand.

> *Dear Talmadge,*
>
> *The weather here is fine. It looks like the tobacco crop will be good this year. My back is bothering me bad though, and I would be thankful for your help. Charlotte wrote that you might be glad of a change. I will look for you as soon as you can get here. —Uncle Richard.*

Talmadge frowned and read it over again. The request for help didn't surprise him, but the mention of Charlotte did. What was Charlotte doing writing to Uncle Richard? If there were no customers in the store, he would ask her immediately.

She, however, pounced on him first. "Where have you been?" she demanded.

He threw the catalog toward her. Some of its pages fanned open and showed pictures of ladies in new hats and shoes. "Down to town," he said. "I picked up the mail."

"It doesn't take two hours to pick up the mail."

"I did some other prowling around."

"Where?" she asked suspiciously.

"Oh, just to the mine and—"

"And you found Lilly Burchett somewhere, I've no doubt."

He feigned nonchalance to hide his shock at her sharpness. "Yes. We talked for maybe ten minutes."

"Talmadge, this has got to stop right now."

He walked around the counter and pulled himself up onto it, facing her, trying to understand this sudden onslaught.

"I looked the other way when you walked her home from church the first few times," she went on. "I thought you were just having fun and nothing would ever come of it. But now I'm afraid it's getting serious. This has to stop. Now!"

He touched the letter in his pocket. "I guess it will," he said slowly. "I had a letter from Uncle Richard today. He wants me to come and help him."

"Good."

"Were you behind it, Charlotte?"

Her eyes flashed. "Yes. I wanted you gone, even if it kills me with loneliness."

"But why?"

"Oh, you're a simple one. Always with your head in the clouds so that you can't see what's going on right in front of your nose. Do you think you would be happy marrying Lilly?"

"We haven't talked of marriage."

"Maybe not. But don't tell me you haven't thought of it." She paused and waited; his silence seemed to condemn him.

"Not exactly," he answered at last.

"Oh?" she said, arching her eyebrows. "That's a pretty fib."

She was right, and he knew it. All the while he had been enjoying Lilly's friendship, the thought of marriage had been growing, hardly acknowledged, but there. Her words exposed it. Maybe he had been foolish, thinking and talking of poetry, but playing at courtship.

"I won't let you marry a mountain girl."

"I don't understand."

Charlotte drew herself up to all of her short, plump height. "Look at me. Do you think I'm a happy woman?"

"You don't seem so," he admitted candidly.

"Let me tell you, I married a mountain boy, and I am living to regret it. I thought I could tame him and civilize him and make him enjoy living in the city. But I couldn't. Here we are in the mountains, though he promised he would never make me live here. It's this foolish duty to his pa that has brought him back, and now he sits at the house with him all day and lets me run the store and put the food on his table."

"You could stay home and let him come. He's offered that you could."

She shrugged angrily. "Oh, I don't want to stay. I'd much rather come here, if I have the choice. I don't know how to take care of his pa. I might as well let the two men sit over there and spit and chew and talk and be lazy."

"I didn't know you felt that way about Joe," Talmadge said in amazement.

"No, you wouldn't. I'm good at pretending, when I want to be."

"Does Joe know you're not happy?"

"Yes. It's really best if I leave him alone and come over here. It's the thought of doing this for years and years that I can't stand."

"Okla might die someday. Then you could move back to Lexington."

"I couldn't make Joe leave, now that he's back where he was born," Charlotte retorted. "I used to think I had some control over him. He listened to me about what to wear and things like that, in Lexington. But now that we're out here, he doesn't care. He's just. . ." She paused, searching for the right word. "He's just torpid. Nothing I say makes any difference. I'll never be able to persuade him to go back. This life is too good. For him."

"I'm sorry," Talmadge said awkwardly. "I know it's been hard for you to adjust."

"Adjust?" Charlotte cried. "You think I just need to adjust? Might as well tell a fish to adjust to living on land."

"Customers coming," Talmadge murmured and slid off the counter.

It was two little girls, come to buy some liniment, and soon they were on their way again.

"So you see," Charlotte went on coldly, "why I won't let you get serious about Lilly."

"No, I don't see."

"I'm thinking about your good. Listen to me. I've discovered what it's like to be married to a mountain man. I want to spare you of that."

"Lilly's not a mountain woman in her heart."

"You think so now. There was a time when I could only see Joe's charm and freshness, and I thought it was romantic to marry someone from the hills. But the charm and romance go away. Doesn't Lilly live in a log cabin?"

"Yes."

"Has she ever seen the world?"

"No, but she wants to."

"Sure. She says so now. Here's what will happen. She would go with you willingly enough if you asked her to. But after living on the farm, or in Lexington, for a few months, she will start moping. These folks that are born in the hills, they can't ever live without the hills. They don't ever acclimate."

"Lilly's different." Talmadge knew even as he said it that it sounded trite and foolish.

Charlotte laughed harshly.

"I thought you liked her too," he added.

"Oh, I do. To a point. But I'm being wise. I know she won't make a good wife for you, so I'm stopping it right here. You're not too much in love with her yet, I hope. Go away before it gets any worse. It will be better for both of you."

Talmadge felt the letter in his pocket again, running his finger along the sharp edge of the envelope where he had slit it with his knife. Lilly came up before his mind's eyes in all her fresh litheness, brown eyes glowing as they talked. Then he pictured the older women that attended the revival services, bowed and burdened by years of hard work, their eyes sometimes dull and apathetic, their thin faces chiseled from rock and seamed by fissures, the bones in their hands distorted, their feet wide and heavy and cracked. Would Lilly look like them someday? He shuddered away from the image.

"You feel sorry for Lilly," Charlotte accused. "You just want to get her away from here, because you think she's a nice girl. That doesn't mean you love her."

"Lilly should get away from here."

"Sure, she should. But as long as her pa is against education, there's not much hope."

Except by marrying her.

Chapter sixteen

This conversation went on and on and on, between customers, all through the long afternoon. Now that Charlotte had started pouring out her own frustration and disappointment, she couldn't stop. Talmadge felt his own defenses of Lilly powerless before her arguments. "I had no idea this would happen when I invited you here," she said, and actually began to cry. "I know you don't believe me. But at least go away for a whole year, and think about it without seeing Lilly. Don't write to her either."

"She'll expect me to write."

Charlotte dried her eyes with vicious swipes of her fingers. "Of course she will. You'll have to explain."

"That will be hard."

"Listen, Talmadge, I'm doing this for you own good."

"She could marry someone else within a year."

"So could you. You're just taken with her right now because you're here. Go away and give yourself time to think. You'll see that I'm right."

Finally, when the sun had begun to slink down into the west, he got up and walked deliberately away from her, out of the store. He went to the copse of birch trees where he had first talked with Lilly, where it seemed that her spirit still lingered, and sat down among them. But after a few minutes, he stood up and moved to the back of the store, where the door opened out of old Mr. and Mrs. Keeton's abandoned quarters. He knew that Lilly would come by soon on her way home from work, and he couldn't afford to see her just now. Not before he had some things settled. He could, of course, tell Lilly that his uncle wanted him and then simply go, with no further explanation. But that would be unjust, even cruel.

Lilly carried the poem book from Talmadge home in the ample pocket of her dress. Once through the town, when she had the road all to herself, she pulled it out and turned the pages slowly. At one poem, a piece of paper fell out and fluttered to the ground. She stopped for a moment and read the poem.

It started,

> *Hope is the thing with feathers,*
> *That perches in the soul,*
> *And sings the tune without the words,*
> *And never stops at all.*

Hope. That was what Talmadge had given her in these last few weeks.

When she got to church that evening, she scanned the crowd for him, and, not seeing him, lingered outside for a while. They had never yet sat together in church, but she wanted to be sure he was there. The singing started inside, and he still hadn't appeared.

"Your beau coming tonight?" Eula asked clearly beside her.

"He's not my beau."

Eula fluttered her eyelids and laughed. "Did you tell him off?"

"Let's go in."

"Sure you don't want to wait for him?"

During the service, Lilly's anxiety mounted. Talmadge came at last, late, but he slid into a back bench, his shoulders slumped. Lilly could hardly sit still, worry gnawing at her now. Had something happened? Bad news from home, perhaps? If he needed comforting, she wanted to reach out and try to give it.

A different look stared out of his blue eyes when he asked to walk home with her. He seemed worn and distressed. But it had only been eight hours since she had last seen him, and she couldn't make sense out of this change.

"Of course, Talmadge," she said.

She wanted to ask him what was wrong, but didn't know how to begin. He had grown so strangely silent, grown away from her into a place she couldn't reach. They walked past the school and entered the woods, where darkness reigned alone. Finally she asked, "Did you mark a poem in the book you gave me?"

"Yes."

"The one about hope?"

"Yes."

"It's a beautiful poem. I read it."

No answer.

"Is something wrong?" she ventured.

"Something is very wrong," he answered dully, without looking at her. "I had a letter from my great-uncle today. He's asking for me to come and help him on the farm as soon as I can get there."

So he would be leaving. She had known this would happen, sooner or later, but never let herself think too much of it. Was he that sorry to leave too, or was there something else, something bigger behind this silence? She felt a creeping dread, but hid it behind bravery. "You always said you would need to go at harvest time."

"Yes. But there's more to it than that." His long arms hung down limply beside him, and his eyes were half-closed, hiding himself.

"What do you mean?"

"It's hard to explain," he answered haggardly. "I think I can do it better in a letter after I'm gone. Can you wait that long?"

Her budding trust in him, and the desire to comfort him somehow, gave her confidence to say, "Yes, Talmadge, I can wait."

He turned to her suddenly, roughly. "No. I didn't mean that."

She stared at him in bewilderment.

"I don't know what folks around here are saying," he went on, "but I imagine they're trying to guess how soon we'll get married. You know as well as I do that we've never talked about that. I thought maybe we would eventually—we think so much alike—but, not now. At least not for a long time. I can't tell you what I mean. But you must not. . ."

Must not what? Although Lilly had just told him that she would wait for his letter, she now wanted to cry out in anguish that he had to explain everything at once.

"I'll write as soon as I can," he promised. "I don't want to hurt you, Lilly. Maybe I can keep from hurting you in a letter."

They walked the rest of the way in a dead silence, the living breath that had accompanied them on so many other walks buried somewhere in the valley behind them. At parting, Talmadge shook her hand with a strange formality. "I'm leaving tomorrow," he whispered. "There's no point in waiting. So good-bye. Don't try to see me in the morning."

"Won't folks talk if you leave so sudden-like?"

"Yes," he said sharply, "they will. They'll think we fought, and I'm running away. But Charlotte and you both know I had to go help Uncle Richard. Stop the rumors the best you can."

Lilly hardly slept that night. And after spending most of the next day in Mrs. Price's garden, she developed a raging headache. She remembered Talmadge saying once that Emily Dickinson had written a poem describing such a headache, but she couldn't summon the will to try to find it.

"I'm not going to the meeting tonight," she told Caroline.

Caroline stood at the mirror in the front room, twisting her hair up into a bun with deft fingers. "Are you sick?"

"I have a headache."

Maybelle called down from the loft, "What shall I tell Talmadge when he wonders where you are?"

"He won't be there."

"Where is he?"

"He left today to go to his great uncle's farm. He had a letter asking him to come."

"Did you say good-bye?"

"Yes," Lilly answered wearily. "Last night."

"It must have been urgent."

"His uncle wanted him to come as soon as he could."

"No wonder you have a headache," Caroline said wisely. "It will do you good to sleep."

As soon as her family had gone, she crept upstairs to bed. Evening sunlight flooded into the loft, rich and golden and warm, and she shut her eyes tight against it. No matter how hard she tried, she couldn't relax and go to sleep. All was silent outside, except for an occasional yapping from a dog, or the distant squeal of a pig. It was so quiet that she could imagine she heard a train in town, a train like the one that had carried Talmadge away from her that morning.

At last she threw back the sheet, went downstairs, and got a slim bottle from the cupboard in the kitchen. Ma had used it occasionally when she had a bad headache, and she figured this headache justified it as well. She poured two swallows of the moonshine into a cup and thinned it with water. This would put her to sleep soundly enough to rid herself of the headache.

She needed to go back to work for Mrs. Price the next day, and she discovered that already talk of Talmadge's sudden departure had filled the community.

"Folks are saying that you must have quarreled, or he wouldn't have gone so sudden," Mrs. Price said pointedly.

"No. We didn't. He needed to go and help his uncle."

"Oh, I heard that too, of course. But I think there's more to it than that. Is he going to write to you?"

"Yes." *At least that one letter.*

"I thought something was going to come of him and you."

Other people talked too, and by one source or another, some of their comments trickled back to Lilly. They speculated where they didn't know and conjectured about his now-dead father, his mother, his step-father, and his uncle. The stories were less than flattering, almost entirely false. Some of the girls whispered that he had another girl at home and had only been playing with Lilly. They didn't say it directly to her, of course, but she understood the insinuations.

Lilly gave Talmadge four days, and then she began stopping in every day at the post office to check for a letter from him. The post master always grinned provokingly as he sorted through the stack. "Well, now," he would say invariably, "it's taking that Talmadge a good while, isn't it?"

Ten agonizing days passed before the letter came. He flipped it casually across the counter at her. "Hope it's good news. There's been a lot of talk about Talmadge."

Lilly took the letter without looking at him and headed straight for the bridge. She had known ever since Talmadge went away that when his letter came she would read it there. In its safety, she stood motionless for a long moment, trying to still the tumultuous beating of her heart, the fear in her throat. Then she opened the envelope.

Dear Lilly,

I have been at Uncle Richard's for four days, doing a lot of thinking, and remembering with fondness our time together. But I must be true to my promise and write you this letter.

We are very different, Lilly. In spite of our similar tastes in things like poetry, you must be able to see that. You have grown up in the mountains, while I'm used to living out here in the flatlands. I hope that once I inherit the farm, I will never need to live in the city again, but we both know that my farm is very different from the farm where you are. Besides that, we are used to dressing differently and talking differently. And we have different sorts of friends.

I will not be so presumptuous to say that you loved me, Lilly, or that I loved you; but I think it could have come to that. It is easy to think that if we loved each other, all these differences would not matter. But I have been doing a lot of thinking, and I'm not at all sure that this is true. I do not want to drag you into anything that will make you unhappy.

Take my sister Charlotte for an example. She thought she loved Joe, but she is not very content with him there in the mountains. If they would move to Lexington, she would be happy, but he would not. Do you understand what I am trying to say? I think it's best for me to be away from you and not to communicate for now. If time and fate should bring us back together some day, then perhaps our friendship was meant to be.

For it was only a friendship, I believe. My heart told me that I would have been in love before many more weeks, and it seemed best to go away and think it over carefully before that happened.

I'm afraid you will think I'm deserting you. Perhaps I left too abruptly. Please do not think it is easy for me to do this. But at this point, it is better that we stay only friends. I can ask for no promises from you, and can give you none from me. I will only ask that you remember me as a dear friend.

Your sincere servant,

Talmadge D. Preston

Lilly read the letter once, then folded it up and slid it back into the envelope with hands that shook. Perhaps later she would read it again, but for now once was all she could stand. He had sounded so formal, except for several spots where he dropped in a gentle word or phrase.

He told me to my face that being nobody didn't matter, she thought wildly, *but he didn't really mean it.*

However, one piece of the puzzle seemed missing and she needed it to complete her pain. Why this change in Talmadge? Surely he had really liked her at one time. Surely he hadn't been merely playing with her. An idea took shape in her mind through that long night and the next day. She stopped in at the store on the way home from work, feeling like a wounded lioness, her hand on the letter that she still carried in her pocket.

"You didn't want Talmadge to marry me," she accused.

It had been only a hunch, but Charlotte's face blanched, and against the whiteness of her cheeks, her lips looked sickeningly red. "Did he tell you that?"

"No. I think it myself. Is it true?"

Charlotte's voice gentled. "I thought it would be best if he wouldn't. I was thinking about his good and yours. I don't want either of you hurt."

"No. Stop lying to me. You wanted to save him from me."

Charlotte sat down and looked at her coldly. "I wanted to save him from the life I have."

"Talmadge is different from you. And I'm different from Joe."

"People who are in love always think their case is different. Someday you will thank me for this."

Lilly stared back at her, coldness for coldness. She felt hatred boiling up in her stomach, hatred for both Talmadge and Charlotte, anyone who could betray her like this. Wordless, she turned and went away.

Stories were not real life, she realized suddenly. If she and Talmadge were living in a story, he would fly in the face of everything Charlotte said and marry her, whether she was backwards and uncivilized or not. He would stand up for the girl he loved, letting the chips fall where they would.

But this was real life, hard and crushing, with more pain and disappointment than Lilly had ever dreamed possible. In this real life, Talmadge would walk out, claiming that this budding closeness between them had been nothing more than friendship. Maybe it hadn't been, but it had been a sweet and satisfying friendship, and this sudden loss, this betrayal, left her achingly empty.

Not caring about supper, she walked on past the house, taking the upper fork of Sand Lick. The weeks with Talmadge had thrown a gauzy veil in front of her face. She had believed in beauty again, had learned to smile and laugh without bitterness. But this letter had wrenched that rudely away from her again, forever.

Betrayal. Abandonment.

Hideous words.

Talmadge appeared now to her as a weak fool who could talk nicely, show off lovely manners, and make everyone like him, but who turned tail and fled when the going got tough. She knew she was judging him harshly, but couldn't stop herself. This new wound opened up the old one of losing Mrs. Riley, Ma, Vince, and Patty, making them all bleed afresh. Life seemed to be closing in like the steep hills on both sides of her, sucking away all that was sweet and precious.

She was blind to the opulent loveliness of the woods in July, not seeing the blackberry brambles hung thickly with fruit, the deep green ferns curling at her feet, the cream-streaked rocks along the creek bank, or the warm forgiving light of the setting sun.

She had learned her lesson the hard way, but she had learned it sure. Never again would she trust someone from outside the mountains. She felt for the letter in her pocket, felt its sharp edges against her palm, and finally let herself cry.

Part 4

Chapter seventeen

Lilly sent one cool, courteous letter back to Talmadge, telling him that she understood what he said. As she expected, no more letters came. In spite of the pain it caused, she continued reading the book of poems he had given her.

Certain verses stood out sharply.

> *I felt a funeral in my brain,*
> *And mourners, to and fro,*
> *Kept treading, treading, till it seemed*
> *That sense was breaking through.*

Or,

> *The heart asks pleasure first,*
> *And then, excuse from pain;*
> *And then, those little anodynes*
> *That deaden suffering.*

She avoided Charlotte whenever possible and, when not possible, dealt with her without meeting her eyes and without talking more than necessary. She threw herself into her work for Mr. Riley and Mrs. Price with a new determination, trying to forget. It was hard when people talked. With keen intuition, everyone was sure that something else lay behind Talmadge's sudden departure. Someone nosed around and came up with the juicy tidbit that there had been one letter, only one, and then nothing for weeks.

Even Caroline broke her customary silence around Lilly to try to get the story. One September evening she asked without warning, "Can you tell me a little of what he said in his letter?"

"Who?" Lilly asked, feigning ignorance.

"Talmadge Preston." Caroline stopped throwing ears of corn into the basket between them, and wiped sweat from her face.

"It was personal."

"Your pa is wondering what happened between you," Caroline added pointedly.

"Let him ask me then."

"Will you tell him?"

"No."

Caroline stripped another stalk of corn and tossed the ears into the basket. She was a slender woman and her dress hung loosely on her shoulders. Lilly found herself scrutinizing her and wondering about her relationship with Pa. The honeymoon stage was definitely over, and occasionally they argued now. He rarely looked at her with that fresh, new love; and she rarely did special little things just for him.

They were all discovering that under her quietness and apparent docility, she had a hard streak of granite that could not be chipped. Sonny called her ma now, a word he had never used with his own ma, since she had died before he could talk. Although it had stung the first time Lilly heard it; she was slowly getting used to it now. Bobby hadn't gone that far, but he seemed comfortable around her. Maybelle disagreed with Caroline sometimes. These clashes never blossomed into all-out fights, because Caroline simply went ahead and did things the way she wanted to do them. T.J. still much preferred Lilly to his step-ma, and Lilly took comfort in that.

As she mused, she worked her way up the row, keeping pace with Caroline, who preserved an unbroken silence after her rebuff. Pa had gone to sleep already, worn out from his long day in the mine. After Maybelle finished up the dishes, she would come out and help them. Bobby and T.J. had been instructed to watch Sonny closely, and Lilly could hear all three of them below her in the yard. They were beginning to feel like a family, she realized suddenly.

The next morning she went down the trail to town with a new lightness in her step. The edge of the pain had worn off, and although she still carried a wound, she could smile again over the goldenrod showing yellow along the trail, the fat furry rabbit that hopped frantically into the woods, or the sound of water rushing through its rocky channel below the bridge. She loitered for a few moments on that bridge, thinking of happy times. She hadn't gone back there since the day she read Talmadge's letter; the spot itself had only been more pain. It had seen so many of her sorrows, but also so much of her happiness; and this time the happiness seemed bigger than the sorrow. She remembered the times she had spun stories there, had dreamed dreams, had dipped her toes in the water and felt the slow, steady sweep of a peace outside herself.

Her stories seemed long ago. She thought of them one by one, lovingly, as a grandmother might remember the days when her children were born. She had to smile to herself over some of them, especially the one about Ramina and Abadash. She understood now why Mr. Ferguson had laughed at it.

She could feel something coming alive in her, something that had gone to sleep when Talmadge walked out. With that feeling in her heart, she decided to give the library a good cleaning that day. She was her own boss in the house, and Mr. Riley let her do whatever she chose. Many times in the last months, she had cleaned the library, but always quickly skimming her rag along the shelves, hurrying to get done, avoiding any titles that would make her think of Talmadge.

Today she took her time. In some neglected corners, she took the books off the shelves and cleaned carefully where they had been. It took her a good part of the morning. After she had eaten her lunch, she returned and stood in the doorway, just to revel in the clean feel of the room. She hadn't yet lowered the drapes at the windows, and the golden late summer sun poured in, lighting up the richly bound books, and the dark walnut shelves, and the burgundy upholstery on the chairs. Lilly thought she had never seen the room looking more beautiful, even when Mrs. Riley was alive. She let the drapes down carefully, and the sudden dimness in the room altered its mood. Where it had been warm and rich and happy, it was now all at once quietly alluring. The books looked darker, full of unhappy secrets that they were reluctant to divulge.

Lilly breathed lightly and thought fast. Did she dare? There was no washing to do today, and she had already cleaned up the kitchen. She only needed to fix something for Mr. Riley's supper, which wouldn't take long. She selected a book gently. Before, she had always sat on the floor to read, uncomfortable in the chairs even while she admired them. But today she felt gentle and feminine, almost ladylike, and she sat in the chair where Mrs. Riley had so often sat, crossed her ankles in imitation of Mrs. Riley, and opened the book.

This was one she had never read before. In minutes she had immersed herself in the story of a girl scarcely older than herself who left family and friends behind and traveled west as a young bride. She could identify quickly with the feeling of loss as the girl left home, and she understood the desire for adventure that ran strong through both her and her husband. She read slowly enough to grasp the whole story, so that she could retell it to T.J. that night.

The prickly feel of a presence behind her at last made her look up, poised, with a page ready to turn in her hand.

Mr. Riley stood in the doorway, his face dark purple-red, his eyes balls of fire, his fingers working the beard that he had grown since Mrs. Riley died. "Lilly. Burchett." He said the two words menacingly, and Lilly remembered that he had a reputation as the most ruthless and hardhearted man this side of the Mississippi. The death of his wife had only increased his hardness.

She was trapped, and she cowered back in her chair.

"Get. Out. Of. That. Room." He said the words through his teeth, making each one stand alone like a separate order. "I trusted you to come in here and do my washing and cooking and cleaning, and when I come home unexpectedly, I find you reading like a lazy lout. Besides that, who do you think you are? These books do not belong to you. They belong to my wife."

Lilly hoped the mention of his wife would calm him; it only seemed to infuriate him more. "My wife collected and loved these books. And a common girl like you dares to come in and handle them, even sits down and reads them."

This was unfair. Lilly wanted to tell him she had never done it before, but she dared not open her mouth. She stood up and moved toward the door, obeying him, unconsciously still holding the book in her hand.

"Put that book away." Mr. Riley was yelling now. "I forbid you ever to do this again. And no wages for today's work."

Lilly had fully expected him to fire her on the spot, and she felt a tinge of relief. But when he had gone out of the house again, carrying a sheaf of papers from his desk, the relief evaporated in shame. He had called her a common girl. She felt that it was irrevocably true; that because she was a common girl Talmadge couldn't marry her, because she was a common girl, she would never get out of the mountains to the life she dreamed of. She sat down limply at the kitchen table.

As usual she got Mr. Riley's supper. As usual she tidied the kitchen and swept crumbs from the floor. As usual she set one place for him at the table, wondering this time what he would think of her while he ate. When she had calmed down enough to think the episode over rationally, she realized that his fury in the library was caused partly by grief over his wife. Still, that understanding did little to lessen the sting of his accusations.

Not until the way home did she realize that she now had no way to finish the story which had captivated her.

Caroline had just set out bowls of corn, fried tomatoes, and beans with bacon when Lilly stepped in the door. They acknowledged each other with a look, nothing more. "Go call Bobby in," Caroline directed T.J. Pa came from the front room, sat down, and leaned his elbows heavily on the table. When everyone had gathered, he led them in a short grace, and then dug into the food.

Everyone ate silently at first, intent only on filling their empty stomachs. But toward the end of the meal, Caroline announced, "My ma was up to talk to me today."

"Yeah," Pa grunted.

"She stayed for a while. We had a nice visit."

"Yeah."

Silence fell again. Lilly took the last roasting ear from the plate and sank her teeth into its buttery goodness. A meal like this helped to take the sting out of the afternoon.

Visiting with her ma must have inspired Caroline to talk. Before long she said, "Ma wanted me to do something."

"Yeah," Pa grunted for the third time. But he had finished his food now and he looked at her. "What was that?"

"Would you be willing, Bernie, to have my mammaw move in with us for a spell?"

She had the sudden, undivided attention of everyone at the table. They all stared. "Are you crazy, woman?" Pa asked.

"She needs a home."

"Where's she living now?"

Lilly tried to think if she even knew Caroline's mammaw. She was probably an ancient woman who never stirred from her own hearthside.

"She's with my aunt," Caroline said, "but my aunt just had a baby and is doing poorly. They don't think she'll live. They need somewhere to go with Mammaw, at least for a few weeks."

"Only a few weeks?"

"I don't know," she answered cautiously. "Maybe."

But Lilly realized by the tone of her voice that it would certainly be longer. Pa heard this too. "And where would we put an old woman in this house?" he asked. "I don't want her sleeping in the front room with us."

"Neither do I. But there would be room for a cot right here." She gestured toward a corner of the eating room, close to the fireplace. "It would be warm for her in the winter. You're handy with your tools. You could put together a cot in two shakes of a mare's tail."

She was flattering him so that he would give in to her. Ma had told Lilly once that the men did well with a bit of flattery, but this was laying it on too thick. Lilly took a gulp of water in disgust.

"No, Caroline, I won't have an old woman sleeping in our eating room."

"But, Bernie, she needs somewhere to go."

"Haven't you got any other cousins?"

"We have a bigger cabin than most of them. And a smaller family."

The way she said this seemed to draw Vince, Patty, and Ma into the middle of the argument. Lilly still had half her ear of corn left, but it looked sickening now. She took a nibble and pretended to chew it.

"My wife and children didn't die so that we could take care of your mammaw." Pa's voice had risen.

How many angry men would Lilly have to see in one day? T.J. started to cry.

"Oh, I know that," Caroline said placatingly. "I didn't mean it that way at all. I was only trying to say—"

"Wait to say it until everyone is finished with their supper."

"Can't we talk while they finish?"

"No one is eating," Pa pointed out.

Bobby pushed back his chair from the table and carried his plate, still holding a few beans, out to the porch. "Come back, Bobby," Pa called after him.

He surely heard, but he pretended not to. Maybelle kicked T.J. under the table. "Hush up. Quit your crying."

"Maybelle," Lilly hissed.

"Time he grows up," Maybelle sassed back.

The delicious supper Lilly had just eaten made a nasty lump in her stomach. She stood up too and began carrying dishes to the kitchen. Unobtrusively, she threw the corn she hadn't finished out the back door. Caroline had quieted for the time being, but Lilly knew that the battle between her and Pa was not over. She knew that Pa would not go to bed right after supper this evening, and that Caroline would find a convenient moment to renew her attack. Lilly wanted to be out of the house when that moment came.

So as soon as the dishes were finished, she called T.J. "Want to go on a walk with me?"

"Where to?"

"Come along and you'll see." She didn't know what had inspired her to show T.J. her spot under the bridge, except a growing conviction that he liked the same things she liked. She wouldn't tell him how often she had been there, only take him and watch his reaction.

T.J. went willingly down the path through the grass, which had turned sere and brown in the dryness. "It's not so hot down here," he said in admiration, and his voice echoed among the pilings. Lilly realized that she had never spoke aloud there.

"The water isn't deep, is it?"

"No, not much. You can wade if you want to."

"Why did you bring me here, Lilly?"

"I wanted a quiet place to think, and I just decided to bring you along."

"Well, it's a nice place," T.J. said decidedly. He waded across to the other creek bank and walked circles around the sturdy pilings, sometimes hopping from rock to rock, sometimes dragging his toes through the mud at the water's edge.

Lilly sat down, cupped her chin in her hands, and, without warning, thought of an almost-forgotten comment from Talmadge. "There's nothing like running water to help you think and sort through things." She felt like she needed some sorting out of herself, after this day. What kind of person was she anyhow? She seemed wavering between two. This morning she had looked without so much pain and regret on her past, cherishing the good times of the past several years. She had looked forward to the future with a reviving of the unquenchable hope of youth that believes there is always a way. She had reveled again in Mrs. Riley's books and thrilled to the touch of them. She had known that life could be beautiful and had felt akin to the green-gold trees, and the hazy opal sky. Tonight, after Mr. Riley's harsh scolding, she felt more like the dead, brown grass that swayed ghostlike along the edge of the creek, the best of her life behind her, only bitterness and sorrow and drudgery ahead.

Lilly felt sure that Caroline would win her argument, and that meant more changes. The one change she most longed for—leaving the mountains—had been repeatedly denied her, while other changes were hurled at her faster than she could cope with them. She wanted nothing more of change now. Just let her live out her life in peace.

Eventually T.J. came over and sat down beside her. "How long are we going to stay here?"

"I don't know."

"Do you think Pa and Caroline are fighting up at the house?"

"Probably." She reached out and rubbed his hair.

"Will they fight all evening?"

"They'll fight until Caroline wins," Lilly answered wearily.

"You mean her mammaw will come live with us?"

"I think so, T.J."

He dug up a rock and brushed the mud from its underside, still thinking. "Do you think Caroline will mind if I come here by myself? It's so nice."

"Oh, T.J., let's keep it our secret."

His eyes sparkled suddenly in a way they seldom did. "Then do *you* care if I come here?"

"No-o. But don't do it often, or the others will wonder where you are."

He nestled close to her and propped his elbows on her lap. "This is such a nice secret to have," he said dreamily, and Lilly was not sorry she had brought him.

"Want to hear a story?" she asked after another spell of silence.

" 'Course."

Lilly became suddenly the story-giver, and she wondered if this was how Mrs. Riley had felt when she read stories aloud in the library or sitting room. T.J. stayed as still as she used to, his eyes half-shut, his usually restless fingers still, while she told the beginning of the story she had read that afternoon, before being interrupted by Mr. Riley.

She stopped at the exact place where she had looked up and seen him, and T.J. asked breathlessly, "What's the rest of the story?"

"I don't know. I only read that far."

"Will you read some more when you go back again?"

"Yes, T.J., I will." She knew suddenly that she would defy Mr. Riley's ire, carefully of course, in order to satisfy T.J.'s hunger and her own. She reasoned that before Mrs. Riley died, the books had belonged more to her than to him; and she would have given Lilly free access to the library.

When she and T.J. at last walked back up to the house through a late summer's dusk scented with clover and dying corn and ripening apples, all was silent. Maybelle was already in bed, the quilt on the floor.

"Did they talk any more after I left?" Lilly whispered after she had climbed in beside her.

"What do you think?" Maybelle asked crossly. "Caroline don't give up that easy."

"Is her mammaw coming?"

"I don't know if Pa quite gave in yet, but he will. She worked on him pretty hard. When I couldn't stand it anymore, I went to the cornfield. Where were you?"

"Out of hearing," Lilly answered tersely.

Chapter eighteen

Only two evenings later, she found Pa outside when she came home from Mrs. Price's, nailing together a rough box shape. It looked chillingly like the coffins he had built last winter, but Lilly knew at once what was going on. He was muttering to himself and did not look at her. She sat down on the grass close to him and drew a long sigh. "When is she coming?" she asked quietly.

"End of this week."

"Where will the bed go?"

"In the corner where Caroline wanted it."

"Who is she? Have I ever seen her?"

"Probably not. She's so old that she and everyone else has forgotten which year she was born in. All anyone knows is that she had great-grandchildren already in the war between the states. She's most blind, but Caroline says she's a sweet old lady."

Lilly watched him hammering for a few more minutes. When he had the basic box finished, he bored holes in the sides so that rope could be strung through to support the ticking. Lilly got up and walked away from him. The graves drew her tonight. All three of them had settled slightly, leaving hollows where sparse grass grew. Vince's stone had slipped backwards a bit, and she straightened it, propping it with a stone. Although the air was cooling, the stone slabs still held the heat of a warm day. She sat down by Ma's and leaned against it.

T.J. came upon her there. "Do you know more of the story yet?" he asked, standing in front of her and looking at her entreatingly.

"No, T.J., I haven't been back at Mr. Riley's since then."

"Are you going tomorrow?"

"Yes."

"Will you have time to read?"

"I'll try to."

And she did, in spite of the uneasiness in her heart. She took more pre-cautions this time, carrying the book into the sitting room, facing the door while she read, and keeping a rag nearby so that she could hop up and begin dusting if Mr. Riley came home again.

But he stayed away; so she read for a full half hour and repeated the story that night to an enthralled T.J.

On Friday evening Caroline's mammaw came.

Lilly's first impression of her was that she looked more like a sack of shriveled-up apples than anything human. Caroline's uncle, an old man him-self, delivered her to their doorstep. Then Caroline took her arm and guided her into the house. The old woman reached out the other hand and groped in front of her for the walls and the furniture.

"We'll walk around the cabin so that you know where everything is," Caroline said cheerily. "We're in the eating room. You'll be sleeping here too. The table is in the middle, and the fireplace here on the left. This is your bed." With each object she pointed out, Caroline laid Mammaw's hand on it to show her where it was. They went on into the front room while the younger children peered in the door, watching. Then Caroline called, "Come here, children. Let me introduce you."

She pulled forward Maybelle, then Bobby, T.J., and Sonny. Mammaw felt their faces and hair gently, noting how tall they were. "Is this all?"

"One more yet. Here's Lilly."

Standing in front of her, Lilly had a good look at Mammaw for the first time. She was bent over like old Rob, but she lifted her face as far as she could. It was seamed all over with wrinkles, some of them fine and webby, some deeply furrowed. Her hair was snow white and so thin that her brown skin showed through on her scalp. Her eyes peeped sightlessly and yet brightly from behind heavy lids. The only thing that seemed young about her was her mouth. It was wrinkled too, but the lips were surprisingly pink and full, and they smiled easily.

"Lilly," she repeated in a cracked, whispery voice that softened some of the sounds through toothless gums. "Is she the oldest?"

"Yes. She's fifteen."

Mammaw held out hands made mostly of knotted joints and parchment skin. She had to reach up to find Lilly's face, and when she touched it, her fingers, though hard with calluses, were gentle as a mother holding a newborn. "Lilly. What a pretty name."

Lilly had been fiercely resenting this intrusion of Caroline's relative. But now, face to face with the fragile woman, she couldn't help softening.

Caroline tucked her into bed and sent the children to the loft. As Maybelle pulled her dress over her head, she asked, "What do you think of her, Lilly?"

"I think she'll be okay," Lilly said cautiously, not willing to commit herself too far.

"Wonder how Caroline will manage to take care of her and all the boys after we both get married."

"What are you talking about?" Lilly snapped. "She'll die long before either of us get married."

"She doesn't look quite ready to die yet."

"And neither of us are getting married just yet."

"No. . . not yet." Maybelle's voice dropped to a conspiratorial whisper. "I heard Caroline telling Pa the other day that she thought it would be good if you got married soon."

Lilly gazed at Maybelle in hurt disbelief. Ma had often embarrassed her by making such comments, but when they came from her step-ma, they were something else entirely. "But, Maybelle, who is she to talk? She had to be nigh on thirty when Pa married her."

Maybelle giggled. "We still don't know exactly how old she is."

"This is not funny. Who did she think I should get married to?"

"Oh, she didn't say that."

"What did Pa say?"

"He told her to quit planning your life."

"Good for him."

They suddenly heard Caroline's voice close to the foot of the stairs. "Girls, I've got Sonny ready for bed. You want I should bring him up?"

The girls gave each other frightened glances. "I'll come get him," Maybelle said quickly.

They tucked him into bed and lay down on either side of him. He was almost two now and was far too good at repeating things he heard. They waited until he had fallen asleep to continue talking. By then, complete darkness had submerged the loft. Maybelle and Lilly both propped themselves up on their elbows, unable to even see each other.

"Maybelle, does she think you should get married too?"

"No. At least—she didn't say so. But don't you suppose she feels like the boys would belong more to her if we were out of the way?"

Remembering the way T.J. preferred her to Caroline, Lilly knew what Maybelle meant. "But they aren't hers," she said.

"Hush, Lilly. Not so loud. She'll hear you."

Lilly could faintly feel Maybelle's breath against her cheek, and her next words came clearly through the black. "They are hers in a way. They came along with Pa when she married him."

"When did you get so wise?"

"Listen, Lilly, you've been off in town, and I've been left at home to watch Caroline and think about all this. You and me are old enough that we'll never really get used to having Caroline in the house. But the boys will."

Lilly had known this for herself, but she had supposed that Maybelle, along with the boys, would adjust, given enough time. Now she realized suddenly that this long-legged girl lying across from her had looked the situation over philosophically, and would probably take her first way of escape from it—the first boy who asked her to marry him. With her thirteenth birthday nearing, this could easily happen in the next year or two. No doubt she expected Lilly to come to the same conclusion and make the same decision. Lilly didn't want to open up a discussion of that just now. Instead she said, stating an obvious fact, "You're not going to school this year."

Maybelle giggled lightly. "School started two months ago. Have you just now noticed?"

"Did you and Pa talk about it?"

"No. I decided it on my own."

"I thought maybe you would want to get out of the house when you have a chance."

"Yes. . . But I think I've had enough schooling. I'll be old enough to marry soon. And it's good now that I didn't go. I think there'll be a baby by spring, and Caroline needs me here, whether she knows it or not."

"A baby?" Lilly asked, shocked.

"Of course. I thought you'd have noticed that she's more tired these days."

"I'm gone almost all the time," Lilly said slowly.

"Well, start watching her and see if I'm right."

This was too much. Lilly lay back down on her pillow, gingerly, as if she had been hurt. She was sweaty with the still heat in the loft, but she held herself motionless.

"One more thing, Lilly."

"What?"

"You'd better not take T.J. down to the bridge too often."

Lilly bit her lip, crossly now. "How did you know?"

"I've known forever that you liked to sit under there. I just guessed that you took T.J. there the other evening."

"And why shouldn't we go there?"

"Caroline will worry about T.J. drowning."

She won't worry if she doesn't know anything about it."

Maybelle sighed and lay down too. Out of nowhere, a phrase from Scripture that Brother Holbrook had often quoted, crept into Lilly's thoughts. "There is nothing hidden that shall not be revealed." She didn't think Maybelle knew everything she had done under the bridge, but suddenly she didn't really care if she did know. Although Maybelle would never understand her fascination with books, pencils, and paper, she was growing up, taking on the airs of a woman, and putting away the nuisances of childhood. Before long the two of them might well be good friends.

When Lilly came into the eating room the next morning, Mammaw was still in bed. Pa had already gone off to work an hour ago, and the younger children would come down later. Caroline had fried mush in a pan on the stove; Lilly helped herself to a slice and poured sorghum over it. She tried to move quietly as she sat down at the table to eat, not sure if Mammaw was still asleep.

"That you, Lilly?" Mammaw asked suddenly.

"Yes, ma'am."

"Come over here a minute, child."

Lilly washed down her mush with a quick swallow of buttermilk and crossed the room. She bent down to lay her hand over the old woman's hand.

"Now listen a bit, Lilly. I don't want you to call me ma'am. All my grandchildren and great-grandchildren and all them other generations, they all call me mammaw. Will that work?"

Lilly nodded, and then remembered that Mammaw couldn't see her. "I would like to call you that," she said sincerely.

"Good. Are you going to be here at home all day?"

"No. I work in town."

"That's too bad. I wanted to get to know you better. I think that we are going to be very good friends." She reached up and touched Lilly's hair. "Tell me what color your hair is. It feels so nice and soft."

"It's brown."

"What kind of brown?"

"I don't know. Just a medium brown, I guess."

"And what about your eyes?"

"They're brown too."

"Medium brown like your hair?"

"Kind of a light brown. Ma called them the color of honey."

"Honey brown eyes. That's pretty. You must be a pretty girl, Lilly."

Lilly didn't know what to say to that, and just then, Caroline stuck her head into the room from the kitchen. "You're still here, Lilly?"

"I'm leaving soon."

"Check for mail on your way home."

"I will." She waited until Caroline's head had disappeared again, then said, "Good-bye, Mammaw. I'll see you this evening."

"Good-bye, Lilly girl."

The memory of Mammaw's warmth lingered with her all day, in spite of Mrs. Price's ordinary grumbles, and in spite of one or two piercing remarks about Talmadge. Mrs. Price thought it her right to know all that went on in other people's personal lives, but she had never figured out Talmadge. She baited Lilly, and teased and conjectured, making her life miserable. And no matter how many times Lilly ignored her, changed the subject, or walked out of the room, she never seemed to weary of the game.

"Has Charlotte heard anything from Talmadge?" she asked this time.

"I don't know."

"You come past the store every day. Seems like she might tell you."

It was doubly hard to stay calm if Mrs. Price brought Charlotte into the conversation. While Lilly's pain over Talmadge had eased somewhat, her hatred of Charlotte still ran deep, dark, and heavy. If anything, it had grown in intensity since the day they had stared at each other over the counter, city-bred perceptions pitted against mountain-bred will.

Lilly remembered to stop at the post office for mail that evening. "Letter for Caroline," the post master said gravely, but his eyes were sparkling with fun, "and a package for you." He drew it slowly off the shelf behind him, delighting in Lilly's moment of suspense. "Maybe Talmadge hasn't forgotten you after all."

Talmadge, she reckoned, had gone further toward forgetting her than her acquaintances had gone toward forgetting him.

The post master winked as he handed it over.

She saw immediately that the handwriting wasn't Talmadge's. She didn't recognize it. "Thank you," she said calmly. When the thought occurred to her that he might start a story spreading, she added, "It's not from Talmadge."

As she walked back out into the sunshine, she held the package between both hands, pressing it with her thumbs. It was hard inside the paper wrapping, like a book. In spite of her words, she felt trembly. Perhaps Talmadge had gotten someone else to mark the address. She couldn't wait until she got to the bridge for the knowing. So when she reached the schoolhouse, she looked around furtively and approached the door with quick steps. It was jammed shut, and she had to kick it at the bottom to get it to slide over the uneven floor boards. She shut it again behind her, securely, and then tore at the wrapping on the package with eager, shaking fingers.

The paper came away to reveal a glossy, black, hard-covered book—a unique book with a lock and key. Lilly turned the key and the clasp flew open, letting her lift the front cover. Inside lay a single sheet of paper.

Dear Lilly,

    My wife found this unusually thick diary and thought of you. I don't know if you are still writing, but I hope you are. I hear through Mr. Riley that your mother died, and your father remarried. My wife and I both send our sincerest sympathies. If this change in your family makes any change in your prospects, let me know immediately. My offer from a year ago still stands. Or if there is any other way I can help, I will be glad to do so.

With kind regards,

Mr. and Mrs. Barker

She noticed next a slender pencil fitted in behind the clasp, pulled it out and turned to the first white page. It stared up at her, nothing but faint lines on its smooth surface, begging to be written on. The pencil felt slim and cool in her hand, and it made a clean, gray line when she touched it to the paper.

"October 3, 1920," she wrote slowly, thinking of how much had happened since the day she kept a sporadic diary under the bridge on discarded bits of paper. "My name is Lilly Burchett, and I live at the Forks of Upper and Lower Sand Lick. In our family there are my pa and step-ma, three brothers, and one sister."

She stopped, feeling suddenly helpless and frustrated. So much wanted to come out of her that it seemed obstructed by sheer enormity, as though she held a giant lake inside her, and it needed to pour all at once through the tip of her pencil. How could she give so many emotions shape and form on the page?

At last she decided to try again another time, shut the diary, and very carefully locked it. That lock made it doubly precious. As long as she hid the key, she could write what she wanted, and no one would be able to read it.

Beyond the schoolhouse, she crossed the bridge, then passed the store and Silas Greer's house. She saw no one at either place, and she hurried on by thankfully. Charlotte she could ignore; but Silva, grown desperate from watching her husband die by inches, would hail her and want to talk. Everyone said that Silas couldn't live through the winter, not the way he already coughed and struggled for breath. Silva knew this too, and no matter how innocent a conversation, she always managed to bring it round vindictively to the mine owners and managers who were responsible for it. Lilly heard this depressing denunciation over and over.

When she got home, she threw Caroline's letter down on the table. "What else do you have?" Maybelle asked.

"There was a package for me."

"A package?" Bobby repeated in disbelief.

"From Talmadge?" Pa drawled.

"From Mr. and Mrs. Barker."

Pa straightened perceptibly. "Them?" His single word held a wealth of contempt.

"Pa. . ."

Caroline looked puzzled, so Pa explained briefly. "They wanted to take Lilly to Louisville and let her go to high school. Train her to be a writer who would make lots of *money.*"

"What did they send for you?" Maybelle demanded.

"A diary," Lilly answered, thinking that this sounded safe. She held it out for everyone to see, and Pa looked a bit less disturbed.

But he asked, "Did he beg you to come to school?"

"No."

"Did he say anything a'tall about it?"

"He said his offer still stands."

"Are you going to write back?"

"I don't know. I need paper and a stamp."

"If you write back," Pa suggested, "tell him that your pa still stands too."

"Let's have supper," Caroline said quickly.

Mammaw had not joined in the discussion, but after supper, while Caroline bathed the little ones in the kitchen, and Pa sat out on the porch, humming an old song to himself, Lilly found her in the front room. She was in Ma's rocker, swaying gently back and forth. Lilly always felt resentment when Caroline sat down in it to rock Sonny, but strangely she felt no resentment now. "Lilly? Is it you?"

"Yes, Mammaw."

"Can I see your diary?" She held out her hand to feel it.

For answer Lilly laid the precious book in her lap.

Mammaw's gnarled fingers traced over the edges of it and curled around the lock. "Do you have a key for it?"

"Yes, I do."

"Have you written in it yet?"

"I tried, but I couldn't think where to start," Lilly confided.

"I used to keep a diary of sorts," Mammaw said dreamily. "It wasn't much, just a bit of a history of my days. Of course, I can't do it since I went blind."

"What happened to your diary? Do you still have it?"

"It washed away in the flood."

Lilly laughed in surprise. "All the writing I've ever done washed away in the flood too."

"Tell me about it, dear." When Lilly hesitated, she added, "We're alone here, aren't we?"

"Yes, Mammaw."

"I think I hear a story, and I do love to listen to good stories. Love to tell them too." She settled her thin shoulders against the curved back of the rocker and smiled up at Lilly.

This was not a tale that Lilly felt like telling at any time, and certainly not to someone she had known for only a day. But with Mammaw waiting, her hands still folded over the diary, how could she refuse? And she found that Mammaw made a sympathetic listener. Lilly tried, awkwardly, to make her feel just how much the stories had meant, and how the loss of them had hurt.

When she finished, Mammaw said, "So it's a story with a sad ending. Some are like that in life. Now tell me about this Mr. Barker who gave you the diary."

"Can I save that for another evening?" She heard childish squeals from the kitchen and thought that Caroline might join them soon.

"All right then," Mammaw agreed, and laughed a low delightful chuckle. "I think I'll ask for you to sit with me every evening." She handed the diary back to Lilly and struggled to get out of the chair. "Then if the stories are done, do you mind helping me to bed?"

Lilly could have lifted her with ease and carried her into the next room, but she took her arm and helped her walk across the floor. She lifted Mammaw's legs onto the corn shuck mattress and pulled a quilt over her.

Mammaw sank down, sighing with happiness. "Now that does feel good.

I believe I'm set for the night. Don't you think you should write some more in your diary now?"

"You mean, here?" Lilly had pictured doing her writing in the loft by moonlight, or under the bridge, not downstairs in the cabin. Her writings had always been very personal, something she felt sure others would laugh at.

"Why not?" Mammaw retorted. "I can't read what you write, that's sure."

To Lilly's amazement, when she opened the diary this time and took the pencil in her hand, the words came pouring out coherently. "It's been a long time since I had a diary. My first and only one was while I was still in school. I saved pieces of paper that weren't full and used them. No one knew where I had it, or even that I had it at all. So I couldn't write every day. I wish I could read over all the things I wrote, but I can't. They're gone forever. I'm going to write down exactly how it happened."

Her pencil raced now, finding the right words to describe the haven under the bridge, the ferns that grew along the banks, the rush of white-capped water across the stream bed. She recalled the slimy algae that grew on the old bridge, the smell of slowly rotting wood, and the thrill of reaching into her crevice for her treasures.

Caroline led the boys through on their way to bed, but she only asked, "Do you need anything, Mammaw?"

"No. Lilly's taking care of me."

After a time, Mammaw lifted her head slightly. "Are you still writing, Lilly?"

"Yes, I am. Do you need something?"

"I'm quite all right. I'm praying while I lie here in the quiet, and it just makes me feel easy to know you're nearby too."

Lilly looked at her thoughtfully. She had said, "I'm praying," in a very ordinary tone as if she had said, "I'm thinking about the story you told me." To know that the woman beside her was praying gave her an odd feeling.

She had not finished everything she wanted to write when she heard Pa coming inside. "The children all abed?" he asked.

"Lilly's down yet. She's with Mammaw."

"Time she gets to bed too."

"I'm on my way, Pa," Lilly said. *I'll finish another time*, she promised herself as she shut the book and locked it.

Chapter nineteen

Caroline tried not to leave Mammaw alone for long stretches of time, and after that first evening, Lilly often got the job of sitting with her when she came home from work. Sometimes the others were around them too, and sometimes they all scattered to do outside chores in the bright fall evenings. Then the cabin was quieter than Lilly had ever known it to be. She and Mammaw would talk for a while, sometimes telling each other stories about themselves. Lilly had found it easy to tell Mammaw about the bridge, but a little harder to tell her about Mr. Barker, and harder still to give her details about the winter of sickness. About Talmadge she said nothing at all. After they had talked, Mammaw often said cheerfully, "Well now, don't you suppose you should write in your diary?"

And Lilly would get her diary from under her clothing in the loft, her key from her pocket, and sit down with a feeling of excitement. As the weeks passed, she wrote much more than just what had happened to her each day. She tried to record her emotions, and often she would slip into the past to relive the things that had happened there.

Silas Greer breathed his last at the end of that month, and was buried with his kin. His was the first funeral Lilly attended after the memorial service the spring before, and it made death seem sinister and close again. One evening not long later, when the approaching winter oppressed her with a feeling of doom, Lilly wrote this:

"Pa is already in bed sleeping. Caroline and the children are out husking corn, and I'm alone with Mammaw. I like it best this way, when it's just us two, of an evening. Caroline is showing the baby more every week. A baby that will belong to her and Pa. Sometimes I can hardly stand the thought. It will be only a half-brother or half-sister to the rest of us. Of course, this happens all the time to people here in the mountains. Why do so many women need to die? Men too? Just last night I heard of a mine accident in Letcher County. Three men were killed. I wonder if they had families."

She got up restlessly and walked over to the window, glad that from this side of the house she couldn't see the three graves with their straggly growth of grass and their rock slab markers.

She propped her diary on the window ledge and went on. "In a few more months, it will be a year since Ma died. Only a year, and already Pa is married again, and his wife is bearing him another child. But a year is really a long, long time, if you think much about it. I am so tired of the mountains. They are nothing but cruel. If they don't kill us women outright, they cripple us, or make us old and ugly by the time we're thirty."

She put her pencil to her lips and relived a scene from the day before. She had been rolling out biscuits for supper at the boarding house when she heard Mr. Riley's car. Curious, she stopped for a moment to watch it go by, since he didn't usually drive out that way in the afternoons. He had two visitors with him in the car, a man and a woman. The woman, pushing her long wavy blond hair back from her face, looked up and saw Lilly through the kitchen window. She flashed a warm smile. They were gone quickly, but not before Lilly saw her white lace sweater, her kid gloves, and a fur coat draped across the seat.

"Who are Mr. Riley's visitors?" she asked Mrs. Price.

"Some gent and his wife from Virginia-way," Mrs. Price answered carelessly. "Cousins of Mr. Riley, I think."

"Are they staying around long? He should have told me they were coming so I could fix food."

"Who knows what they'll do? I sure don't. Their children are all grown up and married and have children of their own. These folks just travel around for the pleasure of it. I suppose they'll stay until they get tired of it here and shove on to the next place."

"But," Lilly said in wonder, "the lady looks so young. How can she have grandchildren?"

"City folks stay young longer," Mrs. Price answered sharply, "and that's a fact. They don't have to work half as hard as we do." She looked around her kitchen, half in frustration, half in pleasure. "You wouldn't catch any of them cooking for twelve men, that's sure. And doing their washing and mending and cleaning besides."

Lilly returned from her memory and read over what she had just written. Then she added to it slowly. "If we lived someplace besides Sand Lick, if we lived in the city, I wonder if we would still be a complete family." She knew very well that people had died in cities too, from the soldier's sickness; but the idea clung to her that maybe away from the mountains, somewhere where there was better food and nicer houses, they would have been stronger to fight it off. She had never written much about the terrible weeks when Mrs. Riley and a third of her own family died. And she couldn't just yet. She slapped the book shut and snapped the key into the lock decisively.

On the bed, Mammaw stirred. "Done already?"

"Yes, I guess so," she said with forced lightness. "For tonight."

"Then come sit close to me. I'd like to have you near."

Lilly sat down and folded herself in half, her knees up to her chin. She felt like a captive, somehow. She wanted to go out, to go far away, maybe along Upper Sand Lick, splashing unmindful through the cold water; or maybe to the ridge where she could lift her eyes to the far hills and try to pierce what lay beyond. She forced herself to sit still.

After some long minutes, Mammaw said, "What did you write about?"

"Mostly about what happened today."

"No stories?" She chuckled. By this time it was a joke between them to call Lilly's recollections stories. But it wasn't wholly a joke, for Lilly tried to make them sound like stories, weaving in details, and making up conversations that she couldn't remember.

This time she answered soberly, "No."

"Tomorrow maybe?"

"Maybe."

Mammaw let silence fall heavy again. Finally she asked, "Did you have a hard one to write, Lilly girl?"

"Yes, Mammaw," Lilly answered quietly.

"Which one?"

"The one about Ma dying. And Vince and Patty. And Mrs. Riley." She had told Mammaw the story, but she had told it on an evening that flaunted fall colors and the scent of corn and apples. She had managed to tell it without too much emotion. Tonight, though, she could not keep the raw anguish out of her voice.

"That is a hard story," Mammaw agreed gently.

Lilly would have left it at that and said no more, but the silence seemed as thick and burdening as the gathering darkness outside. Lilly tried to break it several times, got as far as opening her mouth, and then stopped. When at last she managed words, they were low and tight, filling the room with tension. "It's not fair, Mammaw."

"No, Lilly girl, it's not fair." Mammaw's voice was even lower and more whispery than usual.

"Life is cruel."

"Often it is."

Mammaw was just agreeing to everything she said. Subconsciously Lilly decided to shock her, and she let her next comment fly with pent-up passion. "I hate life."

Mammaw lifted herself up on one elbow and turned her sightless eyes toward Lilly. "Oh, no, you don't," she contradicted gently.

"Well, I. . ." Lilly felt at the moment as if she did hate life, but she was fair enough to remember that she didn't hate it on evenings when her pencil raced across the pages of her diary, or the afternoons when she slipped below the bridge, or the nights when T.J. snuggled up against her at bedtime. "I hate what life is like in the mountains," she amended.

"No, you don't," Mammaw contradicted again.

Something in her voice made Lilly think of summer sunrises, of sturdy pines, of rushing creeks, of violets and goldenrod and iron weed, of apples blushing redly through green leaves, of so many beautiful things in the mountains. "I know it's pretty here," she said defensively. "But life is hard. People die. We work ourselves to death, mostly." She stopped, realizing how loudly and harshly she had talked.

Mammaw said nothing, but something fitted together at last in her wise mind. This was what she had been guessing at ever since she came. This was what lay hidden in the quiet, competent girl that everyone else saw. This was the real Lilly, with her masks off and her pain naked for the first time. Her heart reached out in yearning to the young girl beside her, and she thought perhaps that she was beginning to understand why God had brought her here.

Lilly had no idea of what Mammaw was thinking, and she grew uncomfortable with the silence. "I'm sorry," she ventured. "I shouldn't have talked that way. I—"

"Stop," Mammaw said decisively, her voice no longer whispery. "Are Caroline and the children coming yet?"

Lilly went to the window. She could still see lantern light by the corn crib, and shadowy silhouettes in the dusky dark. "I think they'll stay out awhile longer."

"Good. I have some things to tell you. Will you listen to me, Lilly girl?"

"Yes," she said meekly.

"Then sit down here close to me again."

Lilly sat down, but it took Mammaw awhile to get started. At last she said, "You just told me that life is cruel and unfair. You're right. Life is cruel and unfair."

She didn't say this lightly, and Lilly knew why. She had buried two husbands and outlived most of her own children. More recently she had gone blind.

"So we think the same about that," she went on. "But now I have a question for you. Think about it before you answer. How do you feel about life being cruel and unfair?"

Lilly was on the point of saying, "Very angry," when she remembered Mammaw's instructions to think it over. She tried to analyze her own feelings and realized that she had done little of this sort of probing before. Her feelings were like a well inside her, deeper than she was willing to reach into, and she drew back from the edge.

"Well?" Mammaw prompted after several moments.

"I don't know. I think I'm just angry."

"Is it good to be angry? Does it feel good?"

"I don't know. Sometimes. . . but not. . . not really, I guess."

"Do you know what being angry for a long time does to a person?"

"No."

"I know someone who's been angry for most of her life," Mammaw said sadly.

"Is it someone I know too?"

"Yes, you do. Her name is Silva Greer."

"Silva Greer," Lilly repeated slowly.

"Did you know," Mammaw went on, "that before she was married to Silas, she was married to a man named Frederick? He died after they were married only a year. Part of the mine collapsed, and he was trapped. He died before they could get him out. Not long after that, Silva had a baby boy. He was deformed, and he didn't live long. They lived on the far side of the ridge then."

"I didn't know that." It was a terrible story, but then, not so much more terrible than many mountain women's stories. Lilly remembered Silva as she had looked at Silas's funeral, dry-eyed, her face immobile.

"Those two things made Silva angry, and she has kept that anger with her all her life. Now she's angry because Silas died, and she thinks the mine owners should have kept him from dying. Everyone knows it. Nobody really likes Silva."

Even beyond Sand Lick, Lilly knew, Silva's reputation for sarcasm and self-pity and retribution were legendary.

"I knew Silva when she was young," Mammaw said. "I remember her being born. When she was a girl, she wasn't like she is now. She was happy, and she sang a lot. Everyone loved her. But the Silva that you know is angry about everything. See what it's done to her? She let her anger turn into bitterness, and her bitterness ate up all the good that was in her soul. When I think of Silva, I think of a good apple that got worms in it."

Lilly shivered. What was Mammaw trying to say to her? "But I can't help being—" she began.

"Now, Lilly, we're not going to talk about this any more tonight. There's only One who can take that anger out of your heart. That's God. I want you to go away by yourself sometime and get down on your knees and cry out to God to take the anger away."

"Will He?" Lilly asked, doubtfully.

"Try it, Lilly girl, and see what happens. Then come and tell me about it. I'm going to pray for God to keep after you until you do it."

She wouldn't let Lilly discuss it anymore, and Lilly really had no wish to. She went quietly upstairs and put the diary away and stood at the window for a long time, watching the shifting shapes of shadows outside, her thoughts running in more directions than she could well keep track of.

Mammaw said no more about it the next day, or the one following. But her words, few as they had been, haunted Lilly. They seemed to walk beside her on her way into town, to stay at her elbow as she worked, to get into bed with her, and sneak into her dreams. They shouted most loudly and clearly when Lilly passed Silva's house. Mammaw hadn't said it exactly, but Lilly knew she had meant it all the same. "You'll be like Silva when you get old if you don't quit being angry now."

Mammaw had given her a simple remedy, so simple that Lilly was afraid to try it, afraid that it wouldn't work. But at last, one gray day when a fretful wind blew, she slipped below the bridge on her way home from the boarding house.

"Get down on your knees," Mammaw had said. Lilly had never knelt in her hide-out before, but now she lifted the skirt of her navy dress and knelt down on the bank. Her soul had reached out to God here, even when she hardly knew what she was doing. But she had never prayed quite like this. She thought over Mammaw's instructions again. "Cry out to God." She didn't know how to do this crying out, what words to say, how to be sure she did it right. But she whispered, "Father in heaven, take the anger out of my heart. I don't want to be like Silva."

And she waited.

The wind picked up, and left over sodden leaves came swirling down the current. The clouds broke and unleashed a torrent of rain on the bridge above her. She moved a little to one side to avoid being thoroughly drenched. She didn't quite know what she had hoped for, but certainly something more than rain on the bridge. She imagined herself going back to Mammaw and saying, "I did everything just like you said, and nothing happened."

Then she was aware of a creeping feeling of quiet. It came so slowly that it was all around her before she even knew it was coming. It was not only around her; it was inside her, filling her up, gently, like water in a cup, filling in every hole, even the ones Lilly didn't know existed. She sat back on her heels and let it come.

She sat for a long, long time without moving. The rain stopped. Sun touched the ripples on the creek and trickled through the cracks in the bridge. Someone passed on a horse, then two more on foot.

She let herself think of Mrs. Riley, of Ma and Vince and Patty, of Pa with Caroline, of Talmadge. . . and the quiet feeling persisted. She wondered how long it had been since she had felt so still, so like the creek when it ran full and deep and slow.

When she stood up at last, she had to rub her sleeping legs and let them tingle back to life. Moving with a grace born of what had happened inside her, she climbed up the creek bank and onto the road. Trees and grass glistened from the recent shower. Lilly suddenly loved the trail ahead of her, loved the cabin waiting for her, loved the mountains themselves. She was amazed to find that she felt no fierce desire to leave. Nothing but quiet.

When she opened the cabin door softly and went in, she saw only Mammaw sitting in the rocking chair and rocking demurely. "Where's everyone else?" she asked.

"They went to your Uncle Sandy's for a sorghum stir-off."

Lilly had completely forgotten this, but just now it didn't matter. "They left you alone?" she asked.

"I told them I would be all right. I was sure you would come home soon, and then if you wanted to, you could stay with me. But I don't mind if you run up there with all of them."

"I think I'd rather just stay home tonight. Is there any supper left?" She answered her own question by going into the kitchen and finding some limp fried potatoes and a hearty chunk of cornbread. While she ate at the table, she could hear Mammaw in the front room, humming to herself, her old voice skipping the high notes and faltering on some of the others. Still, it was a beautiful sound.

When she finished her supper, Lilly washed off her plate and then went into the front room again. "Are you ready to be tucked into bed?"

"Not just yet. I'd like to stay in my rocker a little longer."

"Mammaw?"

"What is it, Lilly girl?"

"I did what you told me to do."

Mammaw smiled. "I knew that as soon as you set foot in the cabin," she said simply.

"How?"

"Your voice is different. I sure do wish I could see your face right about now."

Lilly sat down on the floor beside the rocker and put one hand hesitantly up into Mammaw's lap. Mammaw covered it with both of her gnarled ones. "How does it feel?"

"I feel so. . . like I just want to be quiet all the time and never get excited again."

Mammaw patted her hand. "That sounds like peace, to my way of thinking."

"I didn't know it would feel like this."

Mammaw chuckled. "You didn't think God would take away the anger and not give you something in its place, did you?"

"Will I never feel angry again about Ma and the others dying?"

"You've taken the first step, Lilly. The first step is the most important, and sometimes the hardest. But sure, the anger and the bitterness will come back sometimes. Then you just need to pray again."

"It seems so simple," Lilly marveled.

"Sure, and it is simple. But most folks don't want to give up like that. They want to hang onto their bitterness. You have to let it go before God will take it away. He never grabs it from you."

Lilly wondered how many times Mammaw had given up her anger and bitterness in the course of her long life. Probably more times than Lilly would ever know. What if she hadn't done so? What if she had let the anger fester until it ate up the goodness in her heart?

Chapter twenty

During the next weeks, Lilly took to stopping beneath the bridge more often again. Her diary stayed at home, and she spent her time there simply thinking and recapturing the peace when it slipped away from her. She always told Mammaw when she returned if she had been there or not. One day Mammaw casually referred to her times there as praying.

"But I don't really pray," she protested.

"And what do you do, Lilly girl?"

"I just think. . . and. . . sometimes I ask God to take the anger away again, and sometimes I thank Him for things that seem beautiful or special."

"And you don't call that praying?"

"Well, no, I didn't think it really was."

"What do you think praying is then?"

Here Lilly was stuck. "I know that people do it in church. And you say you do it while you're lying in bed, but I. . ."

Mammaw laughed in satisfaction. "If you're thinking about God and asking things of Him, you're praying. It sure don't have to be done just in church. Anyone who really knows God prays all the time."

That last comment of Mammaw's bothered Lilly. But a whole week passed before she asked, "Mammaw, do you think many people really know God?"

Mammaw was already in bed; a light rain was falling outside, and Caroline sat on the porch with the younger children. Maybelle had washed her hair and stood in the doorway brushing it out. Lilly spoke low.

"Well, Lilly, what a question! What makes you ask?"

Lilly reminded her of her words about prayer, and Mammaw's face saddened. "I've lived a long time, Lilly girl. Over a hundred years."

Lilly smoothed the quilt over her thin legs and stood looking down at her. "But I've only knowed God in the way I told you for the last little while. When I was as young as you, I didn't understand it either. I was baptized, and I prayed in church, and I believed in God, and I tried to live right, but I don't think I really knowed God. He didn't seem up-close and like my friend in those days."

Lilly thought of her own baptism, her questions, her blank sense of not knowing quite why she was doing this. She knew what Mammaw meant, but she still waited.

"I think a lot of people don't know God like He wants them to," Mammaw went on. "But that don't mean they can't eventually learn it. God keeps working at every one of us. He's just brought you to know Him sooner than most people do. Thank Him for it, Lilly girl."

"Mammaw, do you like poems?"

"I can't say if I've ever heard one."

"I know one about God."

"Tell me."

Lilly had read this poem again several weeks ago, and it had taken on a sudden sweet clarity. Since then, she had memorized it, and now she quoted it in a whisper.

> "*I never saw a moor;*
> *I never saw the sea;*
> *Yet know I how the heather looks,*
> *And what a wave must be.*
>
> *I never spoke with God,*
> *Nor visited in heaven;*
> *Yet certain am I of the spot*
> *As if the chart were given.*"

"Well, that's nice," Mammaw said when she finished. "That's just the feeling I get when it seems like God is close by."

That year, fall gave way slowly to real winter. Besides rain storms, and frosts that quickly melted, the nice weather hung on well into December. The children went to school barefoot, and Lilly did the same when she went to the boarding house or Mr. Riley's house. At the boarding house, her days were still full, but at Mr. Riley's house, she took time to read books from his library. She had finished the first book, repeating the story in pieces to T.J., and had thought for a while she would stop with one, obeying Mr. Riley's order. Then the longing became too strong again, and she yielded. But she did all her reading in the sitting room, and kept some mending close at hand, in case Mr. Riley appeared. She justified herself by thinking that she never did more reading than Mrs. Riley had allowed her.

One cold morning Lilly burst in at the boarding house, barefoot as usual, but thinking that maybe the time had come to start wearing her shoes. She picked up one foot at a time and rubbed it in her slightly warmer hands. Mrs. Price never looked at her, but kept on rattling the breakfast pots and pans in an alarming way.

"Good morning," Lilly ventured.

"Good morning." Mrs. Price grunted. "I've got another boarder."

"But you're full already."

"Don't I know that? I was in bed last night when he came, and I do hate to be gotten out of bed. I'm sure I don't know why people can't come in at normal times."

"How did he get here?"

"Walked, I suppose." Mrs. Price shrugged one plump shoulder.

"What did you do with him?"

"He apologized for coming in late, and he seemed enough like a gentleman that I let him sleep here in the kitchen. He cleared out of my way so I could make breakfast. But mercy, how that man can eat. It'll be like cooking for two more men. I wish I would have sent him to lay hisself down somewhere else."

"Is he here for a job?"

"Why, yes, I reckon so. He went to the mine this morning."

"Who is he?"

Now Mrs. Price looked over and caught Lilly's eye slyly. "Reckon you might want to know."

For one wild moment, Lilly thought she meant Talmadge had come back to town.

"He's from the bluegrass," Mrs. Price went on, "close to Lexington, I think."

No!

"He looks like an educated man. Might be your sort. His name is Everette Sherman."

Lilly could breathe again. "You won't catch me taking a fancy to a man from outside the mountains," she said haughtily.

Mrs. Price laughed. "Once is enough?"

Lilly refused to let the conversation go there, so she asked, "Is Everette Sherman young?" Immediately she realized her mistake.

"About Talmadge's age, I'd say. Maybe a little younger." Mrs. Price eyed her, meditatively, as though she were a piece of goods to be disposed of on the marriage market. "Yes, this one might just suit you."

Lilly could see long days of future heckling from Mrs. Price unless she took quick and decisive action now. "I've learned," she said with dignity, "that men from off aren't to be trusted. You're wasting your time trying to pair us up, Mrs. Price."

Mrs. Price humphed. "Our own boys is best," she agreed, but Lilly wasn't completely convinced that she had given up this new idea.

However, she let it lie for the time being, maybe realizing that she had pushed her maid as far as she could be pushed. They fixed up a second cot for him in Mr. Rigsby's bedroom that day and prepared extra food for supper.

When Lilly came home, her family was almost ready to sit down for supper. She went over to stand by the fire to warm her chilled hands and feet, and to let her heart slow after running.

"You'd better wear your shoes tomorrow," Caroline said.

"I think I will. It feels like winter's finally come."

Maybelle sat on the far side of the table, her chin on her hands, blinking slowly at her. "Did you hear the news?"

"What news?"

"Pa said there was a new miner on the crew today."

"I heard. He's staying at the boarding house."

"They say he's from close around Lexington. Maybe this time it will work out for you."

Lilly's anger flared and she spat, "I've endured this kind of talk all day from Mrs. Price. Don't tell me—"

A deep-throated chuckle from Pa interrupted her. "The beaus have been a bit scarce around here," he said.

Lilly felt sick. She looked frantically from one face to another, and found that they all thought it was a joke. Mammaw, not knowing the story, was smiling as always. Lilly suddenly didn't want supper, but she knew it would only make a bigger scene if she refused to eat.

Everyone stayed inside that evening, clustered around the fire in the front room. This had been happening more and more often as the days grew colder, and Lilly had little time to talk privately with Mammaw. Usually they still sat close to each other, and Lilly might bring down either her book of Wordsworth poetry or her book of Dickinson poetry and read to her. T.J. always crept close to her then. But this time she took her pink calico dress and a needle for mending it and sat on the far side of the room from Mammaw. She told herself that she needed the lantern light to see by, and almost persuaded herself that this was, indeed, the only reason. But she avoided looking at Mammaw and kept her mouth shut.

Maybelle tried to make up that night in bed. "Honest, Lilly," she whispered, after Sonny had gone to sleep between them. "I'm sorry. I thought you could take some teasing about it by now."

Her kindness hurt almost as much as her laughter. Tears came up and clutched at Lilly's throat.

"I won't even ask you what happened between you two, now that I know how much it vexes you. I had no idea. . . it must have been bad, Lilly."

"Yes. But it wasn't what you and everyone else thinks. We didn't fight. And there wasn't another girl in Lexington. It was something neither of us—" She stopped and changed her wording a little. "It was something that couldn't be helped."

Maybelle asked no more questions. She only sighed in the darkness, rolled over, and went to sleep. Lilly turned to face the wall. She could feel cold air seeping through it, and she pulled the quilts tightly to her. But she couldn't sleep, not even after wrapping herself into a snug cocoon.

Talmadge seemed close again tonight, unbearably close and unreachable. She wondered if he occasionally longed for her companionship like this. No, surely not, or he would never have written the letter like he did. Pa had said that beaus seemed thin around the place, and he was right— Lilly had no desire to speak to any of the boys she knew. She went over a list of them, and they all seemed flat and insipid, compared to Talmadge with his wit, poetry, and gentle understanding. No doubt she frustrated Caroline and Pa by this disinterest, but no one had ever mentioned it. Until now.

Lilly did not see Everette Sherman for nearly a week, but she heard plenty about him. Pa worked near him, and he said, "He works hard. Never seems to get tired." But he did not stoop to teasing Lilly. From Mrs. Price she learned that he felt the call to preach and would surely get asked to do so the next time Sand Lick held a church service.

"He's awful quiet," Mrs. Price continued. "I don't see how he could get the Spirit enough to preach. He hardly talks here in the house."

Lilly saw him first when she was late leaving the boarding house and met the boys coming for supper. She gave him only a brief, cursory glance, enough to know that he had straight dark brown hair, and grave, deep-set eyes. He looked sober, more like a judge than like the other laughing, joking coal mine workers.

And when the church meeting time came again on Sand Lick, and Jeb Cantrell asked him to preach, he preached in the same way, quietly and gently. Some folks said he needed more practice before he got good at it; others grumbled at the contrast between him and Jeb; still others seemed to like his thoughtfulness.

In spite of their differing viewpoints, the people on Sand Lick grew to like Everette Sherman. He had a calming effect on them, and after a week of hard work, they needed this calming. "Never heard a preacher like him before," one man might say to another, but he smiled while he said it.

"Kind of restful-like," his companion would add.

Once he even quoted poetry, just four lines of it, while preaching. Lilly hunted it up the next time she went to Mr. Riley's place, sure she had recognized it as something Mrs. Riley had read. She found it in a book of Tennyson's poetry.

> *For tho' from out our bourne of Time and Place*
> *The flood may bear me far,*
> *I hope to see my Pilot face to face*
> *When I have crost the bar.*

The words were beautiful, but they did not soften Lilly's heart toward him. Talmadge had quoted poetry as well, lots of it.

Everette preached in other churches too, on the far side of a ridge, or up another holler; and Lilly heard many of these sermons as well, since preachers and listeners alike traveled from church to church for more fellowship. As the new preacher, Everette was in high demand.

Mammaw couldn't get out to go to church herself, but she always wanted a detailed account from the ones who went, including how many people had been there, who had preached, and some of the things they had said. Lilly usually gave her these reports. Mammaw seemed interested in Everette too, and Lilly answered her questions dutifully, but said no more than necessary. She knew that she was avoiding Mammaw shamefully these days, and her heart rebuked her for it. But she felt she couldn't talk about Talmadge. She was fighting a battle to put him out of her thoughts, out of her mind. She wished she could put him out of her past, and knew that was impossible.

For a long time, Mammaw let her be. In spite of herself, the Sunday reports got more interesting, because Everette Sherman had started to preach about controversial things. He said that the way people were dressing in the world was an abomination to the Lord, and that he had seen some of the same things in the church. Some people liked his plain speaking, and everyone was used to it, because Brother Holbrook had preached that way. But to hear a young man say it with quiet conviction was different than to hear Brother Holbrook bellow it across the pulpit, loud enough to hear up at the store.

Then one Sunday he hinted that he believed all war was evil. If his sermons before had made ripples, this one made waves. Lots of mountain boys and men had left their homes, crossed the ocean and fought in the Great War in such faraway places as France, Scotland, Belgium, or Germany. Some of them had never come back and others had returned scarred or crippled. One old farmer who had lost two sons stamped out of church before the sermon was over and declared loudly outside that he would never listen to someone who said his boys had done wrong.

"How can he say it?" someone else wondered afterward. "He fought in the war himself."

Lilly noticed a huddle of older, well-respected men at the edge of the church yard, talking and motioning vigorously among themselves. One of them left the group and approached Everette Sherman. "We want to talk to you," he said stiffly. "Over here."

Caroline had stayed home with Mammaw that day, and on the way home, Maybelle asked Pa what he thought. "I think he's gone too far," Pa said. "These folks have suffered a lot because of this here war, and if he tells them now that they shouldn't have been in it a'tall, it's like kicking a man when he's already down. But Everette's all right himself. He's just made a mistake."

Maybelle helped Lilly eagerly with her Sunday report to Mammaw, who listened without comment to the end. "Well," she said; and then again, "Well."

"Mammaw," Maybelle asked, "do you think he's right?"

"I don't know that I ever gave it much thought, child. The war always seemed kind of far away, and I just figured that the government in Washington knew what they were doing."

Chapter twenty-one

When Pa decided to go for a visiting walk up to Pappaw's place that evening, someone needed to stay behind with Mammaw. Several months ago, Lilly would have offered quickly, but no longer.

"I want Lilly to stay home with me," Mammaw said peremptorily.

"Okay, then," Caroline agreed. "She will."

Lilly watched them out of sight down the path. In the silence she put more wood on the fire and got a drink from the bucket by the kitchen door.

"They all gone, Lilly?" Mammaw asked when she came back into the front room.

"Yes."

"Then come over here. It's time we talk."

Lilly sat down, afraid of what was coming.

"It's been a long time since we had us a talk to ourselves, Lilly girl."

The term of endearment began to melt Lilly. Still she hedged, "It's winter now, and everyone's crowded together inside."

"And you didn't want to talk," Mammaw added calmly. "How's the peace in your heart?"

Lilly hadn't let herself take stock of this for a while. "It wears off eventually, doesn't it? I guess I just got used to it."

"You did not get used to it," Mammaw said, snapping for the first time since Lilly had known her. "You lost it."

The rebuke stung. She looked away from Mammaw.

"But I really want to talk about something else right now. Why don't you like this Everette Sherman?"

Mammaw could be so direct. Her age and kindness gave her liberty to be this way, and usually Lilly didn't mind. Tonight it was different. Everything Mammaw said scraped across raw nerves. She didn't want to talk.

"I don't have anything against him," she answered.

"Hm-m." Mammaw rocked back and forth in silence, saying without words, "I can wait until you're ready to talk then."

"Don't you hear the others teasing me about him?"

"Why do they tease?"

"Because of Talmadge," Lilly said reluctantly.

"Talmadge? I've heard them mention him, but I don't know who he is. Tell me about him."

"He's Charlotte Keeton's brother. Half-brother, actually. He was here last summer. Not for long. Only about three weeks."

"And he hurt you in some way, Lilly girl?"

Her voice must have given her away. Time hadn't dulled Mammaw's ears. "We were good friends," she said, speaking low and quick. "And then he had to—go away." Suddenly she was talking, spilling out the whole story of Charlotte and Talmadge, staring at the cabin floor as she did so, talking around the lump in her throat.

Mammaw's gnarled hand came down on her shoulder when she had finished. "Have you let go of your anger and bitterness over this?"

Lilly was thankful that Mammaw couldn't see her, because she was crying. She dropped her head onto her knees and didn't answer.

"I'm sorry, Lilly, truly I am. That's a hard story. But I don't think you want to be angry about it the rest of your life, no matter how unfair Charlotte was. But I'll not say another word about it, only that I think you should go to the bridge and—"

"It's too cold for that now," Lilly protested.

"I'll pray for a thaw," Mammaw said matter-of-factly.

Mammaw's prayers had power with God. A thaw came two days later. The sun shone like spring, although true spring wouldn't come for another month yet. The ragged edges of ice on the creek disappeared, and the leftover mounds of gray-crusted snow melted. If Mammaw had gone to the work of asking God for this, Lilly knew she had better do the right thing.

So she left the Riley house a mite early one day and hurried toward the bridge. It had been a long time since she had visited it, and, unexpectedly, she relished the feel of her haven. This time she didn't pray any audible words. She hardly even thought words. In the silence, it was enough to open her heart and her hands, to let go the bitter grip on pain. She cried a bit, and thought some things over, and was just about ready to leave for home again when she heard footsteps approaching. Out of long habit, she stood very still and waited for them to pass. She had her back turned when the sound of rolling pebbles made her whirl around.

Long legs in trousers hung over the edge of the bridge just beside her. The next moment the rest of the man swung down by his hands and dropped lightly onto the creek bank. Lilly Burchett and Everette Sherman stood face to face, both of them mute with astonishment and embarrassment. Everette recovered his voice first. "I'm sorry, Miss Lilly. I had no idea. . ."

"I was ready to go," Lilly stammered, wondering why he wasn't at the boarding house eating his supper.

"Don't. I can—"

"No, really. I was just ready to climb out when I heard you coming along."

He smiled slightly at her. "Running water makes a good backdrop for thoughts, doesn't it?"

Lilly remembered Talmadge saying something very similar, and she covered up the momentary stab of pain by saying lightly, "Yes, it's restful."

"You come here often then?"

She blushed in confusion. "Sometimes, yes. Not so often in the wintertime."

He must have sensed that to her this spot meant privacy. "I don't want to take it from you," he said.

"I'm sure we can both use it."

He smiled, but his blue-gray eyes held sadness and shadows. "You have things that need to be thought out?"

"Yes," she said quietly. "I do."

He sighed. "Thinking is a good thing, I believe. Something that many people don't do enough of."

This aroused Lilly's curiosity, and she wished he would go on. But it seemed that he had finished, and she felt herself to be in his way. "I'll go and leave you alone to do your thinking," she said.

After that, when she saw him in town, she began to notice how laggingly he walked. "He don't eat as much either," Mrs. Price commented.

"Do you think he's sick?"

"Sick in his soul maybe," she answered sharply. "I hear that he's sticking to what he said in church about war, no matter what anyone else says to him."

"Did the others think it over?" Lilly asked. "Or did they just tell him what they wanted him to preach?"

"Oh," Mrs. Price huffed, "so you're taking his side now, are you?"

"No, I—"

"All the time I pestered you about him, you seemed to hate him. Now when he's in trouble, you take up with him. Contrary girl!"

"No, Mrs. Price. I'm not for him or against him. But I think everyone should be sure they know what they're talking about before they start talking. What if the things Mr. Sherman is saying are in the Bible?"

"Sounds like he's got you under his spell."

Lilly could feel herself getting angry and held in her emotions with an effort. "Of course not."

"You've been meeting him on your way home and talking, haven't you? He's been coming in late for supper times without number."

"No, I have *not*!"

"I thought you said you wouldn't have anything to do with a man from off."

"I've only talked to Mr. Sherman once. Just once. We met by accident."

"Well, mind yourself around him. He's a snake!"

"Mrs. Price!"

Mrs. Price put her hands on her hips in a gesture that dared to be defied. "Talking against his country the way he did! Do you believe what he said?"

"I think," Lilly said cautiously, "that he was trying to teach us how to love each other, but he said some things he shouldn't have."

Mrs. Price breathed a sigh of relief. "Good. I'm glad to hear you say that. I thought maybe I had two of you on my hands."

This kind of discussion was going on everywhere, except that very few people put up even a weak-kneed defense of Everette Sherman, as Lilly had done. For a Sunday or two, he was not called on to preach.

But Lilly had her own problems to work through, and she paid scant mind to him. One evening, Mammaw asked abruptly, "Did you forgive Charlotte for what she done to you?"

Lilly had just tucked her into bed, and she stood looking down at her for a moment. "I think so."

"Does she know it?"

"What do you mean?"

"Have you done anything to let her know you forgave her?"

Lilly hesitated.

Mammaw insisted. "Do you and Charlotte ever talk to each other?"

"Not much. I don't stay in the store longer than I have to."

"If you forgave her, don't you think you should stay and talk sometimes?"

"I—couldn't."

"Why not?"

"She doesn't like me any more than I like her."

"You think she's happy about this hatred between you?"

"She got what she wanted," Lilly retorted. "She should be happy."

"Getting what a body wants don't make them happy."

Lilly and Charlotte had not exchanged a civil word since the previous July. Lilly shrank from the thought of even casual conversation with her. But she decided she could at least take a good long look at Charlotte and see if she seemed happy.

When she did, she was shocked to see the depth of misery in Charlotte's blue eyes. For one long, vindictive moment, she was glad to see it there. Then she loathed the feeling in herself.

"I'm leaving tomorrow," Charlotte said, without looking at her. "I thought you would like to know."

"Leaving?" Lilly repeated blankly.

"I'm going back to Lexington. I've had all I can handle here."

"What about Joe? And Okla?"

"They'll just have to get along as best they can." Charlotte laughed bitingly.

A long tense moment of silence followed. "I had a letter from Talmadge the other day," Charlotte said at last.

She seemed to be waiting for Lilly to ask her about it, but Lilly refused. The two of them were staring at each other again, as they had not done for months. Charlotte blinked once. "He says he's getting married this summer. I thought you should know that too. The girl's name is Frances."

Lilly knew she should say, "I'm glad for him." She wanted to say it, but the words caught in her throat and nearly strangled her. At last she managed, "Thanks for telling me."

Charlotte reached one hand across the counter as if she would touch Lilly's arm. Then she changed her mind and drew it back. "I'm sorry," she whispered.

Sorry for what she had done last spring? Sorry that she was the one to tell Lilly about Talmadge now? Lilly didn't know, and didn't really care.

"You can tell folks anything you want to about me, once I'm gone," Charlotte added. "It won't make me any difference." But in spite of her words, her eyes still held their misery. Lilly knew that although she was leaving the mountains because she wasn't happy there, she would no longer be happy in Lexington either.

And with that knowledge came a tentative sympathy. "I'm sorry," she said.

She left the store, left Charlotte to wonder as well exactly what she had meant by her apology.

She told Mammaw about this, while Mammaw listened and rocked, seeming satisfied, happy even. "And you felt a little sorry for Charlotte?" she asked at the end.

"A little. When I saw how she seemed so sad."

"When the hatred went out of your heart, there was room in there for love," she commented. "Even for Charlotte."

"I don't think I really love her."

"But you forgave her."

"Yes."

"The love will come."

"She's going away. She told me that today too. She's going to leave Joe and go back to Lexington."

"Love is in your heart. It don't matter where she is. She's one of those people that don't know God yet. But He's going to keep working on her too. Keep that in mind, Lilly."

People talked over Charlotte Keeton's departure, with all the usual vigor of gossipers. But after a week or two, the talk died down, and life went on in its normal routine. Only instead of Charlotte behind the counter in the store, it was now the two men, both stolid and quiet. They had moved into the single room behind the store, and seemed to be making out well by themselves.

Sometimes in those weeks, on her way home from work, Lilly overtook Everette Sherman walking slowly along the trail away from town, walking the opposite direction from Mrs. Price's and supper. He was always scrupulously polite when he saw her, taking his hat from his head and nodding to her. Only once did he speak. "Good evening, Miss Lilly."

"Good evening, Mr. Sherman." It seemed rude to go quickly on her way past him, since he had spoken, and she said the first thing that came to her mind. "Won't you be late for your supper?"

"Yes," he answered briefly. "I will be. Does Mrs. Price care?"

"She doesn't know what to make of it."

"I hate to worry her. It just seems like after I've been all day underground, I need the fresh air more than supper sometimes."

"Have you ever worked at coal mining before?"

"No."

"It takes some getting used to. That's what Pa said after he started."

"I know your pa. We work together. He's a good man."

This simple statement warmed Lilly. "He says the same of you."

"He does?" Everette looked surprised. "That's more than most folks are saying just now."

"I'm sorry," she said, responding more to the look in his eyes than to the words themselves. "They just don't know how to take what you said."

"I know," he answered heavily, but without rancor. He stuffed his hands into the pockets of his threadbare coat. "Maybe I said too much, too soon, and they couldn't take it in. Will they forget?"

"I think so. Once they get over being hurt. A lot of the people think you're all right."

She realized suddenly, as she walked away from him, that she too thought he was all right. He had a quiet strength that never turned back from something hard, and this impressed her, no matter what he preached. By now Mammaw had enthusiastically taken up the idea that war was wrong. "He's on track," she said. "If everyone forgave and let go of their anger and bitterness, there wouldn't be any war. I know that's what he's trying to say."

"Maybe so, Mammaw," Lilly agreed.

When he preached now, his listeners always tensed, ready to pounce on anything he said wrong. But he was very circumspect, and they found little to criticize. He preached about things they agreed with—things like the walk of grace, the eternal destinies of men, and honesty.

After that sermon about honesty, Lilly wrestled for a week. Then one day she stayed late at the Riley house and paced nervously up and down the kitchen until Mr. Riley came home.

"You're still here?" he said in surprise when he came in.

"Yes, Mr. Riley, I have something to tell you."

"Well?"

"I've been reading some of Mrs. Riley's books when I'm here, even after you told me not to."

He stared at her out of cold, calculating eyes. "I told you to stop that a long time ago."

"I know, but I've been doing it ever since. I'm sorry."

"You'd better be sorry."

"You can cut my wages if you like."

"Seems like that's my business to decide your wages, not yours."

"Yes, sir."

"That's all you've got to say?"

"Yes, sir."

"Then go home."

It was unbelievably hard for Lilly to stick to her decision. She always went into the library with set teeth and cleaned it as fast as she could. And then T.J. asked her about it. "When will you have a new story to tell me?" He was tucked into his bed in the loft, only his face peeping out above the blankets, his eyes big and pleading.

"I won't have any new ones for a long time, T.J.," she answered gently, while ruffling up his hair. "Do you think we can remember the old ones?"

"Why not any new ones? Did you read all the books in Mr. Riley's library?"

"No, not nearly. But Mr. Riley doesn't want me to read them."

"Why not?"

"Because they belong to him, not me."

"I'll have a library of my own when I grow up," T.J. declared, "and then I'll let you read all you want. But you won't have to tell me the stories anymore, because I'll read them too."

"Then I'll tell them to your children instead."

This made T.J. laugh, and the sad, longing look left his eyes. "I think I can remember the old ones until then," he said.

Only a few days later, when Lilly went into Everette Sherman's room to clean it, she instantly noticed something new on the shelf—a row of books, their spines lined up meticulously with each other. More books that she must clean around without reading. Wordsworth. Tennyson. Milton. Several books about the Bible. One or two that she didn't recognize. Some of them had much-worn covers, almost in tatters. The look of the books made her feel suddenly that she knew the man.

Chapter twenty-two

A yearning that would not be denied grew in Lilly's heart after this. She faithfully wrote in her diary, even though Pa occasionally laughed at her for it, and Maybelle could not understand what pleasure she got out of it. But it wasn't enough. Mr. Ferguson had stayed in town after school let out this spring, taking a job on a lumber crew. She thought maybe he could help, but she had no chances to ask him until the day she was later than usual heading home from work.

She had stopped in at one of the company houses to ask about a pattern for Caroline, and been invited to stay for supper. Evening shadows lay thick across the town when she left, mingling with the ever-present coal dust. She shivered and drew her coat snugly around herself. On damp evenings like this, she hated the walk home, especially when she knew that rains had brought the level of Sand Lick above the stones, and she would need to take off her shoes and socks and wade it barefoot. Then she saw Mr. Ferguson ahead of her, and it became a good evening after all.

"Mr. Ferguson," she called after him.

"Evening, Miss Lilly," he drawled.

"Can I ask a favor of you?"

"You can ask. I'll do it if I can."

"Do you know where I can get some—paper?"

His green eyes gleamed. "I wondered if you would ever come to me for that. Do you need it right now?"

"Yes, please, if you have it."

"I think there might be some left at school. We can walk up there together, if you like."

They walked side by side, excitement quickening Lilly's feet so that she had no problem keeping up with Mr. Ferguson's long strides. But when they came within sight of the sagging building, Mr. Ferguson stopped abruptly. "Look at that, Lilly. Someone's here. There's a light in the window."

It was only a dim light, likely made by a candle. But it wavered out through the shutterless windows, looking very bright in the dank night.

"Step back," Mr. Ferguson warned. "I'll go in first."

He took hold of the warped door and pushed and kicked at it. When it opened suddenly, he stumbled forward, stopped short, and said in amazement, "What are you doing here?"

Everette Sherman sat in the circle of candlelight. He had laid a tiny fire in the stove and it sputtered feebly, warming the center of the room. On one knee he had a book, and on the other a piece of paper.

Mr. Ferguson took one step forward, so that Lilly could crowd in behind him. "When I left the boarding house," he said, "you were up in your room. How did you get here?"

Everette shrugged, but he looked a little abashed as well. "I often leave my room by the back porch roof," he answered in a low, pleasant voice. "That way no one knows I'm gone, and they won't worry if I don't come back till late."

Mr. Ferguson digested this. Then he threw back his head and laughed heartily. "And you come up here?"

"Sometimes. It doesn't bother you, does it?"

"Nope. Don't bother me none."

"It's a lot quieter than the boarding house."

Mr. Ferguson laughed again. "No doubt about that. We'll get what we came for and be on our way again."

"I don't mind a bit of pleasant company," Everette disagreed. "You're more than welcome to stay."

"I can't," Lilly said quickly. "My family will wonder where I've been."

From a drawer in his desk, Mr. Ferguson took out several clean white sheets. "Will this do?"

She took them from him with eager fingers, fingers that could feel the shape of a story just from the touch of paper.

"I thought you said you were never going to write stories again." He smiled slyly.

"I've changed my mind."

"One condition. You have to let me read them."

She wished he wouldn't have mentioned stories in front of Everette, and she dropped her gaze. "I think I can do that."

She began a story that very evening, spinning out sentences with all the old feeling of pleasure, watching words drop onto the page in even phalanxes, to form sentences and paragraphs. She kept adding to the story as she had a chance, and on Sunday, with the feel of spring warm on the hills, she took it outside, folded up and stuffed into the pocket of her dress.

It was the kind of March day made for dreams, and for a time she wandered idly up the holler, past Pappaw's place and Uncle Sandy's new house. Then she crossed the creek and climbed the ridge on the other side to a glade where the sunshine would linger for several more hours. There she took out her paper and pencil. But for a time she didn't write. Instead she soared out over the farthest crests of hills that she could see and imagined a world out there, imagined it so real and vivid and detailed that she would be able to put it on paper.

She was startled by a familiar voice and looked up to see Everette Sherman. "I'm sorry to disturb you," he said.

She was sorry too that he had come, but she couldn't tell him so. Dreams were best lived alone, and he had broken the shape of the one she held.

"It's a pretty afternoon," he added, "and I've been out exploring."

She noticed the book in his hands, and he saw her looking at it. "My Bible," he explained. "Do you mind if I sit down here and read for a while?"

"No. Go ahead."

This high upland was fairly dry, and he sat down a few paces from her on last summer's tangled mat of grass. She stole glances at him and saw him sometimes smiling, sometimes frowning as he read, sometimes moving his lips to the words.

Lilly began to write, slowly. She had worried that she wouldn't know how to write anymore, not having done it for so long, but Mammaw had said,

"Seems to me like writing a story would be kind of like holding a baby, Lilly girl. When you do it and get knacky at it, you don't forget how, even if you don't do it for a long time." And Mammaw had been right.

Everette Sherman stirred. "It's lovely up here. So nice and quiet."

"I love the quiet too," she told him.

"Can I ask you a question?" he queried.

She was suddenly aware that they were alone, and that if anyone else chanced upon them they would assume this was courtship. Her guards went up, but she nodded.

"I need someone to answer this honestly. What are people saying about me these days?"

"They can't find anything to criticize in your messages."

"I don't suppose so," he answered wryly. "I'm preaching about safe subjects. But I get the feeling they're still just waiting for me to misstep. Am I right?"

She decided to answer him bluntly. "Yes."

He shut his Bible with restless hands. "And what will happen if I tell them the truth again about love and hatred? The truth about war?"

"They won't like it."

"I'll have to tell them sometime."

"Why? Why can't you just leave that subject alone if you don't agree with everyone else?"

"Because they need to know the truth."

"I don't quite understand what you mean."

He moved a bit closer to her and asked, "Do you have relatives who fought in the war? Uncles or cousins?"

"Yes."

"Did any of them die?"

"Yes. My uncle Buell."

"Were any of them wounded?"

"My uncle Ernest."

"Does he talk about the war?"

"Only when he's drunk."

"I figured as much. Most ex-soldiers don't, except among themselves.

Their families at home think they went out and did heroic deeds in subduing the Germans. They have no idea."

Lilly felt a chill from the stark coldness in his words.

"War isn't like that at all. War is hell. It's brutal and inhuman. I can't tell you everything, because you're a girl. But I can tell you enough so that you will see what I mean." And he went on to do just that, etching a grim picture of death and destruction and despair, of starving children and terrified civilians and soldiers gone crazy with the killing and being killed. "There's lots of stories of bravery too," he said, "and they're true, mostly. But the times when soldiers are truly brave is when they forget that they're fighting a war and they only remember that they're humans, and that the soldier next to them is just a human too."

He paused, not looking at Lilly. "I fought in some bad battles. When you see death like that, you don't forget."

Lilly had goose bumps all over her arms. The story she had been spinning lay forgotten in her lap. How could any of the returned soldiers live with memories like this? No wonder they didn't often talk of them. She felt sick and wanted to tell Everette to stop. Then he looked up at her with a hint of pleading. "I want you to understand why I feel the way I do. But I . . . perhaps I shouldn't have spoken."

"I do understand," she said.

"Do you think others would understand if I would tell them the same thing?"

"I don't see how they could help it."

"It's hard to talk about freely."

"Be careful," she begged. "Pa said that people are still hurting from losing kin in this war, and if you tell them that war is a sin, it's like kicking them when they're down."

"But I want to show them a better way. There wouldn't have to be war at all, not if people loved each other."

The sun had dipped toward the west while they talked, cresting the pines on the far ridge with amber. Both of them were thinking the same thing, and they stood to go.

"Thanks for listening," Everette said and laughed shortly. "I hope I don't cause you any nightmares tonight."

He had indeed created a horror picture, the kind nightmares were born from. But she could now see what drove him to speak as he had behind the pulpit. "I'm honored that you told me," she answered.

He smiled a smile that breathed sadness, and she thought he had finished all he meant to say. But he asked suddenly, "May I count you as a friend?"

Surprised, she only nodded.

"You know I have precious few of those right now."

She did know it, and because she also knew loneliness, her heart ached for him.

They stayed friends, just friends, as winter let go of the mountains and crept north. Green peeped freshly from the fields and along the stark lines of tree branches. Dandelions bloomed in clumps. Sand Lick swelled with its spring floods and then subsided again to a friendly thing. In April a baby girl joined the Burchett family, and Caroline named her Rose. In June Lilly turned sixteen.

She and Everette didn't talk often. Sometimes he would overtake her on her way home from work, or she would come upon him under the bridge. She saw him then in other moods, sometimes pensive, sometimes happy, sometimes serious, sometimes even excited. They never talked of the war again, but of ideas like love and unity and peace. And inevitably they began to share pieces of themselves along with the ideas. Her perception of Everette changed, until she thought of him as a man of unplumbed depths.

On the day he gave Lilly a Bible, under the bridge, she realized that her feelings had gone beyond friendship sometime during the merging of spring and summer.

"I thought you should have one of your own," he said. "If you can read it for yourself, you will come to love it."

It was a beautiful book, small but neat, with a black leather cover and fine sharp text on its white pages. She loved it even without having read it. But she realized that she loved it as well for reasons other than its holiness. She loved it because of the one who had given it to her. She walked home, holding it with both hands, her heart throbbing strangely in her chest.

She hardly knew what had happened. When had she learned to talk to Everette? When had she told him of her longings to leave the mountains? When had she told him of Mrs. Riley and her library and watched his eyes light up with shared pleasure as she described the rows of books? When had she told him of Ma, and Vince, and Patty, of Pa remarrying, and of the wise things that Mammaw told her?

For he knew all of this now. In return, he had described his family, the mother and siblings that he helped to support since his father had walked out and left them. The need for a steady job was what had brought him to the coal fields at all, and he still sent part of his paycheck home to them every two weeks. He repeated things that he read in his books, and they discussed them. He smiled more often, she thought, and they laughed together when they talked. Something had changed, and she had felt it. Now she knew it for what it was.

Lilly found the house empty when she came home. Glad of that, she went straight upstairs and put the Bible with her other three books. "Wonder what Pa would say," she whispered, "if he knew Everette gave me a Bible." She was very happy as she came back downstairs, but trembly too.

"Any supper for me?" she asked.

"Caroline said to tell you there are some boiled potatoes and biscuits in the kitchen. They're all out in the field. You're later than usual."

"I was talking to Everette."

Mammaw smiled. "I thought so."

Lilly dumped the new potatoes, with their fragile split skins, onto a plate and took two biscuits from the pan nearby. She carried her supper back into the front room in order to eat with Mammaw. "I think," she whispered, "that I love him."

"I wondered how soon you would discover that."

"Mammaw. . ."

"I've been listening to everything you've said about him for the last while, Lilly girl. I could tell that you're learning to trust him more all the time. That's the first step to love."

"Do you think he's all right, Mammaw? Lots of people around here are still suspicious of him."

"He's all right," Mammaw said firmly. "He knows to go to the Bible when he needs answers. That's more important than having everyone agree with him."

"I'm a little afraid."

"Afraid of what?"

"I'm afraid when I remember Talmadge."

"'Perfect love casteth out fear,'" Mammaw quoted calmly. "You've got the love of God in your heart, haven't you?"

When Lilly finished her supper, she asked, "Are you ready for bed?"

"Yes, dear." She stood up slowly, clutching at the arms of the rocking chair.

Lilly guided her into the other room and smoothed the straw tick before she lay down. "As soon as harvest comes," she said, "we're going to have to put new ticking in your mattress. It's going flat."

"That won't matter," Mammaw said serenely.

"But, Mammaw, you're the oldest person in this house. You should sleep on the best."

"By that time, I'm pretty sure I will be in a place where I won't need straw ticks." She sat on the edge of the bed and lay back on her pillow, smiling up at Lilly. "Tuck me in. I like to feel the way you do it, and I don't think I'll have many more months to enjoy it."

"What do you mean, Mammaw?" Lilly asked, although she knew.

"Of course, in heaven, I won't miss no tucking in. Not after I've got to be like an angel."

"Are you feeling sick?" Lilly asked anxiously.

"No, not sick. But I can tell this old body has lived about as long as it's going to. It seems like my spirit is kind of restless, trying to get out. Soon it will. I would like to live long enough to see you get married to Everette, but I doubt I will."

"Mammaw. . ."

"Don't cry, Lilly girl."

"I'll miss you so."

"But you've got Everette now, and your books and your writing."

After the way she had talked, Lilly was afraid Mammaw would die in her sleep that night. But in the morning she woke up like usual and wanted to sit at the table for breakfast. She seemed like herself in every way, speaking no more of dying, and wanting to live as fully as she could.

Chapter twenty-three

Everette Sherman came to call on Lilly only several times at her home. The first time, she feared what her family would say afterward, but although they teased, they said nothing disparaging.

Maybelle commented wisely, "I think Caroline wants you married, and she doesn't really care who the man is."

"What about Pa?"

"Pa kind of likes Everette. He respects him, at least."

This spoke well of Everette, since Pa worked closely with him in the mine. Lilly smiled to herself in the darkness, pleased. "What do you think, Maybelle?"

"Oh, I don't know. I thought he was dreadfully boring at first."

"But he's not boring at all," Lilly protested incredulously.

"He's quiet," Maybelle defended herself. "That's why I thought he was boring."

"He's not quiet when you get to know him."

"Maybe not. I like him better than I did. I like that he thinks before he talks."

In an upstairs room of the boarding house, with the window open and a breeze fanning the flame of a candle, Everette sat on the edge of his cot. He had a paper on one knee, and a pencil in one hand. "Dear Mother," he had written and then stopped.

Outside, the night beckoned to him. With quick movements, he blew out the candle, tossed his paper and pencil onto the bed, and climbed out the window. He carried his shoes in his hands, and walked cat-like across the porch roof, letting himself down over the edge and jumping the last few feet onto the ground. He headed east, out of town, away from the ever-present coal grime. As he went, he tried to formulate the letter he needed to write.

His mother depended on the paycheck that arrived every two weeks. This knowledge, and his deeply ingrained sense of duty, had kept him from considering marriage before, although he had passed his twenty-fifth birthday. Even now, he knew he had not gone courting in any traditional kind of way. His friendship with Lilly had simply happened, as though it was meant to be, born out of her willingness to listen when he felt like he had no friends, and then nurtured by the similarities they found between themselves.

He wasn't quite sure of Lilly yet, but very sure of his own heart. He walked a mile or two beyond town before heading back. And, in his room again, he lit the candle, and wrote the letter in the simplest of words. "I have found a girl here that I love. Her name is Lilly Burchett. She's only sixteen, young yet, but very sweet and mature. I feel sure that you would love her too. I want to ask her to marry me, but before I do that, I want you to know about it and to give me your blessing. Everette Sherman."

On his fourth visit to the cabin, he asked Lilly to marry him. They were standing at the end of the ridge, above the cabin, and they had just finished discussing a new book. Lilly still held the book, but she looked beyond the rim of the circling hills, into the heart of the sunset; and then he said simply, "I'd like to ask you to be my wife, Lilly, but one thing is holding me back. You've told me how much you long to get out of these mountains and live a different life. I believe God has called me to these mountains, and I think they are beautiful. I love the people here, and I want to stay."

Lilly felt a queer tightening of her throat. "Oh, Everette," she said breathlessly, "those longings are a thing of the past."

"Are you sure?" He looked at her searchingly.

Lilly knew that Everette wouldn't mind if she pondered before answering. She thought of the times when Mammaw had pushed her toward genuine freedom, about the times when she had surrendered under the bridge. At last she spoke, choosing her words as she went. "I used to think I was trapped here, and I had to get out to be free. I didn't know I was looking at the wrong thing. It wasn't that I was trapped in the mountains, but that my soul was trapped by being angry and bitter. As long as my soul is free, it doesn't matter where I live." She looked up at him confidently, returning his gaze with joy. "No matter where I am, my heart and mind are my own."

"Then will you agree to be my wife and live with me in the mountains?"

"I will be glad to be your wife, Everette. Right here on Sand Lick, if that's where you want to live."

"It won't be easy," he reminded her. "People still don't know what to make of me. And I can't promise that God is done teaching us hard things."

"I know," Lilly agreed. But the next moment she smiled radiantly. "You know what Mammaw told me the other day? She said, 'Perfect love casteth out fear.' "

When Lilly whispered her news to Mammaw that night, Mammaw only smiled and patted her cheek. And two weeks later she died, going away in her sleep to meet the God she had learned to know so well. Everette preached the funeral sermon for the handful of friends and neighbors who gathered. All of her generation and most of the next were already gone. Her blindness and frailty had kept her at home, and few people knew her. Others lived too far away to make the trip.

Near to where Caroline had lived before she married Pa, they buried her in a family plot. Lilly stood holding T.J.'s hand as they filled in the dirt over the rough pine coffin. She cried quietly for sorrow at another loss. She had only known Mammaw for about a year, but she would leave a gaping hole in her life. She reached into her pocket for a handkerchief and held it to her eyes for a few minutes. When she looked next, the grave was nearly full, Pa was wiping his hands and passing his shovel to someone else, and T.J. had slipped away.

Everette Sherman stood looking down at her compassionately. "She was an important woman to you, wasn't she?"

"Yes," she answered softly. "I don't know where I would be if she hadn't come into my life. Angry and bitter, I'm sure. Probably angry at you."

"Angry at me?" he repeated in disbelief, while drawing her away from the edge of the grave.

She laughed shakily. "Angry at you, and at a whole lot of other things and people. I have a story that I haven't really told you yet. . ."

"I think," he said slowly, "that I'd like to hear it under the bridge."

Don't miss the other books in this series:

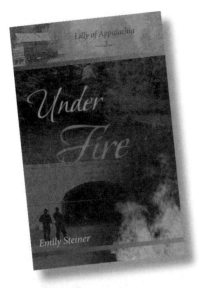

Under Fire

the story of Lilly and Everette
in Harlan County, Kentucky,
a tense story of love and hate,
hope and despair,
trust and surrender.

Under the Juniper Tree

a triumphant story of
faith and hope and
peace in spite of pain
and disappointment.

About the author

Emily Steiner has lived all her life in Eastern Kentucky. She has a love for the hills and valleys, and a fascination with the vivid history of the area. She combines these with an appreciation for well-crafted fiction.

With questions or comments, or to order additional copies of this book, you may call her at 606.495.8090 or email *jemstyle01@icloud.com*.